Also by Justina Chen Headley

Nothing but the Truth (and a few white lies)

girl OVERBOARD

Justina Chen Headley

LITTLE, BROWN AND COMPANY
New York ↝ Boston

Little, Brown and Company

Hachette Book Group USA
237 Park Avenue, New York, NY 10017
Visit our Web site at www.lb-teens.com

First Edition: January 2008

The characters and events portrayed in this book are fictitious. Any similarity to real persons, living or dead, is coincidental and not intended by the author.

ISBN-13: 978-0-316-01130-3
ISBN-10: 0-316-01130-4

10 9 8 7 6 5 4 3 2 1

Q-FF

Printed in the United States of America

The text was set in Berkeley Book, and the display type is Memo.

For Robert, my man for all ages

If you were to ask me why I dwell among green mountains,
I should laugh silently; my soul is serene.

—Li Po (A.D. 701–762), T'ang Dynasty poet

1

The worst part of having it all is having to deal with it all — the good, the bad, and the just plain weird. Like seeing more of my dad when he's on the cover of *BusinessWeek* than I do in person. Like the surgeon whose schedule was too jammed fixing professional ballplayers to deal with my busted-up knee . . . until he heard who my parents were, and miraculously his calendar was wide open. Like the pseudo-boyfriend who was more in love with my last name than with me.

So that full-body girdle waiting on my bed after school today? It doesn't faze me at all. Not when I already know that the body I have isn't the body Mama thinks I ought to have.

I ignore the corset and continue updating my manga-slash-journal as if the most important social event on Mama's calendar isn't starting. Whoever these guests are, they're early birds who want to catch every last minute of Ethan Cheng's birthday extravaganza. Not that I blame them. Considering that people still talk about my dad's sixty-fifth blow-out bash five years ago like it was the party of the millennium, Mama's inspiration at combining his seventieth along with Chinese New Year means tonight is sure to be a once-in-a-lifetime spectacle.

I flip to a blank page in my journal, draw Mama cattle-prodding my big butt with a jewel-encrusted chopstick down our marble stairs, and add her speech bubble —

"*Aiya!*" cries my nanny, Bao-mu, barging into my bedroom without so much as a knock. Her slippers slap against her dry heels as she marches for me faster than you'd imagine a septu-agenarian could move. "You suppose be downstairs." When she sees that I'm still in the shapeless jeans that Mama hates, I earn two more *aiya*s and a distressed "You not ready!"

"I've got ten minutes," I say confidently before I even nudge aside the silk curtains hanging from the canopy of my Ming-Dynasty bed and quick double-check the clock on my wall. "Actually, twelve."

As though I don't hear the doorbell ringing, Bao-mu tells me, "Guests here already." Sighing impatiently, she takes matters into her own hands and plucks the journal out of mine. "Why you have draw now?"

"I just had to prepare," I tell her honestly. Three hours of smiling and small-talking wipes me out more than a day riding the mountain. Or at least how I remember snowboarding be-fore I tore my anterior cruciate ligament back in August.

Bao-mu nods as if she understands how I would need to for-tify myself with some borrowed bravado, but that doesn't stop her from ordering, "*Lai!*" and expecting me to follow. She forges ahead to my closet, the one place in this antique-laden bed-room where I can hang my snowboarding posters and ribbons from local riding contests, relics from my pre-Accident days.

Inside the closet I shed my jeans, sweatshirt, and bra to

tackle the "gift" Mama so generously left me. What starts as a healthy glow turns to an all-out sweat usually seen only in hot yoga classes, as I struggle into this "Torso Bustshaping Body-slip." I suck in my stomach like, yeah, right, that's going to help this lycra boa constrictor down my hips. It takes a full eight minutes of contortions never witnessed outside Cirque du Soleil before the bodyslip finally snaps across my thighs. According to my surgeon, at an inch over five feet and one hundred ten pounds — six pounds over my pre-Accident weight — I'm still smaller than the average American girl, which is why I'll probably feel the pins in my reconstructed knee for the rest of my life. According to the Nordstrom lingerie department, I barely fill an A cup. Whatever the experts say, I challenge any-one to stand next to my mother and not become Sasquatch: huge, hulking, and with perpetual bad hair.

"*Wah!*" says Bao-mu, admiring the miracle of microfiber with a light poke at my corseted tummy.

I'd *wah,* too, if my head didn't feel like it's floating away. I may have shed ten pounds in under ten minutes, but all I can manage are little hyperventilating pants. Tomorrow's headline in the business section is going to read: CHENG DAUGHTER, 15, FOUND MUMMIFIED IN GIRDLE.

My smirk ends in a gasp. "I can't breathe," I tell Bao-mu.

"You get used to," she assures me, although she looks awfully skeptical.

The voices downstairs recede into the living room. Hoping that fresh air might revive me, I hobble over to crack open a window. Below, one of the valets drives off to park a guest's car. If my best friend Adrian were here, he'd identify the type of car just by the way its engine rumbles, but Age is probably still

3

snowboarding on all the new powder at Alpental. This morning, he text-messaged me during History: "Fresh pow. Blow off school."

"No can do," I had surreptitiously messaged back, watching the rain through the classroom windows and imagining the snowflakes layering the mountain. But I couldn't risk being late for Baba's party. Besides, I still have my parents' snowboarding embargo to deal with.

Chelsea Dillinger, It Girl of Viewridge Prep, barrels down our long driveway in her black Hummer. Even before the vehicle's doors open, the shrill voices of the Chelsea clones, the girls I've dubbed The Six-Pack for all looking uncannily alike, shriek about *Attila,* the new teen flick premiering later tonight for the viewing pleasure of the "younger" set.

"Hurry," urges Bao-mu, taking my hand in her wrinkled one and yanking me back to the closet.

It's time for my showdown with the tiny yellow dress that Mama carted home from Hong Kong a couple of days ago. My nemesis of silk hangs like a piece of art in the center of my walk-in closet: a micromini halter dress so short it could pass for a sequined tank top, adorable on Mama, obscene on me. When I was little, I never played dress-up. Why bother when every day *was* dress-up? "She's darling," salespeople would coo at five-year-old me dolled up in outfits that coordinated with Mama's, as if I was a purse or a pair of shoes.

Now, even with the super-suctioning power of the body shaper and Bao-mu's *aiya*-ing, I struggle with the back zipper and catch myself in the floor-to-ceiling mirror that runs the entire back length of the closet.

"Oh, no!" I gasp, the words weak, horrified. Perhaps that was

4

Mama's intent all along: deprive me of oxygen so I won't have the breath to complain about looking like an overstuffed pot-sticker.

"*Ni zhen mei,*" says Bao-mu, eyeing me with pride as if she were my grandmother, one in desperate need of an eye exam if she really thinks I look beautiful with this sequined dragon, flapping wings and all, rising from my hip to my chest.

I turn to my side and correct myself. The dragon isn't flying away; it's being catapulted off the taut trampoline of my girdle. I'd fling myself onto my bed if I could, but in this vise, the chances of that happening are about as good as me sneaking off to catch some Friday night riding with Age.

I turn to my other side as if the view might be better. It's not.

"I need take your picture," says Bao-mu.

"No way. I can't wear this," I tell her, desperate. Downstairs, another doorbell rings and more hearty "good to see you's" are exchanged. Nervous beads of sweat form on my nose, and I wipe them off. I should have tried on the dress Tuesday night after Mama handed it to me.

Bao-mu hurries to my bathroom and returns with concealer, still in shrink-wrap.

"Your mommy want you cover scars on your knee," she says, urging the concealer on me, a makeup pusher.

I can't formulate a single word, not even the two little letters that want to burst from my lips: N-O. No, I won't wear this stupid dress. No, I won't wear the heels. No, I won't slather on makeup. No, I won't hide the scars the way my parents want me to hide my snowboarding dreams.

"Hurry," says Bao-mu as if she can hear my protests that she can do nothing about either, and flies out for her party duties.

Downstairs, Mama calls brightly to guests, lavishing them with her attention, "*Gong hay fat choy!* Happy New Year! Helen, you look brilliant."

Alone in my bedroom, I stare at my pale face. Turning away, I rush over to my bedside table, grab my cell phone, and call Age, wherever he is, ready to beg him to come get me. Bring me to the mountains. To hell with my knee. And my parents.

"You know what to do," Age's voice rumbles before his voice-mail beeps.

Another doorbell, another rash of greetings, another burst of laughter. You bet I know what I want to do. But what I have to do is non-negotiable. Missing a Chinese New Year celebration would be one thing, but my dad's birthday bash? That's impossible. I hang up without leaving a message.

Instead, I upturn the concealer and shake the brushed glass bottle until a drop wells on my finger like colorless blood. I bend down and work the thick, flesh-toned liquid over the red scars leftover from my knee surgery, rubbing until I look as good as new.

2

Perma-smile in place, I stand in the foyer where I've been commanded to stay until the very last guest arrives. The only guest I want to see is Age, but a glance at the grandfather clock — seven forty-five — has me sighing. If Age hasn't shown up by now, he's still snowboarding, which means the new powder's so good, Age isn't coming at all tonight.

My right knee throbs, calling into question Dr. Bradford's pronouncement yesterday that I'm back to normal. This ache is not how I recall normal. No sooner do I perch on the bottom step of the staircase than the front doors bang open. I stand up hastily, wincing at the sharp jab in my knee, and then greet my older half-brother, "Wayne!"

All I rate from him is the barest nod of recognition that he reserves for acquaintances he can't quite place. I, on the other hand, can place Wayne instantly, anywhere, any day. Dressed in a tailored double-breasted suit to elongate his slight build, Wayne's the forty-five-year-old version of Baba, the right age to be my dad. Or my mom's husband.

7

As usual, Wayne ignores me and strides toward Grace, my half-sister who's standing near the pianist, offering a morsel of dumpling to the miniature poodle cradled in her skinny arms. As Grace laughs at whatever Wayne is saying, I retreat back to the foyer where no one can see how much I wish he would be the perfect big brother for me, too.

I lean against the altar table and rub my cheek muscles that deserve a gold medal for party-smiling. Even if I want to dump my hostessing duties, I can't leave to sprawl on the red velvet couches in the theater downstairs with the rest of the kids, commiserate with the girls about being strangled by girdle. Anyway, which girl? And how far would I get before they started asking for something? Say, a personal tour of my closet. Or a joy ride in one of Baba's sports cars. And then they'd snicker behind my back about how I was showing off again.

Over by the bar, a man bloated with self-importance broadcasts to the entire party, "We're about to remodel the garage at our cabin because, you know, we've got to have a place to store the boat."

Be still my heaving stomach.

While I'm mentally retching, a waiter trots over with a tray of bite-sized crab cakes resting on porcelain spoons. "Miss Cheng, anything you need?"

Yeah, I think, reaching for a spoon but stopping when ever-vigilant calorie police Mama shakes her head at me from across the living room before returning to her conversation. *Miss Cheng needs a one-way ticket out of Cheng-ri-La.*

If I sneak out into the January night, I'll freeze. But flirting with frostbite is a small price to pay when I know with my eyes closed, for just a moment, I can pretend I'm free. Pretend I'm on top of a mountain. Who knows? I might even be able to trick myself into believing I'm about to ride with Age, the way we used to before the Accident.

As I push open the front doors, salvaged from some ancient monastery in China, I run right into the Fujimoro trio. Baba's new hire, his pregnant wife, and daughter Lillian should be on meet-and-greet duty instead of me, their handshakes are so hearty-hello-nice-to-network-with-you.

"Good to see you, Syrah. Knee okay?" asks Mr. Fujimoro.

Knee okay, I nod; it's my hand I'm worrying about. He's pumping it up and down so vigorously, you'd think bonuses and stock options were going to spill out of my mouth.

"Good." He thrusts a bottle of — you guessed it — my name-sake wine toward me. "A memorable syrah for a memorable Syrah."

"Thanks," I murmur politely, taking the wine bottle, wishing once again that my name didn't reek like a fermented grape. Honestly, if my parents had to name me for wine, why couldn't it have been sassy, whip-'em-into-shape Shiraz, Australian for Syrah? Age says I should count my blessings. They could've named me Zinfandel. Or Gewürztraminer.

"You girls should catch up," says Mrs. Fujimoro, one hand pushing back her blonde-by-salon hair, the other hand pushing Lillian toward me.

The problem is, we girls have nothing to say to each other. In the two months since Lillian transferred to my school, she's already next in line to be editor-in-chief of our paper and has worked herself into Chelsea Dillinger's Six-Pack clique. In short, Lillian is more Chengian than I am, right down to her figure that defies the need for any body shaper.

Deafening drumming, euphemistically known as Chinese music, pounds over this painful party chit chat. Without a backward glance, Lillian and her parents abandon me to watch the lion dancers pouncing around the living room to scare away bad luck from this Lunar New Year. As Bao-mu would say, this is a sign to grab my opportunity for escape. So I stumble-run outside, past the valets, as fast as I can in my heels, and head for the grounds.

The last time I felt this giddy with freedom, I was racing Age down the backcountry in Alpental a year ago. Not that either one of us would admit it to anyone aside from ourselves, but we'd been keeping score since the first snow over Halloween opened the season early. Bragging rights for being the fastest were on the line since we were tied, and that perfect morning, I had the lead.

"Watch and weep!" I yelled as I screamed past him, thinking life couldn't possibly get any better than that moment. I knew that if I didn't head straight for the base of the mountain, I'd lose for sure, but pillows of fresh snow were mounded everywhere, the kind that you hit on top and they bust open under your board. How could I resist? Even though it'd cost me precious seconds, I jumped, knees rising so high they could have substituted as my earmuffs. Just as I landed on the fluffiest pillow, Age spun around, shaking his head at me like he'd never seen a girl more crazy than I was.

In that split second, I flew around him, and as I soared down the mountain, swerving in and out of trees with Age chasing me, I remember thinking that life rolled out in front of us, one infinitely long and smooth welcome mat.

A sharp stab in my knee returns me to the Garden of Ethan, our version of the imperial summer estates in Suzhou, the

Venice of China. Aside from the rustling of the bamboo around me, the garden is silent, as if it, too, is paying respects to the girl I used to be.

Then the drumming begins again, louder than before, which means that the lion dancers are leading the guests to the *tang*, the Hall of Expansive Dreams, where all of my parents' formal entertaining takes place.

Expansive Dreams. That's a laugh. I cross a bridge that arches over a manmade stream. My dreams have shrunk to the size of a snowflake now that everybody in the snowboarding industry has written me off as a selfish, spoiled dilettante who thought my trust fund entitled me to ride anywhere I wanted at Whistler, even in the off-limit, avalanche-prone backcountry.

No one has ever asked me why I went where I wasn't supposed to go and ended up where I shouldn't have been. No one reported about how the avalanche may have missed my body but iced over my heart. No one knows how the avalanche dog "found" me and ski patrol "rescued" me. But the Real Me, the fearless one? She's still buried under an avalanche of one man's making. I breathe in as deeply as my body shaper allows, refusing to be sucked down into the memory of Jared Johanson, snowboarding camp counselor who wanted me to be his free pass to paradise.

The sounds of Baba's party, muffled conversations and clear laughter, cross the pond, almost camouflaging the crackle of interference on the garden path. Before I can duck into the shadows, Meghan, Mama's favorite event planner, strides swiftly to me, announcing victoriously into her walkie-talkie: "Eaglet captured." Without missing a beat, she nods her head toward the main hall. "Syrah, you're late."

3

Just as the lights dim, I reach the family table, nestled inside the innermost circle of Baba's premier business associates within the bigger pool of his wine-collecting aficionados, his corporate minions, and the Ethan-Wife Number One friends, all gray-haired enough to serve as my grandparents. I swear, Darth Vader is narrating a Hollywood homage to Baba's life, large-screen movie, swelling music, and all.

While Darth extols Baba's humble beginnings, starting with my great-grandfather who moved to *Gam Saan,* Gold Mountain, the Chinese name for America, Wayne makes a big deal of looking pointedly at his watch. "Nice of you to show up," he says.

Give me a break, I want to tell him. But it's safer to ignore Wayne, so I slide next to Grace, who, naturally, keeps focused on the movie.

Another surge of music follows Darth's words: "Like his grandfather before him who helped build America's transcontinental railroad a hundred and fifty years ago, Ethan created Europe's first transcontinental telecommunications superhighway."

A small growl gets my attention. Grace's dog is, as usual, perched on his lap of honor, only now he's trying to wriggle out from under her heavy hand.

"Hey, Mochi," I whisper.

The dog barks, sharp and high.

"It's okay, Mr. Mochi," coos Grace, soothing her little yippy dog with gentle strokes while glowering at me accusingly. I swear, that glorified rat gets more attention than a baby. While the movie credits roll, Wayne stands up in the still-darkened room, Grace following suit. She murmurs to Mochi, "Come on, sweetie, we've got a speech to make."

On the dais, Wayne and Grace give off the same unmistakable vibe of success that Baba does. The Cheng power gene obviously skipped over me, or, more likely, ran out because so much success got concentrated in my half-siblings. Wayne is Mr. I-Graduated-Cum-Laude-from-Princeton. You can't pick up a newspaper without reading about some new deal his venture capital company in San Francisco is brokering in Asia. And Grace's hop, skip, and a jump from Princeton landed her in New York, where she found out she could brag and get paid for it. So now she's the head of her own public relations agency.

Naturally, Wayne takes the microphone first, establishing himself as The Eldest Son, a chip off the gold block. "It's hard to believe that my father is seventy tonight, when he's got the energy of a man half his age. I'm sure all of you know what I'm talking about. His midnight phone calls. Three a.m. e-mails. And multi-tasking abilities." Wayne waits a beat for the next photograph, this one of Baba sitting on an exercise ball in his office, instead of a chair. "The Ethan Cheng Way: why not work and work out at the same time?"

The businesspeople laugh appreciatively. I sweat profusely. I can't remember a single word of my toast. Call me the ultimate case study for the should have, would have, could have chapter in Baba's best-selling book, *The Ethan Cheng Way: From Rags to Richest*. I *should* have practiced my toast more. I *would* have if I hadn't been dueling this dress. I *could* have been more prepared if I were a Cheng cookie cutter kid. But I'm not.

Brevity is not Wayne's problem. His history lecture takes us back to the sixties, when Baba did research for Bell Labs, then moved to Hong Kong against the advice of his colleagues — "No one's going to want to use a mobile phone" — to start his own wireless company. "Naturally, *my* mom's family bankrolled that endeavor," Wayne says, shooting a look at *my* mom, the beneficiary of that endeavor. "We should all be so lucky to look and act half his age. I suppose we all could if we had a beautiful Betty at our side, too."

On the face of it, Wayne's comment sounds innocent enough, but when he says, *"Mei-Mei"* — little sister — and hands the microphone to Grace, I see the look they exchange. The one that says, *Oooh, nice dig*.

Grace's speech is all "we" this and "we" that, making it clear with laughing glances at Wayne that the "we" she's talking about is her and her big brother. "We" were the original beta testers for The Ethan Cheng Way. "We" were forced to be nothing less than excellent. "We" are such wonderful, accomplished, envy-worthy offspring.

I don't know about the rest of the crowd, but I'm feeling a

wee bit exhausted. Once upon a time, I thought being the off-spring of Ethan Cheng guaranteed my place in paradise, too. Who knew that when I rang the bell at the New York Stock Exchange five years ago to start the trading of DiaComm, my life would change so much I'd give anything for a redo?

I'm not proud of it, but at first I gorged on everybody's attention: "Who wants to see my new house, new yacht, new plane?" Age was the only friend from the pre-Initial Public Offering days who had the nerve to tell me I was bragging.

I should have listened.

My perfect starshine luster lasted three months. After Christmas break, everyone in fifth grade was comparing and contrasting their holiday haul, and I blurted out about my gift, a recording studio — just what every girl of ten wants, right? That's when I overheard the derisive laughter and saw Age's pitying told-you-so gaze and belatedly understood his warnings: my classmates didn't like me; they liked my parents' toys. So when Mama transferred me to Viewridge Prep, the best private school in Seattle, I vanished happily, not knowing that however much old and new money surrounded me, Age would be the one person who accepted me, no matter which side of the decimal point I was on.

Too soon, the audience applauds, and Baba nods approvingly at the Original Cheng Children. I stay seated until Mama's meaningful look pierces me from across the table: *Don't shame me.*

On my approach to the dais, I realize that — oh, God — the crowd of two hundred people might as well have supersized into an audience of two thousand. Even though I want to cry now, even though my cheeks ache from grinning at these people, most of whom I don't know, I smile like a good daughter, a good hostess, a good sport. After all, in my family, "face" is everything — how people perceive you, how you act in public. Who would have known that "saving face" would mean sacrificing the girl behind it?

Back at our table, the way Grace rolls her eyes at Wayne, she might as well gloat out loud, *And she calls herself a Cheng?* I knew Syrah couldn't do it.

All around the tang, gazes drop faster than stock prices on a bad-news day. I clear my throat, the sound amplifying horribly in the hall, and spot a familiar army green jacket outside the far window. A red beanie waves at me from above everyone's heads. Age.

Just like that, I remember how Age, my toasting muse, quoted Baba to me the other day. With more fervor than any true Ethan Cheng devotee, I cite that quote now: "As my dad wrote, 'You cannot fail if you have good people at your side.' There's nothing more important in this world than friends. True friends." As Mama makes her way up the stage to me, I look around the hall in my best confident Cheng impression. "Thanks to all of you, the good people at my father's side."

Applause echoes in the tang. Who cares if people are clapping because I've finally said something, or if they agree with what I've said? Next to me, Mama snakes her arm around my waist, and I notice that Wayne and Grace are smiling, too, like we're one big happy Cheng clan. Holding two champagne glasses, Baba takes the stairs nimbly to the stage.

"Thank you, everyone," Baba says. "As you may know, the Lunar New Year is the most important holiday in the Chinese year. Families unite to give thanks together. So Syrah is on the right track, but you're more than friends. You're family." Baba contemplates his champagne glass. "The Year of the Dog is supposed to be one of frivolity and leisure, which is how I'm going to be enjoying my retirement." He grins at the stunned crowd. "Happy New Year!"

Just like Wayne and Grace, and everyone else at this party, I gape at Baba. The only person who doesn't look shocked is Mama. When Baba drops one arm around Mama's shoulders and the other around mine, cold resentment settles on Wayne's and Grace's faces. Even as they lift their champagne flutes along with everyone else in the hall, I can feel the anger behind their stiff smiles as they stare at me and Mama, the two interlopers in their family. I could be three or ten or thirteen again, knowing then as I do now that I'll never be able to break into their inner circle.

Age, standing in front of the window, gives me the thumbs-up sign. He inclines his head toward the garden before disappearing. Like I always do, I push away the hurt (The Ethan Cheng Way: focus on what you can change; change your focus from what you cannot). My inner circle is waiting outside.

4

B ill!" says Baba, clasping the hand of the one CEO whose face is in the news more than his own. This only goes to show that while Baba may consider everyone here tonight family, some relatives are more important than others.

While Mama works the crowd at another table, slimy Dr. Martin oozes over to ours, resting one hand on Grace's bare shoulder instead of mine. "Grace, Wayne," he says.

I take that reprieve as a sign to make my second break for freedom of the evening.

Once outside, I breathe in the cold, fresh air, and hurry along the garden path to my art studio, where Age and I usually hang out. My heel catches on one of the inlaid pebbles in the path. That awful boneless sensation of falling, the same toppling, out-of-control feeling that ended with me blowing out my knee, pulls me to the ground in an all-too-familiar way until Age darts out of the thick shadows to catch me.

I stifle a scream. "Geez, Age! I swear, you must have been a ninja in one of your lives."

"Call me Zorro-guchi, the only Mexican ninja in the world." Letting go of my arms, Age strikes a kung fu pose in front of the old pine tree and a small grove of bamboos.

If my mom were here, she'd scan Age from his perpetually mussed dark brown hair ("That's what a twelve-dollar haircut does for you") to his chipped front tooth ("You really ought to consider cosmetic dentistry") and his oversized army green snowboarding jacket ("That *better* not be how Syrah dressed when she used to snowboard").

But Mama's not here. I grin at my savior in jeans so indigo blue they're black and say, "You made it."

"You think I'd let you enjoy all this fun by yourself?"

I make a face before glancing cautiously over my shoulder in case an overeager event planner is stalking me again.

"That good?" Age asks, grinning.

"That bad. You missed tonight's entertainment. Me."

As I give him the gory details of my toast, we make our way down a covered zigzagging corridor and through a courtyard. "So, Zorrito, how was Alpental?"

"Pretty good," Age says, kicking a pinecone off the path. "I landed a backside seven."

I'm not sure what shocks me more: that Age, who's normally so laid back about his feats on snow, is telling me this, or that he nailed a double rotation trick when pre-Accident, neither of us could even throw down a backside five. A light wind blows through the trees. I pick up the pace, worrying about how far I've fallen behind Age in snowboarding.

"That's so great, Age."

"Yeah, you should've been there." Age's eyes dip toward my knee. "You sure your surgeon said you were up for snow-boarding?"

I can almost ignore the throb in my knee as we cross a hump-backed bridge. Ignoring my own doubt is harder because the thought of launching myself off a twenty-foot cliff into air with nothing but a board under my feet makes me equal parts eager and nauseous.

But a good Cheng never admits fear. "Yeah, Dr. Bradford told me" — I deepen my voice — "'Go snowboard, young woman.'"

Age doesn't answer. He doesn't even laugh.

Silence laden with hidden meaning stretches between us; only I know how to decipher it. Age can see straight through to my self-doubt. "So when are you going to ride?" Age notices me shivering and shrugs out of his jacket. "Here."

"No, I'm fine," I protest, but Age looks at me like I'm an id-iot and spreads his hands out so there's no missing the fleece pullover he's wearing.

"Thanks," I tell him, and take his jacket. "Actually, I was feel-ing a tad naked."

That's when I notice that Age is looking at me as if he's never seen so much of me before. Can I blame him? Frankly, I haven't seen so much of myself in public before either. I nes-tle into his cocoon of a coat, wishing that I were hiding in my usual jeans and T-shirt. Or better yet, in my own oversized, an-drogynous snowboarding pants.

"That bad?" I ask.

"Oh, yeah."

But the way Age says it, like I look that ba-aad, makes me echo: *oh, yeah.*

Geez, where did *that* thought come from? Probably from the same brain-dead part of me that fell for Jared Johanson at my summer snowboarding camp. I duck my head so Age doesn't catch me blushing and keep walking through the doorway that leads into a pavilion overlooking the pond.

I breathe in deeply, wishing my ever-alert symbolism-detector had warned me that Jared was a wolf in snowboarder's clothing. To be talk-show truthful, all the signs were there. I just didn't want to admit to myself that Jared only wanted me to introduce him to my bank account. I mean, like my roommates at camp gloated when they thought I was asleep, "Guess being loaded can make anyone look good."

A thousand firecrackers stitched together on a celebration string pop loudly, just the way they have for hundreds of years to scare off bad luck. *You're seven months too late, boys.* My knee twinges in agreement.

"What's going on?" asks Age.

At first, I meet his eyes and then drop my gaze, knowing that for the last couple of weeks he's known that I felt close to teetering off Gold Mountain, wondering wildly now if Age is finally asking me about Jared. But how would he know about him? Age couldn't afford the snowboard camp, let alone the back-to-back-to-back sessions I attended, and I've never talked about how Jared dumped me. Not with anyone. A ball of red streaks across the sky before exploding, and I deliberately misread Age's question.

"Phase Three in Mama's plans," I say. "A little fireworks action between the shark fin soup and the oysters."

"I meant —"

Luckily, that's when Meghan and her ever-present walkie-talkie head our way. She's my perfect excuse, one that I grab as if it were a leash, not letting it get away.

"Come on," I urge Age, as scarlet and gold sparkles dive into Lake Washington. He takes my hand and we run down the path, me on the balls of my feet so that my spiked heels don't hook any stray pebbles.

A cheer rises from the great courtyard outside the tang where the guests are now gathered to watch the fireworks. Another whiz of green bursts overhead, as Age and I cross under the round moon gate, that symbol of ever-lasting happiness. I cast another glance over my shoulder, but don't see Meghan any-more. She must have been paged on a more important mission than tracking down a runaway daughter.

"Up here," I tell Age, veering to the side of the building.

"Where?" While he's barely breathing hard, my forehead is beaded with sweat. I assure myself, it's not because I'm out of shape; I'm just anxious about making a speedy getaway.

"Here," I say, stopping in front of the steps outside of the pavilion, hewn right into the stone, that lead up to the moon-viewing terrace on the roof.

"You kept this from me," says Age.

He has no idea what else I've kept from him. I simply shrug and say, "A girl has to have her secrets. Maintains our air of mystery and all that." *Maintains our sanity and all that.*

As if he heard my thoughts, Age asks, "What's going on with you?"

"Gentlemen first."

"You first. Move it."

I know he wants me in front of him in case I fall. Anyway, my protests die when my heel scrapes along the uneven rockery of the first step.

On the roof, Age and I can see straight down to the barge on the lake where the master pyrotechnician flown in from China moves gracefully, like one of the black-robed *Bunraku* puppeteers who once performed in my house for some charity fundraiser. The fireworks guru leans to his right, and suddenly, there's a sharp crack. A flash of orange squiggles into the overcast night before it fans out and showers droplets of gold.

Age is focused on the sky as if that's where he wants to be, carving in and out of the sparkles, these phantom moguls. Moguls that I need to be able to skim over and call fun again.

Without taking his eyes off the fireworks, Age leans closer to me, resting his hands on the wood railing, and quotes, "'The only people for me are the ones who never yawn or say a commonplace thing, but burn, burn, burn, like fabulous yellow roman candles. . . .'"

"Who's that from?"

"Jack Kerouac. He's my man."

What I want to ask Age is, *What happens when the only person for you burns out?* And just like that, the sky goes blank with blackness, mirroring what I'm thinking, how I'm feeling. Blank is the way I feel when I think about snowboarding and flying off uncharted cliffs. The way I feel when I think about a future *without* snowboarding. The way I feel when I think about the articles parsing my "incident" in all the snowboarding magazines. A rocket blazes a shrieking path, reaching higher than any of the other fireworks before it explodes, burning a hole into the night just as Jared did through my head and heart.

The fastest way out of dwelling on Jared is dwelling on anything else. So I tell Age, "My parents probably won't let me ride, no matter what Dr. Bradford says." The loud blast of fireworks can't drown out the sigh of relief in my head; I can keep blaming my parents for stopping me from facing the slopes.

Even if Age doesn't hear my words, he knows what I'm saying because he turns to me, his dark eyes missing nothing. Not even my rationalizations. He bumps my shoulder with his.

"God, this is so stupid." Looking away, I wish Age didn't see me tearing up, because I'm scared to ride and more scared not to. "I mean, I'm not good enough to go pro anyway."

"No, you're not good enough. You're great. What did that one rep say? 'You've got potential.'"

"You're the one with potential. You just won't compete."

"Could you take a compliment for once? Look, it's not like your parents will ever know if you snowboard."

I shrug, knowing he's right. They're barely home enough to remember what I look like.

"And Bao-mu's not exactly going to follow you onto the mountain," he says with a grin.

I laugh, imagining my nanny, who's even older than Baba, picking her way through hip-deep snow. But Age has a point; Bao-mu has never spied on me the way my parents think she does, keeping tabs on all my minutes when they're away. So unless I want them to know, my parents won't have a clue if I blow off school to ride or not. If I slack off on my graduation requirements — say, those thirty hours of community service I'm supposed to have done by now or not. If I fall in love with the wrong guy or not.

"Yeah, but . . . ," I say.

"But what? Why do you need them to bless your snowboarding?" He keeps staring at me, ignoring the fireworks that flare out before dripping red down the sky. "Or are they a convenient excuse?"

I bite my bottom lip and study the night stars like I'm divining my future. How does Age do that? Eavesdrop on my secret thoughts . . . at least some of them?

"Have you ever showed them your video?" he asks me, more gently now.

"Are you kidding? The last thing I want to show my parents is my video," I tell him, shuddering to think about what Baba would say if he knew how many hours I spent over the last couple of months editing since I couldn't add any footage. See, any serious snowboarder readies a video résumé, bait to hook a sponsor. And that — being paid to ride — is the Holy Grail for everyone, including me.

"All I'm saying is maybe it's time to show them," Age says.

"Yeah. Like that would go over well."

"Your father's Ethan Cheng."

"I know I'm related to the Cheng-ulator, thank you very much."

"So negotiate with him." Age quotes my dad, "'There's nothing I like better than a worthy opponent at the negotiation table.'"

"You are so . . ."

"Wise? Insightful?" He pauses. "Worthy?"

"I was thinking, more, frustrating."

"Thank you." Age waits a beat before he continues, "Why don't you broach it with them at the World Championships? You're still going to Wicked at Whistler, aren't you?"

25

"That's the plan." As much as I complain about having Ethan Cheng, billionaire, for a father, I know there are more advantages than disadvantages to being his daughter. For one, I don't have to worry about whether my parents can afford my activities, say, snowboarding, which isn't exactly a low-cost sport. To snowboard, Age has to work part-time at a local board shop. And then there's Baba's position on Nokia's board of directors, the company sponsoring the world's biggest snowboarding competition over winter break. As chairman, he has to represent the company at Wicked in Whistler, which is why he presented me with those VIP tickets at Christmas. I tell Age, "I wish you could come."

"Another time," he says easily.

I shove my hands into his jacket pockets, feeling who-knows-how-old crumbs in the seams. When, realistically, will his "another time" come? Classical music blares from the elaborate sound system rigged up around the garden. Only my parents would ask the fireworks guru to choreograph an entire show to music that's better suited for a symphony hall.

Gratefully, I change the subject. "Ever seen fireworks set to Mozart?"

"Could be worse."

"Like how?"

"Could be country music." Age grins down at me when I laugh hard because he knows there's nothing more jarring to my ears than a country twang, ya'll hear?

See, that's another good thing about friends. They make you laugh when you want to cry.

"Anyway, I'll be helping Natalia over winter break," he says casually, but I notice how he's looking everywhere but at me.

"Natalia?" At the mention of Age's ex-girlfriend, the one who couldn't stand how one word could trigger so many of the same memories between him and me, I realize that friends can make you want to cry, after all.

"Yeah, she asked me out next week."

"She did?"

He nods. So does my ice-clad heart, adding a *See? See? I told you, you can't trust anybody.*

"We're helping out Chill," he says. "It was Natalia's idea. She was short on her community service hours."

I bet it was Natalia's idea. The way to Age's heart is through his snowboard. Hooking Age up with Chill, Burton Snowboard's program to give back to the community, is a brilliant maneuver. I can practically hear Sun-Tzu, Baba's hero who wrote *The Art of War* two thousand years ago, applauding Natalia in his grave.

"Do you want to come with us?" Age asks. "You were talking about how you haven't done squat on your own community service hours since school began."

He's wasting his breath; I'd stopped listening at "us." "Us" has always been me and Age against the world, or at least against our elementary school playground, where we bonded over being teased as the two shortest kids in third grade. Our "us" was cemented when Age's dad taught us to snowboard. "Every kid needs just one sport he's good at, and the bullies will stop harassing you," he'd intone while driving us to Snoqualmie every weekend and accompanying us on the winter ski bus every Wednesday after school. Amazingly, Mr. Rodriguez was right. The harder we rode, the more kids respected us. It was my first taste of fame.

"I didn't think you wanted to get back together with Natalia?" I ask, watching another explosion scatter gold dust in the sky.

Age pushes off the railing and faces me. "She accused me of cheating."

"What? You don't even cheat in Scrabble. So how could she think you cheated on her?"

"Not on her. On you. With her."

"Oh." I take a step away from Age. If I tell myself the truth, it had felt like he was cheating on the two of us when he was going out with Natalia. And maybe that's why I don't feel like I can tell him about Jared.

"So," he says, staring, staring, staring at me. "'Life is daring adventure, or nothing.' Helen Keller said that."

"She did?"

"She did."

I study first my feet and then the fireworks, everywhere but his toffee-brown eyes. But there it is, the are-we-or-aren't-we pause, the one I swore I'd never experience again. The last time I was in this determine-the-relationship conversation, Jared was standing opposite me, claiming that I had misread everything, that he had never planned to break up with his tall, skinny, red-headed waif of a girlfriend for short, dumpy, frumpy me.

Even if this is Age in front of me, I don't want to go to that messy space again. So what if I have to bunker forever in the crawl space between scarred and scared? I laugh like Age has told me a great joke.

"God," I say, "that's so stupid since we're just friends."

Age's expression flickers like he's been memorizing *The Ethan Cheng Way*, and has prepared for my dodging him. "Syrah —"

28

Why chance turning Age into a here-today-gone-tomorrow boyfriend who makes you cry when all you want to do is laugh like you were still perfect for each other? I become my mother, superconversationalist to the rescue, able to block unwanted intimacy with a single comment, smooth over social awkwardness with a turn of phrase.

"You guys are great together, Age," I chirp my lie to him. "She's really perfect for you."

He's silent for a moment, and then finally, gruffly, says, "We should get you back."

Even though Age is walking at my side, intent on delivering me safe and sound to the reception hall for the rest of Baba's party, I can sense the void growing between us. Here's the thing. Falling in love is a lot like landing blind: carefree and fun while you're gaining momentum, uncertain and risky when you're supposed to commit to that backward rotation, unable to see where your feet are supposed to land. Or if there's land at all. Been there, done that, not doing it again.

Still, standing at the back door of the tang, I can't take this tension accumulating between us. I shrug out of his jacket and hold it out to him, an olive branch of Gore-Tex. "How about we ride Sunday?" I ask the way "just friends" would. "My parents are leaving tomorrow."

There's a long pause before his answer: an easy shrug as if spending time with me is no big deal. "I'll call you," he says. As Age walks away, all the secrets I've tamped inside myself make me feel like I've gorged on food that's much too rich.

5

A few minutes before six thirty on Sunday morning, late according to Cheng standard time, I'm lounging in bed. There was no early-morning check-in phone call from Age yesterday. He didn't even return my calls at his work, the way he usually does when business is slow. My palms grow slick as I watch the clock. But minutes tick past six thirty, and the phone remains silent; there's no "hey, it's me" this morning either and no confirmation of our snowboarding plans.

Instead, all I hear loud and clear is my last conversation with Age — *show them your video . . . Natalia asked me out . . . life is a daring adventure.* With all these competing thoughts banging around my head, I can't ignore them for another second the way I did all day yesterday, and now, I have to shake them into my manga-slash-journal.

Authentic manga is read from the back of the book to the front, Japanese style, which is how I've sketched my journal. The panels start on the top right-hand corner of the page, sliding over to the left and then down. Across the top of the right page, I write: *Life is a daring adventure* . . . The only daring adventure I've wanted, at least since the moment snowboarding became as natural as walking for me, was to become a professional rider. A snowboard girl who's paid to ride the mountain, money I earn on my own so I'm not beholden to anybody. So meet Shiraz, my manga–alter ego, a character I created after I couldn't snowboard post-Accident. My warrior girl catches such big air off the dais that she sails on her snowboard over a bewildered Grace and Wayne. I smile to myself, tapping out the dots of water that spray off Mochi as he yanks his wet face out of a fishbowl.

On the next blank page, I print the end of the quote in tiny letters: *or nothing.* The only part of Shiraz visible on the leftmost edge is her dark hair streaking above the tail of her snowboard. Even if I don't draw the guy she's riding to, I know exactly who's waiting on the other side of the blank page. My friend for all ages.

At last, the phone rings: 6:45 a.m. I grab for the phone off my nightstand, and there it is, the familiar "Hey, it's me."

Relieved, I sink back into my pillow. "Age!"

"So eight today?" His voice is brisk, as though this is a business transaction.

"Sounds great. You doing okay? I was worried about you yesterday."

There's a long pause, and then like he can't wait to get off the phone with me, Age mutters, "I gotta run," and hangs up.

I hold the phone in my hand, forgetting to hang up, too. How am I supposed to keep Age within the no-heartbreak-zone of my heart when it's breaking my heart that he's pulling away?

o   o   o

Come ten thirty, I'm playing a game of chicken with a mountain. If you believe my father, there's one and only one way to overturn your fears, and that's to win. Who am I to say that the million people who bought his best-selling business book are wrong? So on this trail in the backcountry of Alpental, I force myself to gaze down the slope to my right. Big mistake. Blame it on being land-bound for so long, but the open bowl looks so steep, I could almost trace a straight line down to the snow-glazed evergreen trees and dead-end cliffs. All I want to do is throw myself facedown in the thin layer of fresh powder, cling to this ridgeline, and beg the mountain, *Don't break me again.*

My fear billows in front of me in the cold air like I'm Puff the Chinese Dragon. Age must hear me huffing behind him, because he calls over his shoulder as if the last day of no conversation hasn't happened, "Yo, Syrah, need some help back there, girly-girl?"

Pity or not, I'm just glad we're talking normally again. Even though I feel like I'm on the verge of hyperventilating, I bat my eyes at Age as if I'm one of those pink-outfitted, fashion-before-function girls. "You going to carry me and my gear, burly-burly man?"

"Nah, you snowboard chicks are more kick-ass than cute."

"Gee, thanks."

Like always, Age's answering grin is one hundred proof wicked, one hundred percent welcome, Natalia or no Natalia. He nails me, not with a snowball or a comeback, but with the one question I've been asking myself since we left the high-speed quad: "You sure you're up for this?"

Age's battered goggles may mask the concern in his eyes, but

I can tell from the dip of his head that he's looking at the knee I'm unconsciously massaging through layers of Gore-Tex, sweat-wicking long underwear, and neoprene brace.

I straighten quickly. "Pick up the pace, Zorrito." He doesn't budge, so I say, "Really. I can do this."

Liar, liar, snow pants on fire.

For a second, Age studies me like he's debating whether to call ski patrol to toboggan me down to the base of the mountain. Been there, done that. Time may have healed my knee, but it does little to dull the humiliation of being strapped in and carted down a mountain in front of everyone. Including Jared, the only one who knew why I had taken off by myself that morning.

Even as I trudge faster, three boarders hike wordlessly around me as though I'm nothing but one of the small clumps of powder they're kicking through. The guy bulldozing ahead in the lead is the wonder kid of Alpental with sponsors up the yin-yang for ripping mountains, half the time high. Following the Pied Pothead wasn't how I imagined my comeback moment.

My knee twinges in reproach. Or my downfall.

"Hey, that's Syrah Cheng," says one of the guys, casting a look at me over his shoulder.

Wonder Kid snickers, pulling ahead, but I can still make out his words: "Maybe we should call ski patrol now."

Age whips around. "Don't listen to them."

I nod, but the damage is done. The snowboarders may be drawing farther ahead of me, but I hear the echo of their disdain: *Call ski patrol now.* Pretty soon, all the guys, Age included, are leaving footprints, pockmarking the feathery snow.

One-two, one-two, I focus on that rhythm while plodding through the glistening snow. It's a lot more uplifting than the other chant frozen in my head: *mis-take; mis-take.*

Another sharp jab needles the back of my knee. Matadors might as well be prodding me with those barbed sticks they use to rile up bulls before their showdowns.

"Come on," I tell myself, and flip on my music, hoping a strong bass beat will rev me up and drown out my doubts, those guys' words.

Up ahead, the snowboarders splinter off, lobbing down the run that'll drop them straight back to the chairlift.

"Hey, we can take Snake Dance, too," Age says.

I nod my head toward our regular run. "No way, let's go."

After fifteen more minutes of power-trudging, we finally reach our sweet spot, just past P-Pass, so named because it's where guys pull over to do their business up here. Let's face it, guys have superior equipment when it comes to outdoor relief.

"Untouched pow," I say, pointing down to the pristine white, powdery snow on Alpental, our home mountain known for its steeps and natural terrain.

Age grins at me. "Yeah, no thanks to Little Miss Slowpoke."

"So do you think snowboarders have the same primeval instinct that makes dogs pee on every telephone pole?" I pound my chest in my best caveman impression, lowering my voice: "Me here first."

"For some guys, probably," says Age, seriously. "But it's all about blank pages, isn't it?"

I nod because that's what virgin snow is: a fresh start, a beginning, a brand-new daring adventure.

"I mean, can you believe this?" Age says, getting to his feet, reverential. That's what I love about Age. This mountain is his winter home, yet the pitches and fallen trees and cliffs are always new to him. Even this season, which started late with barely any snow until recently, Age has managed to get up here at least ten times since early January. "Who needs a half-pipe? I wish Mobey'd get that."

"He's been on your case again?" I ask, remembering all the times that Mobey's badgered Age about making his own video, schmoozing a sponsor, becoming a Someone on Snow.

"He just doesn't get that, for me, snowboarding needs to be pure. You know what I'm saying?" Age breathes out heavily. "Who cares if you're a tenth of a second faster than the next guy or get paid to ride?"

"So you say until I beat you."

Age bumps his shoulder against mine. "You wish, Gidget."

"You're good enough to go pro, that's all."

"As if I could really travel around the world now. Who'd take care of the ankle biters? My dad?" Age snorts, not that I blame him. Ever since Age's mother died two years ago, his dad has been a workaholic recluse, outsourcing all his parenting duties to Age.

But Age has a point. Serious snowboarders either go the pro route, getting paid to ride and eventually starring in edgy snowboarding movies that are shot around the world. Or they hop on the Olympics track, the way Jared is doing, and go for gold. Either way, it means making a full-time commitment to snowboarding.

"Besides," says Age, staring at me, "if it's all about racing, I'd rather take you on."

Unless I'm mistaken, there it is again, the define-the-

35

relationship moment that most girls in my class seem to hurtle toward. Just as avalanche patrol can read the conditions of any mountain, I know the slide paths of my heart intimately — the chutes created by my parents' everlasting absences, the run-off gully carved by Jared.

"Come on," I say, quickly buckling into my snowboard. "Before anyone else gets here."

Age holds his hand out to me, helping me to my feet. Standing there, looking down the mountain I once called home, all I want is to feel invincible and whole again.

"Welcome back, Cheng."

"It's good to be back."

"You can say that again." Under the ratty red beanie I gave him a couple of years ago, Age's long brown hair spikes out at odd angles. His mahogany eyes sparkle the way they do whenever he's about to do something crazy on the mountain. For a moment, I let myself linger in his gaze, because that look, more than the big view and the mountain air that smells like Christmas, makes me believe I'm really back after a too-long absence.

I'm back . . . but am I still bad?

"Okay," I say. Another deep breath and I drop into the bowl, right foot forward. My board slides easily down the steep slope, picking up speed way too fast. My breathing quickens, and I carve hard into the powder, swerving to slow down. Over the *whoosh*ing of my board on snow, I hear Age: "Yeah, baby!"

Pressing first forward on my toes and then rocking back to my heels, I'm relieved that my muscles remember what to do, even if my courage seems to be stuck in reverse. Age darts into the trees, sliding down a fallen log, crusted with snow. I follow. Not five feet ahead of me is a rock topped in an afro of snow.

Perfect to ollie over. The trick to a good ollie is to get as much snap as you can from the snowboard tail. I lean into my left leg and pop it up, lifting both knees high over the rock, and then sink into my landing with my arms out.

"Smooth," calls Age. He straight-lines down the slope, flying past me to a huge snow-crowned boulder. He jumps over it, twisting his body effortlessly.

"Nice," I say, blowing out an admiring whistle. Age has always made it look so easy. There's a real prettiness and elegance to his riding, though he'd blush if I ever described it in those terms. The way he rides, confident and smooth, leaving a few strokes, reminds me of the priceless Chinese paintings and scrolls my parents collect. Three deft brushstrokes, and a crane miraculously takes shape, floating off a canvas of white just like Age is doing now.

At the last second, when I approach the same car-sized boulder, one I would have flown over before the Accident, I veer to the right, take an easy chute down instead and skid to a stop. Shivering in my jacket, I wonder if I'll ever look or feel like I belong to the snow again. I make a big show of cranking up my tunes as though that's the reason why I stopped.

Age is waiting for me, but he doesn't pull any of that "you can do it" pep talk or "what're you scared about?" crap. He knows that there's nothing worse than having second helpings of pity when you're already stuffed from feeling bad about yourself. After his mom died, he'd stare anyone down who made the mistake of labeling him as "that poor motherless boy."

"So you think this place is haunted?" he asks now.

"Yeah, right," I say, rolling my eyes. Last year, a skier got lost around here, didn't carry any supplies, and was riding by himself.

Three strikes, and Mother Nature threw him out. Just the way I should have been hurt more seriously up at Whistler. Now, even with the avalanche transceiver and shovel in my backpack, a small part of me questions why *I'm* out here, tempting the mountains again.

Age breaks into creepy moaning right when the wind rasps as if it's the dead dilettante's last breath. We look at each other, nervous as eleven-year-olds, when we used to scare each other with grisly stories about snapping ropes and other gondola disasters. That was before I knew I could break without warning, too.

Suddenly, Age takes off. *Chase me,* his riding practically dares, but he's going fast, too fast, and I lose him in the trees.

Another wind rattles the evergreens, sending shivers through the boughs and freezing my exposed cheeks. *Ghosts are on the move,* I can almost hear Bao-mu mutter. She is so Chinese-superstitious; if I took her seriously, Age and I would be cursed for the next couple of lifetimes since we've disturbed so many trees that supposedly harbor souls of the dead.

A gust blows snow off the upper limbs of a tree, showering me in feathery dust. I hate to admit it. The branches aren't the only things quivering on this mountain. I used to think that a little nervousness while riding was a good thing. It means you're pushing yourself. But as sweat collects between my breasts and I stare at all the trees I need to weave around, I know I've traversed beyond "scared" and am well into uncharted "scared shit-less" territory.

A moment later, my walkie-talkie crackles in my chest pocket, and I pull it out of the boy's jacket I'm wearing.

"Syrah, easy ten-foot drop ahead. Do not speed-check," Age says. "Do you copy? Do not speed-check."

I can do this, I assure myself. Petrified or not, I have to go down this line and claim it as mine again. My palms are slick inside my mittens. There are so many butterflies in my stomach, I half-expect to levitate. The thing is, if I can't fly on these mountains, then there is no place on Earth where I am completely free. Where I can be me. Or at least the me I used to be.

Resolved, I point my board toward the cliff, but my memory does a Benedict Arnold and auto-replays the Accident. The twang I felt when my ACL tore. The pain that even two doses of Percocet couldn't dull after my surgery. The way I had to lie on my back for two weeks, strapped in a torture device that bent and straightened my right leg.

I narrow my eyes in concentration, trying to ignore the wind that's blowing me toward another accident. The snow-bent trees around me look skeletal enough to be ghosts incarnate. "Do not speed-check," I hear Age warn again over the walkie-talkie. But I can't help it. I can't get hurt again.

And that's the problem with snowboarding. You need to commit to your speed, to your jump, when you ride. Hesitation costs you on the slopes. That moment of doubt, that deliberate braking, is how accidents happen. I'm too slow going into the jump. When I should be floating in air, challenging gravity, I'm flailing and dropping to the earth way too soon.

"Watch out, Syrah!" Age yells, I barely make out his army green jacket below as he scrambles to get out of my accident-in-progress.

God, how much is it going to hurt this time? I wonder before I hit the ground. Without any time to flatten out my snowboard, I catch an edge and lose my balance. I slam hard on my shoulder, tumble a couple of times, a human snowball. Finally, I stop, face up. Branches from the surrounding trees are shaking snow onto my face, ghosts trembling with laughter.

Who am I kidding? I don't belong here any more than that dead dilettante did.

The cold seeps through my beanie, chilling my neck. All I can think is, *Oh, my God, did I hurt my knee again?* But it's not my knee that's throbbing. It's my shoulder. And my pride.

"You okay?" Age asks, hovering over me, wearing his concern the way most guys wear their machismo.

No, I'm not okay. The sad truth is I don't know if I'll ever be okay. At least not the okay I was before my accident. Even as I touch my tender shoulder and force out an "I'll live" and sit up, I realize the most dangerous falls aren't the ones involving cliffs, missed jumps, snowboards and surgeries. They're the ones where your heart free-falls in disappointment.

6

Like a good little Cheng-ling, I get to my feet, ready for round two. My shoulder could be sprouting a second head, it's throbbing that much. But I brush the snow off my limbs, trying not to wince when I rotate my arm gingerly, and nod at Age as if I'm still one tough snowboard chick.

"Race you to the bottom," I tell him.

"You are *loco*," he says, shaking his head at me.

Age is right. I'm crazy to be up here, but not crazy enough to speed down, heedless, the way I would have once.

By the time we reach the chairlifts, the lines are so long we could be at Disneyland, except everyone's sporting parkas and snow pants. The hardcore riders are clustered around the vendors' booths, not to learn about the latest and greatest snowboards, goggles, and bindings, but to score free product and the ultimate prize, a coveted sponsorship.

"Hey, there's the crew," says Age, pointing toward the fray around RhamiWare.

B.J. is easy to spot, all long neck and longer arms, and as

usual, he's engaged in a lengthy conversation with the rep who once upon a time thought I had what it took to be a Snowboard Girl. Next to B.J. is Mobey, better known as Mobey Dick for obvious reasons. Some study reported that guys think about sex once every fifteen seconds. If the researchers had included Mobey, I swear he would have knocked a good three to four seconds off that average.

After my dismal performance, the last thing I need to hear is how the guys are "this close" to getting sponsored. Before I can make a break for the bathroom, B.J. lopes over with Mobey trotting beside him to keep up.

Apparently, Mobey's got more than sex on his brain this morning because the first thing out of his mouth is, "Let's session a kicker."

I lift an eyebrow at him, since it'll take a couple of hours to build the ramp, even with four of us shoveling. "On a powder day?"

"Some of us need to add footage to our video résumés," Mobey retorts. He spreads his thumbs and forefingers to frame the mountain behind the guys, leaving me out of his Kodak moment. "You in, Age? Syrah can shoot us, right?"

Before the Accident, I would never have been the de facto videographer. "Yo, Cro-Magnon Boy," I say, "Age doesn't need a video, and I'm riding today."

Mobey drops his hands, now assuming what our crew calls his Only Child negotiating stance. With his chin sticking out obstinately, his mom usually buckles. "You are?"

"That would be why I'm wearing my gear." Witness the superwoman effect of wearing snowboarding gear. If only I could bottle up this all-powerful feeling, and stomp on anything and anyone in my snowboarding way. Too bad a girl just can't go through life clomping around in her snow boots.

"Why do you need to add to your video?" Mobey asks belligerently, his tone signaling that I'm just moments away from his usual riff on why my wanting to be sponsored is basically stealing food out of a needier person's mouth — say, his.

"I'll shoot you guys," says Age, intervening.

While B.J. and Mobey compete in their usual testosterone game of one-upping each other about the sick tricks they're going to pull, Age lifts my goggles so he can look me in the eye. He says softly, "It's your first day back. It took you almost six weeks to learn how to walk without a limp. So cut yourself some slack today, will you?"

Whatever Age says, I choked on the mountain. I nod, *yeah, yeah,* but he won't let me go until I say the words out loud.

"Get a room, you guys," says Mobey.

Guiltily, Age drops his hands off my arms, and I step back from him. Without another word, I head toward the bathrooms down the hill. My legs are moving so slowly, I might as well have gained fifty pounds. Mama is right about one thing. Cellulite is impossible to lose, especially when it's dimpling your self-confidence.

My skip to the loo is stopped by the reigning empress of Viewridge, Chelsea Dillinger. Banish all those images of blue-eyed, size-nothing baby dolls who rule the high school roosts in movies. Chelsea is Barbie after bingeing on a one-month ice-cream diet. The heiress to an old-time Seattle real estate empire, her last name might as well be tattooed across her plump shoulders the same way it's chiseled onto the new library downtown.

"Syrah Cheng!" Chelsea sings down the line of girls waiting in the hall for the bathroom. Her brown ringlets bounce, she's waving at me so hard. The curious and the envious turn around as I clomp down the stairs.

God, what does she want now?

I kick myself for not keeping my goggles on to conceal my face. Too late, too late. Girls stare at me with that mixture of awe and envy I've been used to seeing since Baba hit the Big Time. Someone in front of me says, "Oh, my God, do you know who that is?" A meaningful pause, then: "Ethan Cheng's kid," my father's name filling in all the blanks about me. "I heard her dad makes her ride with bodyguards ever since that avalanche."

If it weren't for needing a toilet desperately, I'd have run for the great outdoors and escaped these stares, especially Chelsea's hungry one. For a time, I hoped that Chelsea and I would be friends, she being the one person who might actually understand my life and all. There just aren't many people who'd commiserate when you complain about your mother's couture shopping spree for your school wardrobe because you'd rather dress in Old Navy than Narcisco. Or who understands that having parents perpetually missing on business is better in theory than reality.

That was before I knew Chelsea wanted to display me — and all nine zeros of my dad's net worth — the way her father mounts deer and moose heads in his living room: a trophy for all to admire.

Naturally, Chelsea gives up her place in front of the bathroom door to slum it in back with me. "Your dad's birthday party was so great, Syrah!" she says, standing so close to me, I swear, her perfume seeps into my pores. "That *Attila* screening was so cool, didn't you think?"

"I missed it," I grit out quietly.

"Really?" says Chelsea, who obviously didn't miss me in my home theater. She grips my arm as if confiding a girlfriends-only secret, but the just-you-and-me effect is blown when she booms not-so-secretively, "Well, I was telling my dad, *Attila* is so cool, he ought to take all the people at Dillinger Development to see it."

A dull ache centers in my abs, too low to be mistaken for indigestion from Chelsea's company. I look around for anyone I could beg a Midol off of, but all the girls are bent together in the kind of static electricity that only gossip generates. Just once, I'd love to be on the gossiping side with girlfriends instead of the one being gossiped about. While Chelsea does her "my dad this" and "my mom that" monologue, I keep my eyes on the flyers tacked to the scuffed wall. That's when I spot the snowboarder on the Wicked in Whistler poster, catching such big air, helium must run through his veins. There is no mistaking Jared's sultry come-mess-with-me stare.

"Omigod," I murmur. Damn it, the only reason why I was excited to go to Wicked in Whistler was because I had checked and Jared wasn't listed, which meant that I wouldn't run the risk of bumping into him.

"I know — I'd compete if he was the grand prize," says Chelsea.

Me, too, I echo, and then chagrined, shift my gaze to a different flyer, because I can't stand looking at Jared and remembering how he made me believe that I had jumped off Whistler and landed in Wonderland. The counselor assigned to my group of four girls wrote us off as no-ops: girls with no promise, no potential, no opportunities. He might as well have been a babysitter for all the tricks that he taught us. Then a snowboarder flew over our heads as we iced our butts on the side of the mountain. And just like that, Jared rescued us.

Eighteen and already pro for three years, Jared was back from filming in Europe. "Come on, dude," he told the counselor. His hair, sandy brown, glinted in the sun. "They're here to ride, not catch rays." And he looked at me. "Follow me."

None of us needed more than that invitation, even as he took us down a fifteen-foot drop that came out of nowhere. How could I have been scared of falling when I was already flying? No one was more surprised than I was when Jared lifted my goggles at the end of the first run and told me, "Syrah Cheng, how many kids here have the grace of a girl and the guts of a guy? One." He tapped me gently in the middle of my chest like he didn't want me ever to forget. The problem is, I learned his lesson so well, now I can't forget the teacher.

"Erik Johanson is so hot," says Chelsea, poking me with her elbow. "Don't you think?"

Erik? I look up and realize I've mistaken Jared's older brother, the five-time world champion and Olympic hopeful in boarder cross, for him. If I react that way to a poster, what would I do if I ever saw Jared in person? I shudder, grateful that the bathroom line moves me away from the Jared look-alike.

Chelsea pronounces, "You're so lucky, Syrah."

This, I have to hear, and I brave brunette envy to ask, "How's that?"

"Because," Chelsea says, her voice flattening to a single note: DU-UUUH!? "I mean, my parents would never buy a chalet in Whistler just because I was into snowboarding."

That almost makes me laugh out loud since the chalet in Whistler had everything to do with portfolio diversification, not Syrah gratification. As soon as Baba realized the Winter Olympics were going to be staged in Vancouver and Whistler, he predicted skyrocketing real estate values. Within a day, Mama pinpointed all the prime neighborhoods. Three months after that, Chalet Cheng was signed, sealed, and decorated.

"Trust me, they didn't buy it for me." My knee twinges as I take another step forward. *Or my snowboarding.*

"Horstman or Pinnacle Ridge?" asks Chelsea relentlessly.

Maybe I can manage another run without using the facilities, after all. As I'm about to escape this inquisition about my parents' assets, Lillian Fujimoro bounds out of the bathroom, so peppy she must have springs in her snow boots. Instantly, she breaks into girlfriendese, where every word escalates with shrill excitement. "Chelsea! No way!! You didn't tell me you were riding today!!!"

Chelsea cocks her head to one side as though she can't quite place the girl, the newest addition to The Six-Pack, filling in for Kirsten Anderson whose parents pulled her out of Viewridge for the personally enriching experience of attending a "boarding school" in Italy. Translation: Kirsten was so drugged out, her parents imprisoned her in one of those exclusive boot camps for the young and the rudderless.

Right now, Chelsea's deliberate coldness reminds me painfully of Wayne and his perpetual Syrah-amnesia. I feel sorry for

Lillian, even though she's put herself in this position of always being the seeker. What's worse, I wonder, being a social climber on Chelsea's ladder or being social quarry for her wall of fame?

"Hey, Lillian," I say.

"Syrah!"

I earn a fluorescent smile, and wish Bao-mu were here to order Lillian to turn down her studied chipperness a couple of watts.

Chelsea pulls off her gloves to run her fingers through her hair and then ticks off on her manicured nails. "I would've thought you'd be helping neglected children. Figuring out a solution for world peace. Or snagging a Pulitzer."

Lillian flushes. One does have to wonder if having no girl-friends is better than having destructive ones, the kind who pick, pick, pick at you until you feel as worthless as they want you to believe you are. But then again, Lillian's smart enough to have calculated the price of admission into The Six-Pack. Too steep for me.

"Syrah was just telling me all about her place in Whistler," says Chelsea.

I was?

"We're going to get together there for winter break," she says.

We are?

"Are you taking your jet?" Chelsea asks, her eyes glazing over like she's already en route with me to Chalet Cheng. "God, I wish we had one. It'd make traveling so much more convenient."

Too convenient, I want to tell her. There's no obstacle to make you think twice about picking up and leaving again and again. Instead, I grasp for any other topic but me, my parents, and their plane to interrupt the rich-want-to-get-richer fantasy unfolding rapidly in Chelsea's head. Thankfully, I must have good bathroom karma because just then a stall door swings open. I swear to God, Chelsea is a half-step into my stall before I sigh. "A little privacy?"

The last thing I see before I close the door are the girls behind Chelsea running their eyes down my body, U-turning at my hips.

Halfway through unsnapping and unzipping, I hear one of them ask in sotto voce, "Like, why would she wear boys' clothes when she can buy anything she wants?"

Part of me wants to tell Judgmental Girl, "Um, see how these metal walls don't go all the way up to the ceiling or down to the floor? Not soundproof." The Shiraz in me wants to demand, "So you mean, why aren't I Miss Pretty in Hot Pink like the rest of you? Because I'm not trolling for boys when I ride."

Instead, I tell the truth, "Because I can move in guys' stuff."

In the uncomfortable silence that now hangs in the bathroom, I lower my goggles and pull my beanie down, hoping that I'll be unrecognizable again. I hustle away from the sink and back to the girl-free zone of my snowboarding crew, but the guys are hovering around Natalia, all pretty in her pale pink snow pants and silver body-hugging jacket.

"Hey, look who said she'd video us," says Mobey, his arm slung around Natalia, comfortable in a way that he's never been with me.

Yeah, look who's not meeting my eyes, I want to snap back when Age studies the RhamiWare booth as if he's seriously reconsidering a professional career in snowboarding. Reality is, he's caught between Natalia and me in an emotional tug-of-war I didn't realize I was participating in until now.

Before I can help myself, I ask Natalia, "I didn't think you rode?" I mean, this is the same girl who was so scared of heights, she made the chair lift operator stop when we were just five feet above the ground the one time she came snowboarding with us last spring.

"The way you guys went on and on about snowboarding, I didn't want to miss out anymore," Natalia says, shrugging like she and her thick fluttering eyelashes don't have a clue how crazy-jealous she's making me. "I spent so much time practicing indoors over Christmas break at Mini Mountain, the guys there kicked me off the carpet and told me to get on the real thing." She grins impishly at Age and grabs his arm with her pink-mittened hand. "So I'll just hang on tight during the chairlift."

While I follow in Natalia's footsteps to wait in line, it dawns on me that during my exile, a new Queen of the Mountain has been crowned.

7

Even when it's back to just me and Age on the drive home, Natalia might as well be wedged in the seat between us, his truck feels that overcrowded.

"So," says Age as we finally reach the gate separating The House of Cheng from The Rest of the World. "Used, bruised, and abused."

I glance at him quickly, wondering if he's talking about me post-Jared, but he starts to reach for my banged-up shoulder, thinks better of it, and lifts his own instead.

"How's it feel?" he asks.

"Like a couple of sumo wrestlers have been slam-dancing with it."

"You're officially back." He grins crookedly before punching in the security code to open the gate.

"Yeah." As soon as Age pulls up to the garage, I duck out of his beater of a pickup, more rusted than red. My knee nearly buckles when I put my weight on it. How can I be pushing sixteen and falling apart? I smile automatically at Age when he hands me my snowboard and murmur a quick "thanks," watching him drive off hurriedly like he can't wait to escape our uncomfortable silence, too.

As I limp inside the garage to put away my board, I rail to myself: *God, why did I go to camp? Why did I tear my ligament?* Every step from the garage to the kitchen jolts my knee, and I need to ice it. My heart, it's already numb.

Finally, up in my bedroom, I collapse onto the floor, wriggle out of my snow pants, and strip off the neoprene brace that I picked up at a sporting goods store. No wonder Dr. Bradford said that this cheap thing was only a placebo.

What this girl needs is more than a placebo, and I scoot back on my bottom — no, not the most graceful locomotion method, but I'm too tired to stand — over to my desk, where I place an SOS call to Dr. Bradford's answering service: "Hello, this is Syrah Cheng." Within a minute of throwing around the Cheng name, Dr. Bradford himself is on the line, never mind that it's a Saturday.

"Syrah, how are your parents?" he asks in his growly voice.

"Great. It's me that's not doing so wonderful," I say, rubbing a finger along the largest of my scars, still angry red.

"Did you reinjure your knee?"

"I went snowboarding today, and you're right. This neoprene brace doesn't do anything. Dr. Bradford, I really need a custom one." Even as I cringe at how I sound every bit the spoiled brat everyone thinks I am, I can't stop begging. "A kid at my school has one and he skis with his all the time."

The doc doesn't answer so I prepare to launch a second

assault, but then he says, "One, you don't need any brace. Your knee is ninety percent back to normal, as strong as it's going to get with your hamstring graft. I don't think I need to remind you why I recommended doing a patella graft instead."

"No." God, why did I let Mama override that graft, which leaves a longer scar but stronger knee, in favor of the hamstring graft because it heals prettier?

"And two, braces are just crutches. Before long, you'll think you need it for everything."

"It'd just be for snowboarding," I say, wincing at the whine in my voice. I swallow and try to channel all the Ethan Cheng control I can. "I just need a little extra stability for my landings."

"Syrah, I'm sorry —"

"But it's not the same. Nothing is the same."

"Nothing is ever the same."

Thank you, Dr. Bradford, but right now, I don't need a primer on Zen Buddhism and how the one and only thing that doesn't change about life is that everything changes.

He continues, "So I'm telling you, braces are more psychological than physiological support. Keep doing your exercises. Other muscles will compensate for your compromised hamstring."

Something tells me that a billion lunges and leg presses and squats won't get me back to where I left off. With a "thanks" so polite that Mama would have approved, I hang up the phone and drag myself to the bath, thinking I can multitask: ice my knee while I soak my muscles and brood.

As the water runs in the bathtub, I step on the scale. One bit of good news — I lost a pound. Even so, when I catch my reflection in the mirror, I yank my eyes away so I don't linger on my stomach or my thighs. Even with my eyes closed, I can see the bruise already mottling my shoulder, as dark and tender and reproachful as the realization that you can't return to the good old days no matter how hard you try.

8

With the oasis of winter break shimmering on the horizon, the teachers are cramming in as much work as they possibly can in these last two weeks. Especially Mr. Delbene. My journalism teacher's lecture today not only defies all the normal laws governing time, space, and speed, but it's building suspiciously to a Big Project.

"So I was thinking," says Mr. Delbene, rocking up and down on his Birkenstocks, one foot stockinged in red, the other white. "What is my legacy going to be?" Pinching the last issue of our newspaper between thumb and forefinger like it's a dirty diaper, he asks, "Why isn't anyone reading this?"

Easy. Can you say, *Cure for insomnia*? When the *Wall Street Journal* reads like a gossip tabloid compared to your high school newspaper, something's terribly wrong. I glance around to see if the rest of the class have caught the undeniable stench of impending homework, but no one's paying attention. That is, no one's paying attention to Mr. Delbene. They're all occupied with messaging each other about hooking up at Sun Valley or the Bahamas or wherever they're heading for winter break. I'd be right with them except the guy I'd be messaging hasn't called me once since we went riding on Sunday. Obviously, Age is being quarantined, Dr. Natalia's orders.

Thankfully, Mr. Delbene has terrible eyesight and an even worse sense of direction in his lectures. So while everyone else is messaging and I'm manga-ing, he veers off mid-thought, this time meandering away from his personal contribution to history and over to history at large. "Amazing, isn't it," he mutters, "that the fifteenth century Ming Dynasty nurtured the fine arts, just like the Medicis in Renaissance Italy?"

Mr. Delbene's monotone lulls me into a meditative state, and I start sketching Shiraz at Wicked in Whistler. An unexpected, excited rise in Mr. Delbene's voice bumps into my musings. He pulls away from the whiteboard, not noticing that his pilled-up cream sweater is speckled with blue and red dry marker.

"If you could change anything in our paper, what would it be?" Mr. Delbene's hands circle in big arcs like he's swatting away the confused fog spilling out of our heads.

Around me, a couple of kids finally get an inkling that Mr. Delbene is about to load us down with a project over winter break. I angle my head thoughtfully as if I'm considering his question in case his eyes land on me.

"Where should we focus?" He strides to the front row, the poor sacrificial lambs. Standing before Alexander, whose grandfather was a football jock way back when, Mr. Delbene demands, "Kill sports coverage?"

Whether we're fourth generation old money (whose grand-fossils made their fortunes chopping down trees in the name of timber) or new money (whose parents made a killing in the tech boom), we're all short-changed on ideas.

"Randy." Mr. Delbene swivels suddenly to the boy on my right. "What would you do?"

"Huh?" For the last fifteen minutes, Randy's thumbs have been glued to his BlackBerry.

"Think," Mr. Delbene prompts urgently. "You've got to have some ideas." Wild-eyed the way a Tang horse would look in a losing battle, Mr. Delbene considers us one after another. "Someone in here must have some plans to turn this rag around?"

No one answers, not even Lillian, who for once is gazing out the window instead of paying attention. Mr. Delbene looks panicked, seeing his future as a senior citizen and not liking it. Oh, great. Just great. His bugged-out eyes settle on last-resort me. "Syrah?"

Usually, I keep a low profile during classroom discussions. I mean, who am I to disappoint everyone who expects me to shoot out pithy, wise, Ethan Cheng–worthy aphorisms whenever I open my mouth? Like now. Even as I try to formulate some intelligent, creative idea, Mr. Delbene drifts to the next victim as though he knows that none of my plans are going to come to anything.

"Next Tuesday," he intones with such unusual decisiveness that everyone shakes out of their pre-Valentine-winter-break haze. "Bring in at least one viable, somewhat creative, out-of-the-box idea to turn this paper around."

A few minutes after the final school bell rings, it's down to a couple of stragglers outside in the bus circle. All the buses have already left. So have the private vans and the cars of those few parents who bother to drive rather than delegate that job to the hired help. A red Mercedes rounds the circle, nearly dousing me with dirty puddle water, and I watch enviously as a sullen sophomore, mortified that his dad has picked him up, slouches down low, becoming a human iceberg. Only the top of his head is visible through the window. That kid has no idea how lucky he is that his dad showed up.

Obviously, Mama isn't picking me up the way the daily schedule left on the breakfast table informed me she would. She must have found some new store in San Francisco that she just had to scope out, and in her state of shopping nirvana extended her trip. The clouds release a rain shower, and I pull my hood over my head as if that'll hide me from the truth: the van is long gone, and I'm stuck at school.

Oh, joy, The Six-Pack are descending the staircase, two-by-two, Noah's representatives of the Proud Crowd, chosen to be saved from this great deluge. One problem: their ark is nowhere to be seen.

"You sure your dad's picking us up?" Chelsea asks Lillian, frowning because she has to (gasp!) wait in the rain.

"He's coming," says Lillian, sounding anything but sure. She bites her lower lip uncertainly and repeats, as if she needs to hear her own reassurance, "He's coming."

"Good, 'cause my hair's going to get all frizzy out here." Chelsea pats her brown curls, comforting them.

Adults-in-training, Lillian flips on her phone, and I return to my own high-tech appendage, pretending to everyone on the sidewalk that I have calls to return, messages to check. Why, this snippet of free time is a veritable godsend in my busy, important life, except that I get a direct dial to Mama and Baba's voicemail. My own is empty — just checked and still not a peep from Age.

"When does that party start again?" asks Chelsea, not caring that, one, I haven't been invited to said party, and, two, I can hear perfectly fine since she's standing no more than two feet away from me.

"At five. We've got an hour and a half," says Lillian, checking her watch. "No worries."

"So, I've been wondering, how does it feel to have" — Chelsea points a finger at Lillian — "your dad work for" — the finger aims at me now — "her dad?"

Sorry, but according to The Syrah Cheng Way, business hierarchy doesn't translate into a social one, especially not the high school variety. Even though I keep my voice mild when I tell Chelsea, "They all work for someone. My dad's accountable to all the investors," I raise one eyebrow a la Wayne when he wants to make it painfully clear to me how stupid I am. Surprise, it works on Chelsea, too. She shuts up.

The rain pounds so hard now that it bounces off the cement sidewalk to douse our feet a second time on its way down. Nice. So it's a mass girl exodus to the overhang, as we all huddle in our jackets. Seattle gets thirty-six inches of rain a year on average, but no one carries an umbrella at school ever. I suppose you get used to drizzle the same way people on the waterfront stop hearing the Argosy ships with the tour guides commentating over loudspeakers: "And if you look through those windows, you'll see a real T-rex skeleton that the Microsoft exec who lives here personally excavated. And just across the lake over there is the home of the man you can thank every time you turn on your cell phone: Ethan Cheng."

Lillian's dad swerves into the parking lot. So what if he's too busy talking on *his* cell phone to acknowledge the daughter waving at him? He showed up and that says everything.

Trying to look busy is hard to do when rain is dumping, and I have nowhere to go, and no way to get there. Just as the rest of The Six-Pack hightails it to the dryer ground of the minivan, Lillian turns around to ask, "I don't suppose you'd want to go to Children's Hospital to help with a party?"

"Children's Hospital?" It's ridiculous but I feel relieved that what everybody's been talking about isn't another Viewridge party I learned of after the fact, or worse, been invited just to foot the bill, kegs and all.

"It's going to be a zoo today, which I guess will be good since it's our party. So yeah, you're probably too busy, have other plans for Groundhog Day," Lillian rambles nervously, as she hurdles over guardrails that are surrounding me for good reason. Quickly, she backtracks to the safety of being virtual strangers when I don't answer right away. "Okay, so I'll see you tomorrow at school."

"Come on, Lillian!" hollers Chelsea out the open door.

Lillian sighs so softly I bet she's not even aware she's making a sound. But I hear that release of breath as if it's been broadcast around me. I know that sigh, that sound of resignation and frustration. It's the way I feel when Mama and Baba drag me to one of their black tie events to socialize with people I "ought to know." I study Lillian curiously. Maybe she isn't just another Chelsea girl-bot, but a Six-Packer who wants to break free of the plastic ties binding her to that group. I throw her a lifeline that I've always wished someone, say, Grace or Wayne, would toss to me: "So, a Groundhog Day party?"

She smiles sheepishly. "Another guild already had dibs on Valentine's Day."

"I'd love to help," I tell her.

"Really?" Lillian's voice climbs up a high-pitched scale, reaching disbelief but not the upper climes of girlfriend shriek. Still, it's close enough.

I nod. "Really."

9

Frankly, hospitals freak me out. The last time I was in one, I awoke from my knee surgery to learn that (big surprise) my dearly departing parents had left the hospital for some conference in Paris, assured that all went well. And the time before that, I was with Age, the day his mom slipped into a coma. So despite the two lilac-spotted giraffe statues posed outside like greeters at an exotic boutique hotel, Children's Hospital is still a place for the sick, injured, and scared.

Apparently, Lillian isn't afflicted with my hospital-phobia, because she marches as though she were a regular through the double glass doors and past the mural of elephants and giraffes drinking at a watering hole. A man and a woman, both in shapeless function-before-fashion scrubs, overtake us. The Six-Pack are nowhere to be seen.

I ask Lillian, "So how often do you volunteer here?"

"Volunteer? Not all that often," Lillian answers without breaking her stride. Even at the elevator, she's all impatient movement, jabbing the up button and tapping her foot until the doors open. Even before I'm all the way inside, she's pressed the button for the fifth floor. "My mom started a new guild with a bunch of the other moms at school. So I got dragged in to co-chair this party with her." Lillian quickly appends, "Not that I mind. This has knocked off my entire service learning requirement for the year."

Blame my own zero community service hours on watching one too many fashion parades at black-tie charity events where helping the poor, the hungry, and the weary takes a backseat to showing off brand-new designer outfits that could feed a village for a year.

"Here we go," says Lillian, a tour guide when the elevator opens. Down the long hall we charge — until I spot the large charcoal Plexiglas plaque commemorating the Cheng Foundation. I stand, transfixed, not by my parents' names, but mine sharing the same line as Wayne's and Grace's.

"The Founders' Circle," says Lillian, gesturing at the sign that explains that these are the donors who've given more than a million dollars to the hospital. "You guys do so much."

I nod as if I know all about how involved my family is in the community, but feel like the ultimate imposter, especially when down the radiology wing I can't look at the young boy locked in a wheelchair, his head lolling to the side. Not Lillian. She calls like he's any other kid, "You coming to the party at five?"

"Yeah," he says, his little voice all excited.

The only time Lillian actually stops moving is at the column of orcas fronting the Sound Café, where she takes a deep breath, girding herself, but for what? Suddenly, she lets it out in a hurricane rush at the sight of her mother and her bulging pregnant stomach standing on a chair, an oversized cake topper.

"Oh, geez, what is she doing?" mutters Lillian, hurrying to her mother. "Mom! Get down from there."

"Lillian, you're here," Mrs. Fujimoro says, relieved. The streamers behind her are already wilting, a tired bouquet. Whatever glow pregnant women are supposed to have, it's not emanating from Mrs. Fujimoro, whose skin is more green than white. Still, she manages a wan smile. "Syrah, what a pleasant surprise. Maybe we'll get your mother to join our guild yet."

Lillian casts me an uncomfortable, apologetic look, like she wants me to know that I'm not a stepping stone to Mama, and then she grabs the spool of crepe streamers from her mom.

"We'll finish setting up," Lillian assures her mom, as she helps her off the chair.

"Definitely," I say. "Shouldn't you be resting?"

"Resting . . ." Mrs. Fujimoro sighs at that unknown concept. For a moment, she clenches her jaw as though she's going to throw up, but then peers at Lillian. "If you can handle this . . ."

"Go, Mom. I got it under control."

Mrs. Fujimoro blows out a grateful breath and swallows hard, convulsively. "All this sugar. Who would've known that morning sickness would rear its ugly head with just a month to go?"

By the way Lillian watches her mother waddle out the cafeteria, I can tell that she wishes she could leave, too. I know the feeling, that desperate need to escape, and would have relieved her here, but a screech of laughter erupts from the table where The Six-Pack are parked, chugging lattes like they're at a coffeehouse with nothing more important to do than gossip.

"He is so just using her for sex," cries Chelsea, digging into a 500-calorie scone.

"Honestly," huffs Lillian who, like a Bao-mu in training,

marches to The Six-Pack. Heedless of what this will do to her social status, she hisses, "There are kids here. So do you mind?" Not waiting for an answer, Lillian flips around, but there's no chance she can miss the girls' cackles, their mock "Ooooh, we're so scared." Concerned because I can feel Lillian's bravado faltering, I hurry to meet her halfway.

"My mom's going to throw a fit because I did that," mutters Lillian, rolling her eyes, as The Six-Pack cracks up again at their table.

"Why?" I glance over my shoulder, meet Chelsea's eyes and stare her down, wondering what kind of hold this girl has over Lillian. "They were being totally inappropriate. *I* should have said something."

Looking troubled, Lillian shrugs my question away. So I steer her to the dining room and say, "Come on, don't worry about them, Warrior Girl. We've got a party to host."

Most of the women in the guild have that lethal leanness of second wives who run in Mama's circle. They come to pay respects to me, the visiting dignitary at this party.

"Why, hello, Syrah!" says Chelsea's mom, smiling with such intensity she could be a model for teeth brightening systems. "Will we be seeing you at the Evergreen Children's Fund dinner next week?"

"I'm afraid that's not on my calendar," I tell her.

"Really?" Her eyebrows lift and she steps closer to me, a telltale sign that she's preparing for The Ask, the moment when she'll request that I put in a good word to my parents. See, this is why I stopped going to the gym. Strangers would approach me while I was trapped on the treadmill, downright pleading that my parents donate a couple of thousand here, a couple of thousand there.

Luckily for me, Lillian's grim announcement — "We've got forty-five minutes before the kids descend" — saves me from making party chitchat. The next half hour passes in a flurry of flinging streamers, table rearranging, and "fluffing" the dining room until the national colors appear to have been changed to red, white, and pink. Apparently, the guild hasn't gotten over being bumped from hosting the Valentine's Day party.

How ironic that I, the girl with the most backward fashion sense, get assigned displaying duties for the cookie-decorating tables, as if genetics have conferred me with Mama's primping skills. As Mama points out in her pre-party conferences with her event planner and their post-party critiques, presentation is everything. You simply would not throw down food in — *quelle horreur!* — plastic platters and call that a display, would you? Which is why I'm artfully "merchandising" individually wrapped and pink-ribboned cookies that look vaguely like groundhogs.

"You're great at this!" Lillian says on her third inspection round before groaning when a woman saunters in, clutching a bouquet of balloons. "No latex allowed! How'd she get past security?"

As I finish stocking the workspace with more frosting and hundreds of plastic knives (pink, of course) so that the kids don't double dip and create a watering hole of communal germs in these canisters, the sound of children — loud, excited, and boisterous — echoes in the cafeteria. They spill into the dining room on crutches, in wheelchairs, and with IV poles.

Demonstrating innate party skills that would make Mama proud, Lillian jumps into action, directing a few to the beanbag toss and pointing others to my station.

"You can take a cookie and decorate it over here," I explain to three kids. As I help them unsheathe the cookies from their cellophane wrappers, the telltale yelp of a scared kid pierces through the cafeteria hubbub. Glancing up, I spot a little boy with outrageously long eyelashes burst into tears, fear at first sight of the clowns. The red-wigged wonders duck-walk toward him. He cowers. The clowns freeze. It'd almost be a comical standoff except the boy's mother snaps at him — "Stop it!" — which infuriates me, because, clearly, he can't stop whimpering. And I don't blame him. In my book of horrors, clowns rank right up there with hairy spiders and hairless dogs.

Still crying, the boy hides behind his mom, a frowsy woman whose thick legs are made thicker in shapeless fleece sweatpants. Unfortunately, the kid's tears start a downward spiraling trend. A little girl emits a full-throttle shriek.

"Oh, my God," says Lillian, who's now at my side, wearing what Age calls my *ay-dios-mio* look of mingled stress and despair. "What do I do?"

"I said, stop it," the boy's mom repeats sharply, impatiently shaking him off her leg.

Years of being Mama's hostess sidekick has trained me on the finer details of party crisis management. I tell Lillian to man my station and hurry over to extract the distraction, not a moment too soon.

"Over there," I order the clowns, who slowly back up in the face of this toddler terror and veer off to a group of pro-clown children.

The kid with the eyelashes sucks down a huge gulp of air, like he's suffering from post-traumatic clown syndrome, and his mom's eyes narrow as she gears up for her second eruption. My approach doesn't stop her from snipping, "Big boys don't cry."

Ignoring her, I bend down to look straight into the boy's eyes and confess, "I'm afraid of clowns, too, and look how big I am."

Our mutual clown phobia wins the boy's confidence. After he wipes his nose with his hand, he slips it in mine. My first instinct is to pull my hand away, rub it on my pants, and sanitize my skin with hot, sudsy water, but there's nothing but trust in his big hazel eyes. I forget about the germs transferring to my skin.

"What's your name?" I ask him.

"Frank."

"Well, Frank, come with me."

A father and his sniffling daughter are steps away from leaving the cafeteria. Not on my watch.

"Wait!" I call. The man stops, looks at me questioningly, as I gaze around, desperate. To the side, The Six-Pack are spectators in my fiasco, showing no intention of leaving their gossip to help me. And this is how they define "community service"?

The dining rooms to the side of the cafeteria are empty, and I commandeer one. Heading into the private room, I tell them, "We're going to have our own party here."

Announcing an impromptu party is easy compared to figuring out what to do with two kids, a mother, and a father who are now staring at me around the conference table. I have an awful déjà vu feeling of being back in Mr. Delbene's classroom without a plan or an inkling of an idea. I glance around for inspiration, but come up only with a TV monitor mounted to the corner of the room, a whiteboard, and a wheeled computer rack.

According to Mama, the host is supposed to please her guests' senses, entertain them, create an unforgettable party. It is unforgettable, but not in the way Mama has ever imagined. I wipe the sweat off my nose. The two kids begin to sniffle; the adults shuffle uncomfortably.

Frank's mother raises an eyebrow at me and then slings her body against the back of her chair, challenging me to get myself out of this one. Plaintively, as if she's personally footing the party bill, she demands, "Well?" But she doesn't wait for my answer, apparently writing me off as a dud, and instead hefts herself from her chair, which releases a sigh, relieved of her load. Halfway out the door, she remembers Frank and asks, "You want a cookie?"

Yeah, load him up with sugar, I want to throw back at her. *That'll make him less scared. Right.* No matter how much I stuff or starve myself, it doesn't change my fear of failing or make me feel like I'm enough.

Outside, in the main dining room, the rest of the party crowd are laughing, probably at some clown antics. Thinking fast, I ask, "Do you know what I do when I'm scared of something?"

The kids shake their heads.

"I draw. Wait here for a sec," I tell them, and retrieve my backpack from under the treat table, which The Six-Pack are now visiting, giggling while slathering on thick, half-inch layers of frosting under Lillian's disgusted gaze.

"Doing okay?" asks Lillian, as I run past her.

"Great," I say over my shoulder. The truth is, I'm more worried about her being caught in the eye of The Six-Pack hurricane than about me.

When I return to the private dining room, a tall bald boy whose lanky build mirrors his IV pole has joined our anti-clown crowd.

"This is Derek from the *third floor*," says Frank, looking awed.

"What's the *third floor*?" I ask, mimicking Frank.

"CCA," says Derek, his mouth set hard like a man's rather than a boy who'd look at home at my high school.

"CCA?"

"Cancer Care Alliance." Derek looks at me defiantly, his glare daring me to utter one "sorry" or think "you poor kid."

Luckily, Frank points at my backpack on the table. "What's in there?"

Glad for a subject change, I draw out my notebook, the one I've never shown to anyone. Not even Age. I tell them, "My journal."

"Hey, that's manga," says Derek, leaning across the table to get a closer look at my journal. I fight the urge to slam it shut and cast a cautious glance out the door at The Six-Pack, who I definitely don't want nosing into my private world, but they're too busy devouring their cookies. "Did you draw that?"

I nod and flip forward to more panels of Shiraz riding the mountain, her private snow park. "See, that's me snowboarding," I say. "Or at least, the me I was before I tore up my knee and had to have surgery."

Derek nods solemnly, not only understanding but approving

how I've made a glorified version of my old self. He points to the frame where Shiraz launched into big air over Grace and Wayne back at Baba's party.

"Can you draw the me before I got sick?" he asks.

"Me, too," says Frank, his eyelashes still spiky with tears.

"Do him first," says Derek, nodding over to Frank, volunteering him as the human guinea pig in this test procedure.

So I study the little boy for a moment and then turn to a fresh page, sketching out a three-paneled frame, two little boxes offset within a larger one. As I draw, Frank sidles up to me, so close I can feel his warm breath on my hand. A lion takes shape under my pen.

"See? You read manga from right to left," I tell him.

"Instead of this way," Frank says, tapping the left hand page.

"Smart boy."

He beams at me as if I'm some kind of angel-hero, and I have to force myself back to his manga. In the leftmost panel, I zoom up to the lion, snoring in a hospital bed. In the one below that, his eyes bordered with lashes the exact length and curl of Frank's, crack open. I draw a clown's bulbous nose poking into a thin frame running the length of the paper on the next page. And then beside that, the lion roars loudly. All that can be seen in the very last panel are the undersides of the clown's big shoes as he runs away, afraid.

"Cool," Frank whispers.

"My teacher says we're not supposed to write with curlicues," the little girl tells me solemnly as I add swirls to the letters in Frank's name.

"We're all allowed to break rules every once in a while," I say. Meeting Derek's gaze — one that's hungry for attention but too cool to ask for it, too insecure to risk possible rejection — I ask, "So what should I draw for you?"

Before long, a choir of munchkins, all singing "draw me," are clustered around the conference table. There's almost nothing left of my manga-journal when the party winds down, half the population at Children's, it seems, are skipping back to their hospital rooms, clutching drawings of themselves as dinosaurs, giraffes, elephants, monkeys.

Derek holds his, a baseball dude, gently, as though he doesn't want to wrinkle this image of himself. "So, thanks," he says awkwardly.

"Any time," I tell him before he leaves, dragging the IV pole behind him like it's the shadow of his old self. I don't hear Lillian come up behind me until she says, "So the clowns are grousing that you ruined their party. But you saved mine." She holds out a tray of cookies to me. "You must be hungry."

"No, thanks. I can't afford it."

"You've got to be kidding, right?"

As much as I appreciate her vote of confidence about my body, I shake my head and flex the fingers on my left hand. "If your party had lasted three minutes longer, you would've had a mutiny on your hands. I exhausted my repertoire of animals. What the heck is a chiru?"

Lillian laughs, shrugs, and places the cookies down to look at my now-depleted journal.

"You're a great artist," she says seriously. "I had no idea."

I toss my pens into my backpack, pleased at her compliment. "This was fun."

From the cafeteria, laughter follows after a woman swats her friend with a wad of crepe paper.

"Do they need help cleaning up?" I ask.

"Nah, they're the clean-up committee."

As I zip up my backpack, I think about the times I sneak into the kitchen late at night, eating when no one is watching, and mindlessly I murmur, "They can snack on the leftovers with no one knowing." Lillian looks at me funny, so I change the subject by asking, "Where's The Six-Pack? I mean, your friends."

Confused for a moment, Lillian starts laughing. "You mean Chelsea's crowd? Didn't you see them leaving halfway into the party?"

"I guess I was too busy drawing poison dart frogs. And a chiru, whatever that is."

As we leave the private room, Lillian says, "Thank you. Really, thanks for helping."

"It was nothing."

"It wasn't nothing. The Six-Pack ate and ran."

"You mean, they ate, traded sex tips, and ran."

"Well, yeah. And you didn't just show up. You stayed and helped. That's everything."

"No way," I tell her. "I should be thanking you."

"Why? For subjecting you to clowns?"

"Okay, not the clowns." I lift one shoulder, a half-shrug. "For letting me help."

"We make a good team." Lillian grins at me. "When you took on that mom and those clowns . . . God, who would have thought someone as tiny as you could be that ferocious."

"What about you? Lecturing The Sex-Pack . . ."

"The Sex-Pack!" Lillian convulses with laughter. "That's

73

good." She casts me a sidelong look. "You know, you're not exactly what I thought you'd be."

"Right back at you. And, for the record, this isn't how I envisioned spending my Groundhog Day."

"What? You didn't picture yourself celebrating at the hospital with me as a date?"

"Sorry, no."

"Have a consolation cookie," she says.

So I do, trying not to calculate all the calories I'll need to work off tomorrow after school. But for the record, I don't need a single speck of sugar to feel good, not right now.

10

Aiya!" Bao-mu's anxious, exasperated voice erupts so suddenly in my bedroom a few mornings later that I mar my near-perfect page with a dark, jagged line.

"Oh, hey, Bao-mu." Sighing to myself, I erase the mark, blowing the rubber dandruff off my journal where I've been drawing Lillian telling The Six-Pack to take their advanced birds-and-the-bees lesson elsewhere. It's either illustrate that or dwell on how I snuck out after school to go snowboarding with Age, his brothers, and Natalia yesterday. Wouldn't you know it? I wiped out on my shoulder again — on the easiest green run — to Natalia's "Wow, graceful" commentary.

"You know what today is," Bao-mu demands, eyes glittering above dark circles, advancing on me like Fa Mulan, the warrior woman, grown old.

"It's Saturday, your day off." I swear, sometimes Bao-mu forgets that as a senior citizen, she's earned the right to take it easy. "Shouldn't you be resting?"

"How I rest when you still in bed?" The sheet of paper she

waves at me isn't a white flag of surrender, but a matador's cape that should have me vaulting out of bed. "Don't look at me like that." Bao-mu imitates my wide-opened look of innocence. I laugh because it's like watching the most brilliant person on Earth playing dumb. Bao-mu is as canny as they come. She doesn't smile back but scolds, "You want Grace and Wayne take everything?"

Bao-mu holds the paper a scant two inches from my nose. If I didn't already know what was on it, I'd have gone cross-eyed trying to read the blurred words. But it's the same as all the other memos I've received every fiscal quarter since I was ten:

From: Ethan Cheng
To: Betty Cheng, Wayne Cheng, Grace Cheng
Cc: Cindy Cheng, Jack Cheng, Syrah Cheng
Re: Winter Quarter Cheng Family Meeting Agenda

Please find below the agenda for the Saturday meeting in the teahouse. Be prepared to provide your investment recommendations and the status of your respective business concerns.

7:30 a.m.   Agenda review
7:45 a.m.   Announcements
8:30 a.m.   Cheng Family Holdings financial review
1:00 p.m.   Lunch
1:15 p.m.   New investments
3:00 p.m.   Cheng Foundation, project review
5:00 p.m.   New projects
7:00 p.m.   Dinner

"I'm not even on the 'to' line," I tell Bao-mu, and that, as far as I'm concerned, means my presence is requested, not required. So I plan to no-show yet another family meeting to go over all the Cheng holdings: the cellular business in which Baba still holds a controlling interest, the family investment arm that Wayne runs, and the foundation, which funds philanthropic work.

"Anyway," I say, shading in Shiraz's hair, "I don't have to go to one of those until I'm eighteen."

Wrong answer. Plucking the pencil out of my hand, Bao-mu switches to Mandarin, hot and sharp, the language of her lectures: *"Ni shi Cheng jia ren."* Her nose flares wide in her insistence that I'm part of the Cheng clan. Back in English, she snaps, "Just like Wayne. Like Grace." In other words, I am just as much Baba's rightful heir as Wayne and Grace, his other children. Not on the same lower-rank cc line as his grandchildren.

Trust me, if there's one person who should never be angered, it's Bao-mu. Let's just say that Bao-mu was put on probation from my kindergarten classroom after she saw a boy whose name I've forgotten snatch a crayon out of my hand. It's been, what, ten years, but I'm fairly confident that Bao-mu remembers his name, the color of his eyes, and his height. "You not take from Syrah!" she had snapped and yanked the crayon out of his trembling fingers.

Bao-mu perches on the edge of my bed, closes her eyes, and breathes out, releasing all the air in her lungs the way she taught me to do when I was little and missing my parents. At her next breath, she studies me solemnly.

"Syrah, your daddy said he retiring," she says, reverting to

English, wanting me to understand her perfectly. To make sure I'm paying attention, she tugs the journal out of my hands. "Life going be different now. Business different. You need know what going on or Wayne and Grace take it all."

But that's just it. Part of me wants them to take it, maybe not all of it, but a big chunk would be just fine. Then, I'd be a regular kid who wants to be a Snowboard Girl. Not a rich kid-poseur whose custom-designed Prada snowboard, a gift from one of Mama's favorite designers, would get me laughed off the mountain if I ever used it.

Bao-mu waves one wrinkled hand around my room. "You not want this. But money let you do whatever you want later." She taps my manga-journal. "Draw. Travel. Start your own business like Grace."

"I know."

"Even snowboard."

"Hmmm," I murmur doubtfully.

Bao-mu nods, not as though she believes my parents will let me snowboard again, or that she's satisfied that I finally understand the importance of what she's talking about. But like she knows something she doesn't want to tell me. Her eyes drop to my journal before she returns it to me.

"No," Bao-mu says softly. "This wrong." She shakes her head at the page, smooth and white against her age-spotted hands. "Life not daring adventure, Syrah. Life is survival." Heavily, Bao-mu gets to her feet, back bent until she can straighten painfully. "If you want something, you have to take it." Her hand balls into a fist and she yanks it toward her waist, hard, fast. "I not always here to make sure you get what yours."

11

Once Bao-mu leaves me with a final admonishing look, I try to return to my manga-journal, but it's no use. The clock on my wall ticks away, a metronome that doesn't slow down Age and Bao-mu's duet of advice playing in my head: *Just show them your video. If you want something, take it.*

I flip back to the page where I sketched Natalia doing just that. She faced her fear of heights and took back Age's heart. So what do I want? More than anything, I used to want to go pro. Now, all I want is to reclaim myself. As if I really need to check that I'm alone, I glance at the door before printing in letters so tiny a mouse would need a magnifying glass to read them: *I want to ride hard again.* Then I draw a snowboard around the words, place Shiraz on top of it, she of the self-confident stance.

I swing my feet over the edge of my bed and stand. "You'll get your balance back soon," Liza, my physical therapist, promised me after the ankle-to-hip brace finally came off about six weeks post-op, but three weeks later, I was still limping. "Muscle memory. It'll come back."

Once I stash my journal back in its hideout spot in my closet, I feel safe from any potential prying eyes, including the housekeeper's. After having my accident dragged all over the press, I figure, the less fodder the better. But as I shove the journal onto the top shelf, it snags on the plastic shrink-wrap covering one of my snowboarding magazines. After my accident, I couldn't bear to read any of them, since the pictures made me so homesick for snowboarding.

Easing the magazine out, the face I can't hide from, not even in my sleep, grins at me from the back cover, standing just behind his big brother. Jared's grey-green eyes may be covered by the goggles he and Erik are hawking, but I'd know that bad-ass grin anywhere, that heart-shaped freckle a star over the skyline of his upper lip. *Stop the B.S.,* I tell myself. He's the real reason why I haven't kept up with the snowboarding magazines, much less the videos.

See, after all these months, I still need a rehab program, because thanks to muscle memory and a weird codependent relationship with my memory, my heart swells at the thought of Jared. What I remember now is how Jared would always take the street side of any sidewalk when we were walking together, as if he were protecting me. And how he'd lean down to me, not wanting to miss a single expression on my face, which made me feel witty and wanted and just a little bit wicked.

"There's a wild side to you that no one knows about," Jared told me after I tore after him on a slope that wiped out the rest of the girls in my summer camp. "I like it." He held my gaze so steadily, so piercingly, that I swore, my entire body prickled as if I had been asleep, gone numb, and his words prodded me awake — sharp, sudden, and somewhat painful. Painful, because

I so wanted to shed my Heir Cheng reputation that I didn't even think twice about slipping into the ready-made bad girl image that Jared had conjured for me.

No matter how fun my reverse Cinderella transformation had been, it ended badly, and my knee twinges now in reproach. So I jam the journal and Jared back onto the shelf.

My hand comes away, shaking and empty, and I realize that since my accident, everyone's moved on to a better place: Natalia who mastered more than snowboarding. Mama and Baba who are venturing to a new phase of life together. Jared and his skyrocketing career that didn't need the boost he hoped the Cheng name could provide. Even Shiraz is about to land in a better place in that last panel I drew, safely out of reach of Grace's and Wayne's velvet-covered taunts.

I start to close the closet door, glimpsing as I do the picture of me and Age at Snoqualmie after our very first snowboarding run seven years ago. As third graders, we looked so sure of ourselves, me with my hands on my hips and Age holding his above his head. A petty part of me wants to point out that once upon a time, long before my knee injury, I used to be better than Age. What did Jared say? "God, you've got a lot of guts, for a girl."

Jared. I block out what he said once he realized he wasn't going to get what he really wanted, not my trust but my trust fund: "Look, I do what it takes. Not everybody gets everything handed to them."

I'm tired of being a Qué Syrah Syrah girl, the one who's left behind in the cold snowdrift of memories and pretends that's okay. The girl who's too afraid to read about someone else's adventures because it magnifies how distant her own dreams have become. On my stepstool, I reach for the topmost shelf where I've stashed my video résumé. The CD case in my hands feels too slight to contain the best minute and fourteen seconds of my snowboarding tricks. Too slight to be the compilation of two years' worth of bruises and falls before sticking perfect tricks.

Not wanting to chicken out, I hastily slip on an oversized black sweater and my fat, size four jeans, because I feel bloated just looking at the tiny new skirt Mama brought home yesterday from San Francisco, draped on the slipper chair next to the full-length mirror. Clutching my CD, I head past my bookshelf, backtracking to grab a stack of manga and sandwich them protectively around my résumé in case I can't bare myself to my family. Armed, I rush out to crash my first family meeting and take what I want from the executive committee of the Cheng clan.

Ancient East meets Modern West, at least that's how Mama described our estate in *Architectural Digest*. Whatever it is, our estate is made up of many separate buildings scattered over two acres, sequestered from the rest of the world by the Great Wall of Cheng that runs along the perimeter. Our main house is a modest three thousand square feet, minuscule by billionaire standards. Baba's refuge, The Pavilion of the Next Big Idea, lies immediately beyond the first courtyard, closest to the house in case inspiration hits when he's home. It's in his *zhai,* office-studio, where the quarterly Cheng family meetings take place.

Even though it's raining lightly, I take the scenic detour all the way around the property — past the tang, Mama's bonsai house, my art studio. Before I know it, I'm outside Baba's door, my hand on his prized scholar's rock made of *lingbi*, the sandy-colored stone pocked and twisted into a large question mark.

For hundreds of years, scholars in China contemplated these misshapen rocks, signs of how unpredictable our world is. Like now, when the drizzle turns to snow so wet, it more resembles raindrops than snowflakes. But it is snow, a good sign. At least that's what Bao-mu would say if she were here and about to shove me into Baba's office. Anointed, as though I have every right to be here, I open the door and step inside.

From his seat at the head of the table where he always sits, regardless of whether he's in a dining room, boardroom, or tea-room, Baba nods at me, pleased.

"Syrah," Mama says, smiling because I've finally expressed some interest in the business of family.

Not smiling is Wayne who's to Baba's left, nor Grace who turns in her seat, Mochi to her cheek. She arches one plucked eyebrow at her brother.

"If I had known Syrah was attending," Wayne says stiffly, "I would have insisted that Cindy and Jack come, too."

"Last-minute decision," I say airily.

"Have some breakfast first." Baba nods to the antique table loaded down with dim sum, little morsels of food that are supposed to touch your heart. "The *law bock* is especially creamy this morning. Grace, anything else you want to add to the agenda?"

The review of Cheng family holdings continues behind me as I place the manga and CD on an empty spot on the food table. I'm not hungry, too keyed up about my announcement. Still, I scoop a tablespoon of rice and place a sliver of *law bock,* fried turnip cake, its scent pungent and comforting, onto my plate.

When I return to the conference table, I realize I've made my first tactical error. Mama's plate is clean of everything except for her five daily vitamins, lined up in a neat, soldierly row. Before Grace are three uneaten orange segments, artfully arranged and meticulously peeled of white membrane.

Feeling every bit the fat pig, I set my plate next to Wayne's spot at the conference table.

"Anyone want anything else?" I ask as I start back for a cup of tea.

"No, no," Baba demurs, but when Wayne comes over to help himself to a Coke, I think I overhear his "Your butt is getting big." Ever since I can remember, Wayne has had no compunction about providing me with "feedback" in the "spirit of improvement," whether it's about my future or my figure. But today, his stoic expression doesn't betray whether he's insulted me. Not that it matters, really. My usual insecurities, the ones pecking around my head, sound like Wayne, too.

Either way, I'm self-conscious now and return to the table with a glass of zero-calorie water — instead of ten-calorie tea — and my manga.

"Comic books," says Grace flatly.

"Manga," I correct her. "Otherwise known as graphic novels."

Grace looks decidedly unimpressed. Truly, with her tiny animal *chibi* sidekick, Mr. Yippy Dog Mochi, perpetually slung over her shoulder, the two of them could be characters straight out of girls' manga, *shonin*.

"Whatever you call them," says Wayne, his lips drawn back with distaste, "you're not getting into Princeton by reading pabulum. At your age, Cindy and Jack were reading Greek classics."

"Five hundred million manga are sold in Japan alone every year," I counter softly.

"That doesn't mean it's literature," he snaps back.

"*Maus* won the Pulitzer." Honestly, anyone else and I'd inform him that I'd rather be in good company reading so-called trash than be a pompous ass, but I simply sit down. Pathetic, I know. It's just that I've talked myself into thinking that if I play the adoring little sister long enough, then maybe, just maybe, Wayne will adore me back.

As usual, he has no qualms about dispensing with his role as nurturing big brother. Wayne glowers at me. "You're so intellectually lazy. When Jack and Cindy were your age, they had already earned enough college credit to skip freshman year."

God, the way he talks about his kids, you'd think they were years older and infinitely more Chengian than I could ever aspire to be. Reality is, the last time we all got together for an unhappy family reunion, let's just say I discovered how much Cindy and Jack enjoy dabbling in mind-altering substances. I would, too, if I had Wayne for a dad.

Just as Wayne gears up to further the distinction between his kids' classics-enhanced brain cells and my comic-diminished ones, Mama murmurs, "I just read in the *Wall Street Journal* that manga is the fastest growing segment in the book industry."

"That's right, and manga is picking up traction with cell phone distribution in Japan," says Baba. He points to the display case of old cell phones, a retrospective starting with the toy Dick Tracy wrist phone, the one that started Baba's fascination with cellular technology. "Sometimes the best ideas come from unexpected sources. You should learn that."

Flushing but chastened, Wayne falls silent. I can practically hear him and Grace busily calculating their profit and loss statement, deducting all the wrongs done to them because of me and Mama. Thanks to Baba's support, I've just earned myself another enormous loss. When Mama catches my eye, it's not to wink at me, her conspirator, but to make sure I know that she doesn't appreciate how I've nearly shamed her.

"Any other announcements?" Baba asks, looking around the table.

My mouth feels too dry to talk so I lift my glass. In the space of a sip, I lose my opportunity.

"All right, then, on to the financial review," says Baba, making a neat tick next to the agenda item. "We know how Wayne did." And by the telltale dip in Baba's voice, if we didn't, we do now. Wayne must have logged another deficit. "So Grace, tell us how you increased revenues way over budget in Q1?"

"Wait," I say softly, but my plea is as weightless as a single snowflake. Baba's peering down his glasses at his notes and no one pays attention to me. So louder, I say, "I've got an announcement."

Baba smiles indulgently at me. "Well, what is it?"

Just tell them what you want, I hear Bao-mu. Uncomfortably aware of Wayne and Grace smirking, I'm about to blurt out, *I want to be a professional snowboarder.* But Wayne breathes impatiently, and beats me to the punch: "You're not about to talk about your snowboarding career, are you?"

How does he know? That's what I get for confessing my dream to his kids the last time we got together before I left for snowboarding camp. Out of my mouth, straight into their dad's ears.

Wayne glares at me, unable to believe that someone this

86

stupid could have sprung from his same gene pool. "We didn't fix your knee, much less spend a million dollars rescuing you, so that you could go out and break your neck the next time."

You would think that I just declared my intention to be an exotic dancer, the way everyone is staring at me.

"I thought you were more ambitious than this," says Wayne.

What? I want to say to him. *Like making another couple of million at the end of the quarter is supposed to make me feel fulfilled, good about myself?* Naturally, adoring little sister says not a word.

"I'm just being honest here," chimes Grace. "There simply aren't many companies who'll sponsor a Chinese-American girl, much less one who was skewered for her snowboarding. Look at Kristi Yamaguchi, who, I hate to say this, is more . . . media-genic . . . than you are. She didn't get half the endorsements that the other figure skaters did, even with her gold."

Endorsements. I grab that word as if it's an avalanche probe. "Actually," I say, thinking fast about how Natalia's community service project did double duty, introducing at-risk kids to snowboarding and reintroducing herself to Age. And about Frank at the hospital with his spiky wet eyelashes. And Derek from the third floor cancer ward. "I was thinking about organizing some sort of charity snowboarding contest for Children's Hospital."

"Fundraisers are a lot of work," says Mama, folding her hands in front of her on the table. "The last auction I chaired was practically a full-time job. Even with the Evergreen Fund's staff helping me."

Wayne drops his pen onto his legal pad, where it rolls off and lands on his agenda. "This is just Syrah trying to get us to sponsor her."

"It isn't," I protest.

His "no chance in hell" is set in his stony stare. "What are you going to do once your so-called career is over? Teach snowboarding?" Wayne's tone is so ridiculing, his words so realistic, I look away, sliding my video résumé and manga under the table and onto my lap. "You'd make more in a couple of hours on this," he taps the Cheng family memo emphatically, "than you would in five seasons on the slopes. With or without endorsements."

Just as aware as I was in the split second after I heard the unmistakable *whump* of snow cracking under my snowboard in Whistler, I know I've bungled it now.

"Your time would be better served studying for the SAT," agrees Baba. And then in his ultra-controlled patient voice, the one he uses when he wants to make sure there's no mistaking his message, Baba continues, "Syrah, I can understand how you might want to snowboard again, but if those rescuers hadn't found you when they did, you'd have died of exposure. So it's just not possible."

I wait for the second verse in his statistics-filled monologue. How the number of snowboarding injuries are on the rise every year. How more snowboarders are getting killed in avalanches in the backcountry where I love to ride.

Instead, Baba leans back in his chair and touches his fingertips together in a steeple. "However, it's a moot point," he says finally.

All I want to do is run for cover, clutching my résumé, so I don't have to hear his pronouncement that I'm never, ever to touch a snow-covered mountain again. That the only mountain I'm allowed to ride is a gold one named Mount Cheng. Instead,

I sit still, focus on the dragon robe displayed behind Baba, rich yellow and embroidered with the twelve symbols of imperial authority, including the sun, moon, constellations, and twinned dragons. And I wait for his judgment.

Baba places his hand atop Mama's and smiles at her. For a moment, I wonder why Grace thinks that I'm the beloved one when their Royal We doesn't include me, either.

"We're moving to Hong Kong," he says.

12

B ut I don't want to move," I say.

Those six little words rip the tenuous ligament connecting what is allowed to be said and what remains unsaid in this family. Support for Baba's strategies to further the Cheng name, increase the Cheng fortunes, gild the Cheng legacy: glory, glory, hallelujah! Sing your praises to the high heavens for all to hear. But an issue or a complaint? Those treacherous thoughts are locked down, never-to-be-uttered outside the privacy of your own head.

The pavilion falls silent: Baba and Mama because I challenged their plans; Wayne and Grace because I'm getting another Golden Opportunity they didn't have as kids during the Ethan Cheng, struggling entrepreneur era.

"We're moving in September. Right in time for you to start the International School," Baba continues smoothly as if I haven't spoken up.

Grace and Wayne exchange another eyebrow-lifting look:

Hey, if we talked back like that when we were Syrah's age, we would have been pelted with rebuke.

But Baba's cell phone rings, cutting off any further protest on my part and any potential grousing on theirs. "Yes?" he answers impatiently. Nodding his head once, he trots upstairs to his private office, phone to his ear.

How many times have I seen jealousy at school and camp gain momentum like an avalanche? It's no different now. My new so-called opportunity releases an entire block of pent-up resentment in Wayne.

"I've already warned Baba that you're spoiled rotten," he says, eyes narrowed. The way Wayne's jaw works, I get ready for his you-were-born-with-silver-chopsticks-in-your-mouth tirade. He doesn't disappoint. "How many kids get a chance to live abroad? You'll improve your Cantonese and be trilingual. So what are you complaining about?"

What am I complaining about? I blink at Wayne in disbelief. Honestly, in this family where money is the official language, I might as well be speaking Mandarin since no one aside from Bao-mu understands me anyway.

"That's an excellent point," agrees Mama, nodding, all eager agreement. "Being trilingual would be such an asset in business."

My breath catches disbelievingly at my mom's words. She's the one who forbade me from using Mandarin, because my grandmother complained that it was corrupting my Cantonese, their mother tongue. Even though I guzzle my glass of water, that sharp piece of irony remains lodged inside my throat.

"If I had this chance when I was your age," Grace says, stroking Mochi, "I would have grabbed it."

"You would have wanted to move during high school?" I ask Grace, noting that she goes quiet.

"Of course, she would have. How can you be so shortsighted? Jack and Cindy would move in a heartbeat," says Wayne.

In my frustration, I drop my adoring little sister act. "Then they should."

"Easy for you to say," Wayne says, low and lethal.

My gaze falls to my lap where my hands are clutched over my CD in a tight, punishing ball. Sink or swim, those are your choices in an avalanche. Do the breast stroke and break to the surface fast, otherwise you risk getting sucked down and buried in snow the consistency of cement. The problem is, just the way I felt alone in the benched cliff at Whistler, I'm a girl overboard, and no one's riding to my rescue. Mama's muted "Wayne" sounds more weary than warning. Still, he reacts like his younger-but-not-wiser stepmother has ripped into him. His chair scrapes across the hardwood floor, and he slams the door behind him so that I hear the "bitch" in its echo, loud and clear.

"Can't I just stay with Bao-mu?" I ask Mama softly.

Mama plays with her enormous jade pendant, the one she never takes off, the one that Grace snickers is so apropos. After all, a jade is an adulteress, no? Foreboding expands balloon-like in my belly until I can't breathe as Mama swings the pendant from side to side, hypnotically. Finally, matter-of-factly, she says, "Bao-mu's granddaughter is having a baby. She's moving to California to take care of her."

"What?"

"Excuse me," she corrects me before answering, "Any day now."

"For good?"

"For good." As if she has just informed me of nothing more important than a forecast of rain, Mama skates one of her youth-enhancing vitamins around her plate, unconcerned.

A life without Bao-mu is far worse than a life in Hong Kong. She has been the one constant in my home since I can remember. Other nannies have come and gone, a blur of girls who hauled me around since driving is the one thing that Bao-mu is afraid to do. At my first sniffle, Mama breathes out impatiently. So I blink away my tears.

"Bao-mu's too old to take care of a baby" is my last-ditch protest, and I ignore Grace's loud sniff that insinuates I'm infantile myself.

"It's her decision." Mama busies herself with a piece of imaginary lint on her jacket, flicking it off like it's Bao-mu, gone in a moment. "She gave me her notice."

"When?" I demand.

"A few weeks ago."

A few weeks ago. My life for the last month has been nothing but glittering surface hoar, that gorgeous layer of downy snow that slides once anything breaks through it. Which just goes to show that beauty is as deceptive as it is dangerous.

The most beautiful woman in the room now shakes her head at me, her long, glossy hair gleaming under the overhead lights. "Close your mouth, Syrah. It's unbecoming." Mama picks up another vitamin. "We'll live in Hong Kong during the school year only. Summers in China are too hot and humid." Her thin body shudders delicately as if the mere thought of humidity is melting her thick surface hoar of makeup. A vitamin disappears between her red-lacquered lips.

"Summers?" I repeat numbly.

"One? Two?" Mama answers, throwing her hands up, a care-free girl celebrating Hong Kong, an adventure we've all been waiting for. "Your father wants to leave it open-ended."

This time it's Grace who sputters in surprise, "He does?"

I don't blame her. Our dad has been known to play a single game of Go, an ancient strategy game, for two years, plotting his moves as if he were Sun-Tzu, his hero of a military expert from two thousand years ago.

"Your father is really embracing retirement. Isn't it wonderful after all his years of hard work?" asks Mama, her smile so decidedly bright, I realize that she has no idea she's derailing my snowboarding dreams. I tighten my grip around my video. There will never be a good time to show them, to make my case. "We can summer in the south of France. Or Barcelona."

Mochi yelps, a piercing sound as if Grace has squeezed him too tightly. Grace's geisha girl mask of serenity doesn't slip. But I know. I know exactly what she's thinking, just as Mochi knows what she's feeling. The last thing I want to be is the poor little bitch girl the way Grace and Wayne think I am.

No sooner does Baba walk down the stairs, Wayne returns inside, pretending he's just stepped out to take an important call himself. Grace announces, an incredulous look on her face, "Europe, Wayne. Betty's thinking about summering in Europe."

"Yes, how does that sound to you, Ethan? A villa? We can have our summer meetings there. A family reunion overseas," says Mama, her eyes gleaming with possibilities. Another home to buy, another place to decorate, more things to shop for.

"Why not?" says Baba, squeezing her bony shoulder before taking his seat. "We can talk about it on our way to D.C. tonight."

94

"D.C.?" I repeat.

"Your father's been asked by the CTIA to help open Asia for American telecom companies," Mama says proudly like she's the one who's been asked.

Both my half-sibs look impressed at the real reason for our move to Hong Kong. Over dinners with the bigwigs in the Cellular Telecommunications and Internet Association, I know that the international trade organization has been courting Baba to take the helm again and fulfill the group's mission: expand the wireless frontier.

Excitement glitters in Baba's eyes at this new challenge, yet all he admits to is a modest, "A small project for my retirement. We'll kick it off at the World Economic Summit in two weeks."

"Luckily, that's in Hong Kong so we can look at properties at the same time," says Mama, pleased as if this is a sign that our move is meant to be. "Our next month is crazy. I have to squeeze in another trip to San Francisco, too."

That'll be the third, or is it fourth, trip to San Francisco in the last couple of weeks. Oh, no, we wouldn't want to infringe on Mama's shopping time. Not even when it means breaking her promise to me.

Without thinking, I say, "But that's winter break. I thought we were going to the World Championships."

"God, what's more important?" asks Wayne, his hand snaking around his teacup as though it's my neck he wants to strangle. "A snowboarding contest or a meeting with world leaders?"

Tears prickle my eyes again. I'm kicking myself for believing that my parents were actually going with me to Whistler. For hoping that they'd watch the snowboarders and see why I loved riding the mountains. See that these kids aren't aimless punks with no future. See that I was good at something that had nothing to do with them. See *me* for the first time.

I think of ice so I don't cry in front of Grace and Wayne. The cold, ice-packed crud that trashes snowboards. That I need to become right now. I ask, "Can't someone else drive me?"

"What? Everyone should drop their plans to help *you*?" Wayne asks incredulously. So I drop my suggestion to ask the house manager or Lena the chef to drive me.

"Unless . . ." Mama looks over hopefully at Grace, bypassing Wayne altogether. It's obvious that he'd never help me out, even if he lived right here in The House of Cheng with us instead of in California near his mother, the first Mrs. Ethan Cheng.

Grace immediately checks her electronic scheduler as if she needs proof that she's always too busy for me. "I have a trip to Tokyo then. A very important client pitch." She pauses for maximum impact. "A two-million dollar account."

Ah, money soothes the savage beast, and Baba nods, understanding perfectly well the all-important call of money.

So does Mama, because she changes tactics. "Tokyo. Well, maybe Syrah could go with you?" Her wide help-me look might work with Baba, but it has the opposite effect on Grace.

"Not possible," says Grace.

Mama tries again. "She could go shopping while you're at meetings."

The Princess of Passive-Aggressiveness, I lash out at my convenient whipping girl, "I'm not going to Tokyo with Grace."

Even as I say it, I'm half-hoping that Grace will answer, "Sure, you should come with me!" That she'll tell me she's wanted to get to know me better and this is a perfect opportunity for some sister-bonding time. One look at Grace's tight lips, and I know the chances of that happening are equal to the odds of a miracle taking place right here.

Grace spouts off one of her PR sound bites, a simple tagline that her intended audience of one will remember forever: "Find your own solution."

"Grace, can't you change your plans?" Mama's wheedling tone makes me cringe. "Syrah would have such a good time with you. You know all the right places to go."

If Grace still hates us after sixteen years, buttering her up isn't going to soften her any. We're still her home wrecker. Even so, I'm not sure if it hurts to see Mama trying so hard because it makes her seem so pathetic or if it's because I don't rate half the effort.

Grace breathes in. Her black eyes go so cold, I swear I feel crud frosting my entire body.

"Some of us have to work. Besides," she says, delivering the ultimate coup de Grace, "Syrah's not my problem."

The fact is, I'm not even Bao-mu's problem anymore. I bite the insides of my cheeks. Shakily, I lift a mound of rice to my mouth with chopsticks.

"No rice," Mama snaps, glowering at her enemy, simple carbohydrates. "Hong Kong girls are so skinny."

My hand jerks, scalded, and the rice ball drops onto my plate. We must keep Syrah on a strict low-carb, non-fat, no-food diet so that her hips and stomach don't balloon into obese American-sized proportions.

Baba ends all further discussion with his decision. "Then Syrah will stay home for winter break. She can help Bao-mu pack. Now everyone, take a look at the P and L. . . ."

Cheeks flaming, I keep my eyes on the *chuun hup,* the teak tray of togetherness, untouched on the long conference table. Not one morsel has been eaten. Not the chocolate gold coins for more wealth or the dragon eye for sweetness. Not the coconut for good relationships.

13

The Chengs are nothing if not efficient. Our meeting ends a full hour early. Scant minutes after the last agenda item is checked off, everyone evacuates as though the end-of-trading bell has rung, Wayne and Grace for their private debrief of the meeting, and my parents for their private jet awaiting them at Boeing Field.

On my way back to the main house, I can't help but replay my impromptu plea, horrified. Even to my untrained business ears, I sound inane. A girl who deserves Wayne's condescension. I wouldn't invest in myself. The life path my parents want me to follow is as set in stone as these Chinese poems etched on the walls and on rocks to point out vignettes visitors might otherwise miss in our garden. As I stop to trace one of those poems, I realize that my forehead might as well be tattooed:

> Dutiful child of the great Ethan Cheng
> Bends to her father's will
> Even if she breaks.

Now it just seems so stupid, so naïve, to think I stood a chance of impressing my parents, Wayne, Grace, all the kids at school who ridicule me behind my back. That all of them would watch me ride, awestruck at my skill, my style, my daring.

Frustrated, I stomp back to the house, head for the kitchen. Show me a carb I won't eat right now. Fury overtakes me when I pass all the museum-quality antiques inside this shrine to Mama's style. Oh, no, there will be no reproductions in this house. Ironic, yes, when not a single person in The House of Cheng feels real. Least of all me.

The kitchen is dark, just the way I want for my solo pig-out.

"Done already?" Bao-mu asks.

So startled, I drop my CD, which clatters out of its safe case and onto the cherry wood floor. Quickly, I bend down to scoop my résumé up. How can I possibly still care?

As soon as Bao-mu sees my face, she sets down her tiny teacup, her eyebrows knitted together into an accent mark of concern. "How go?"

I wish I were little again so I could nestle against her warm body and inhale her strength and believe her when she told me that I was special. That I was destined to do great things, whatever I wanted.

"Everybody had to leave early." A surge of misplaced anger rises inside me and I glare at her. "Just like you're going to. How come you didn't tell me you were leaving?"

Bao-mu abandons her bowl of hot and sour soup at the kitchen table and turns on the light. She bustles to the refrigerator, removing saran-wrapped platters, a feast I no longer feel like eating because *she* wants me to. Irrational, immature, I know.

"Learn now, learn later," Bao-mu says, pulling a clean plate out of a drawer. "Doesn't change anything." She heaps so much steaming rice on the plate that Mama would have gone into diabetic shock if she saw. "You need eat."

"I'm not hungry," I tell her obstinately. My stomach growls in disagreement.

Naturally, Bao-mu has ears only for my stomach. She uncovers every single platter to scoop tofu, Chinese broccoli, and sautéed green beans until there are more calories on that one plate than Mama eats in two days. Maybe even three. Just looking at Bao-mu's lumpy knuckles that I used to trace like roller coasters makes me feel guilty, guilty that I've been abrupt with her, even more guilty that she, a little old lady of over seventy, is serving me. Over her loud *aiya* protests, I recover the platters with saran wrap and carry them to the refrigerator.

As I do, half of me wants to tell Bao-mu, *Yes, it's time for you to retire, to stop taking care of me.* The other half wishes she'd never leave.

"Sit," orders Bao-mu, placing my trough of a plate on the table.

I sit because four feet eleven inches of female power are glowering at me. For all I get embarrassed about people finding out that I still have a nanny when I'm nearly sixteen, I love Bao-mu.

"I was hoping you would move to Hong Kong with us," I admit because it's easier to hide the truth from myself than from Bao-mu. "Remember how you used to tell me you were taking the next plane back to China?"

Bao-mu laughs. "That only when you so naughty. China was just talk." She pauses from wiping down the counter. "And it work. Sometime, you too good girl."

"What do you mean?"

"You always stop when someone tell you to. Right away." She sighs, a creaky breath of regret. "You never tell them stop."

Every tear I've dammed up for seven months presses on my eyelids. I want to deny it, tell her she's wrong, but how can I when I know that she's right? I don't stop Wayne from harshing on me. I didn't stop Jared.

Bao-mu says, "I so old now."

"You look so young for sixty."

Usually, Bao-mu has a good laugh when I say that, but tonight she sits heavily next to me. "I too old to move to China now. I used to America. You not need me anymore. You such big girl."

What I want to say is that I still need her. But I don't want to sound like a baby when God knows, I'm not pure and innocent like one. Instead, I nod my head as though I'm agreeing; because Bao-mu looks so severe, I know she's on the verge of crying, too.

"You need eat dinner," insists Bao-mu, nudging my plate even closer to me, food-medicine for my breaking heart. "You want disappear like your mama?"

As a matter of fact, I do.

My stomach rumbles with a hunger I don't want to feel, my mouth bitter with aftertaste from my first family meeting.

"This so delicious," says Bao-mu, tantalizing me with a crisp green bean between her chopsticks, not in that weird way that Mama's friends push fattening food on each other because they want each other to gain weight, to feel superior since they've got stronger willpower and the fat-free body to prove it. But Bao-mu offers food out of love. "Taste."

So I take a small bite. And it tastes hot and sour, salty and just a tiny bit sweet.

"My cooking the best," says Bao-mu, who has never forgiven my parents for hiring Lena, our professional chef, a few years ago.

"Yes, it is," I tell Bao-mu, who's been more of a mother substitute than her nickname could ever have promised. I take another bite. "You are the best."

Upstairs, lying on my full belly in front of my bookcase, I flip through my manga-journal to the last half-drawn image of Shiraz. As usual, my snowboard girl is flying down some amazingly steep run, living my dream. I sit up, and close the book on Shiraz, unable to finish her. My dream is as far away as Hong Kong.

God, I can't believe that we're moving eight time zones away from Age. All at once, I need to talk to him, need the reassurance that we're still friends, best friends, here in Pacific Standard Time. Without thinking, I spring to my feet, wincing when my knee buckles from the sudden movement.

As I wait for Age to answer his phone, I massage my knee on my chair, and spot the new *Snowboarder* in my in-box, still embalmed in shrink-wrap just as all the other issues are since my accident.

"Hey," says Age, his voice surprising me because, I guess, I'd been expecting his voicemail.

I sit up and dispense with any greetings. "So what's a chiru?"

"What?" he says, and I'm relieved to hear the laugh back in his voice, the way he sounded before Natalia's grand re-entry into his life. So I tell Age about going to the hospital with Lillian and The Six-Pack.

"If you really want to know," he says, "a chiru is an antelope. Endangered. In Tibet."

"God, Encyclopedia Zorrito, I'd ask how you know."

"Except you don't have to."

"Because you've got the world's weirdest brain."

"One man's trivia, another one's treasure."

"Who said that?" I demand.

"Me."

"Quoting yourself." I shake my head, wishing he were next to me so I could poke him in the shoulder. "Some people would say that's kind of, I don't know, egotistical."

"What can I say? I'm great."

I laugh and lean back in my chair. "Okay, Exalted One, so what do you think? Instead of being a Cheng business-bot, I could be the first sidewalk manga artist in Seattle."

"Oh, yeah, I can really see you sitting out on Broadway with a can for donations by your side."

"Don't forget my sign that says, 'Let me show you your inner animal.' You think my parents will be cool with that?"

"About as cool with you flipping burgers all day."

"Or going pro." As soon as I say it, I wish I hadn't, because snowboarding reminds me of Natalia, which reminds me that Age has been an absentee friend for the last couple of days, which reminds me of moving.

As if we're operating on different planes, Age says as excit-

104

edly as the kids at the hospital, "So the new Mack Dawg movie came into the store today."

"Come on over," I tell him, willing to break my ban on all things professional snowboarding if it means hanging out with Age. "We can watch it in my studio."

"I can't," he says.

I know the girl behind his can't: Natalia.

"What time is it?" Then Age swears, making me tense, because I know what's coming. Sure enough, he sounds like Wayne, who has a million things on his agenda more important than me: "I'm fifteen minutes late. Natalia's going to freak."

"Just because you're a little late?"

Age coughs, and I translate that to mean, *No, because talking to you made me late.* He says, "I'll call you later."

In a moment, I'm listening to a *click* as Age hangs up. Breathing out in disbelief, I place my phone on my desk, shove back in my chair, but then stop. Recklessly, I rip open the plastic covering the snowboarding magazine. What do I see on the first page that I open to? Naturally, it's a full-body shot of Sonora Bremen, blond and thin, two years older than I am, and the girl who hooked up with Jared right after snowboarding camp. She didn't last long, either.

What would it be like to be her, or any of the snowboard girls who've made it, are under contract with some big-time companies, and are traveling the world? Girls who get to design their own line of boards and clothes and goggles. Girls who everyone aspires to be.

I open my desk drawer, rummage for a pen to manga-journal, and instead feel the framed photograph of me in my snowboarding gear where the housekeeper or my mother or her interior decorator must have stashed it, placing it in solitary confinement for having clashed with the décor. I can barely remember how I used to picture myself in a snowboarding movie, amped up music in the background. How I'd ride the skies into history. How people would breathe my first name in awe — not my last. How I would be Age's first-string-pick riding partner forever.

The antique mirror hanging above my desk, the one that Bao-mu gave to me to ward away evil, is supposed to reflect ghosts. But in the mottled glass I catch my reflection and gasp. That's what I've become: a barely-there girl. God, when did I disappear? I peer more closely into the mirror and wish I hadn't. My cheeks look rounder than ever, my eyes smaller than they are. I'm bloated from overdosing on the Wayne Cheng Kool-Aid, the kind that brainwashes me into thinking that I can't do anything right.

Oh, Syrah Cheng? She could have been great if she didn't chicken out. If she hadn't screwed up and let herself get screwed over big-time by Jared Johanson.

I rear back from the mirror and head to my bookshelf, where I shelved a box with all my ribbons. Standing on my tiptoes, I reach for it, but as I do, a book falls from the shelf like snow sloughing off a cliff. I wince as it smacks the crown of my head.

"Ow," I moan, my hand rubbing my skull.

I bend down to hurl the book, vent all my frustration on it. If I ever doubted Bao-mu that ghosts fly in breezes and topple otherwise stable glasses from shelves and wipe out hard drives, my skepticism vanishes the moment my eyes land on Baba's book, *The Ethan Cheng Way: From Rags to Richest.*

A sign, Bao-mu would say. *You suppose learn from this.*

After it was published last year, I had glanced through Baba's bestseller, called that half-assed effort good enough, and shelved the book out of sight, out of mind at the top of my bookcase.

Putting it in Chenglish, I was ambushed at the family meeting, and I was ambushed by Natalia. Maybe I couldn't help her moving in on Age, but it was my fault for not being prepared for the Cheng assault.

Sitting down, I hold Baba's book in my lap, wondering if the ultimate how-to lesson is somewhere within. What I need is a step-by-step plan to win over my parents, Grace, Wayne. And myself. That's what I find in the table of contents. To paraphrase the great Ethan Cheng, 99 percent of negotiation is preparation (introduction). Identify your goal (chapter one). Select your partners (chapter two). And then obliterate your obstacles (chapter three).

Looking up from the book, my eyes graze over the ghost-detecting mirror. I think about how everybody else takes what they want. They don't stop whatever they're doing. Right away. Why don't I grab what I want, this once?

Slowly, I get to my feet, thinking about my goal; how after tonight, I'd just love to prove Wayne wrong: I can be a snowboard girl, one who's so successful, my busy career will be just as all-consuming as everybody else's in my family. Hong Kong? Hardly. My schedule is going to keep me busy flying around the world for competitions. I'll be the one that other girls like Natalia wish they were.

At my computer, I open the spreadsheet I started a year ago, the one with the list of companies, their local sales reps, and addresses. I find the one I'm looking for, the man who asked to see my video after I finished it. It's as if all my ambivalence and insecurities about snowboarding disappear. My fingers strike each key hard as I type:

From: Syrah Cheng
To: ralph@rhamiware.com
Subject: Checking In

Dear Ralph,
You gave me your card after I won three events at Alpental last year and wanted to see my video résumé. I'm sending you a CD tomorrow. I'd love to talk when you have a moment.
Syrah

My hands feel as icy as if I've been standing on a mountain in skin-burning cold. When you approach a cliff, you can't over-analyze, you can't stall. So before I get scared and talk myself out of it, I hold my breath and hit Send.

14

Come Tuesday morning, I wake from the same dream I've been having since my first day back on the slopes, the one where I'm snowboarding, whole again, only I'm wearing a leash, the kind that kids who are learning to ski sometimes wear. The thing is, I don't know who's holding my reins, slowing me down, but I've got a good suspicion. She's bubbly, wears pink snow pants, and rides with her arms poised in second position like a ballerina. And she's the reason why Age hasn't called to check in yet again this morning.

With my eyes still closed, I breathe out the sensation of being tethered and inhale deeply, catching the scent of my favorite soy sauce eggs. The last time Bao-mu fixed those eggs was before Mama declared it was time for me to lose my baby fat, and lured a fancy American chef away from the top spa in Scottsdale. Another inhale. As a way of returning to my reality, this isn't so bad, even if it means that Mama and Baba must have extended their second trip to D.C. in a week. That's the only explanation for why Bao-mu would dare the wrath of Lena the kitchen warlord and whip up anything with the artery-choking fat content of (the horror! the horror!) eggs.

I open my eyes slowly and remember that it's Bao-mu's birthday. We'll both be eating eggs this morning to wish her long life, and Bao-mu's probably waiting for me. But I can't resist checking e-mail — no response from RhamiWare, and definitely no message from Age. Bao-mu's gift is behind my snowboarding gear, and I wince when I bend down to grab it, because my shoulder is still stiff from falling on it four nights ago.

Before I can head downstairs to the kitchen, where I thought she'd be, Bao-mu surprises me by opening the door to her suite. "I been waiting for you," she says. Bags under her eyes mar her normally unlined face, her mouth puckered with sour worry.

The birthday wish dies on my lips, and I rush over to Bao-mu, demanding, "What's wrong?"

"Christine call last night. My granddaughter had baby yesterday. Too early. Baby not ready come out yet." A frown wrinkles Bao-mu's smooth forehead. "I need go. Today."

"Today?" I repeat faintly. Wait, I want to say, I just found out that you were leaving. But she is leaving. Bao-mu's suite, which is typically a study of neatness with every book, frame, and plant in its place, looks like the aftermath of an earthquake or the mess made by an overwhelmed person who doesn't know where to begin, abandoning one project to start another and another. Random piles of books and papers dot the bamboo floor, creating a sporadic tree line. Only the middle shelf of her bookcase has been cleared off. A few paintings, including the best of my elementary school art projects, lean against the far wall.

"You didn't sleep," I accuse her. "Why did you cook those eggs?"

I know why she cooked them instead of sleeping: because she loves me and knows how much I savor every bite of those forbidden salty eggs.

Bao-mu maneuvers slowly around her coffee table, stacked with clean teacups, looking around helplessly, lost and unsure.

Seeing Bao-mu like this, as if her age has caught up to her over the course of a phone call, makes me want to cry. According to the chapter in *The Ethan Cheng Way* I read last night when I couldn't shake the fear that I'd never regain my feeling for snow, sometimes it's better to act than to do nothing.

I figure, this is one of those times. Besides, I've traveled so much, packing I can do with my eyes closed.

Huskily, I tell Bao-mu, "Let's pack your clothes first."

Bao-mu nods and follows me into her bedroom.

A large suitcase lies open on her low platform bed.

"Okay," I say decisively, "you need enough clothes for a week. Three pants, four shirts, a sweater, a jacket, and underwear." Out of her drawers, I pull out the elasticized pants Bao-mu's so fond of wearing, no matter how many custom-made slacks Mama brings back for her from Hong Kong.

"And this," says Bao-mu, handing me the cashmere sweater I bought for her two Christmases ago, the one she's never worn even though it's her favorite color, tangerine. She strokes it lovingly the way Grace does Mochi or a mother might a beloved daughter's hair. "I been waiting for special occasion wear this.

111

When Christine see me in this, she say, Mama, you look so successful."

I want to ask her why it matters what her daughter thinks, her daughter who has never taken the time to call on Bao-mu's birthday or remember Mother's Day. Her daughter who Bao-mu sees only when she visits California, and never the other way around. Bao-mu always demurs with a "Christine medical doctor. She so busy."

As I place Bao-mu's underwear inside the suitcase, I notice her precious treasures on the bed: the black-and-white photograph of a much younger Bao-mu and her husband, a stern, unsmiling man. Her daughter, surly, wearing graduation robes. But when I pick up Bao-mu's cell phone, the one Baba gave to her that she rarely uses because she says the sudden ringing, ringing makes her think a ghost is calling, I know she's truly going for good.

"You call me anytime," Bao-mu says before turning abruptly to the closet. She walks slower than usual, like she's the one who was used, bruised, and abused.

As she stands on tiptoes to grab her shirts, I nudge her gently aside. Since I have studied with the master and commander herself — Bao-mu the Great — for the last fifteen years, I order rather than ask, "Just tell me what you want."

"I be okay," Bao-mu replies, but to my relief retreats to her bed, her weight a bare suggestion, hardly indenting the mattress.

"Which shirts do you want?"

"It not matter."

So I reach up to select a few, holding my breath when my stiff shoulder protests. On her bed, I fold the sleeves one over the other so they hug themselves.

"There so much work," says Bao-mu, glancing wearily around her bedroom.

"I'll take care of packing the rest of your stuff after you're gone. Just let me know where to ship it, okay?"

"You just like your daddy."

"What? Bossy?"

"You always know what to do," says Bao-mu stubbornly.

That unwavering confidence in me makes me tear up, and to distract myself, I hand Bao-mu her present. "Happy birthday, Bao-mu." Where Mama is stressful to shop for, what with her ever-changing brand hierarchy with each new season — Prada is good, Chanel better — Bao-mu is a challenge, because she says at this time in her life, the best present is having someone listen to her talk. Out of habit, Bao-mu unwraps her present so carefully, she doesn't tear the paper, good enough to reuse.

"*Wah!*" says Bao-mu. Her fingers run gently across the cover of the baby book inside the box. "This so beautiful. You make?"

I nod and tell her, "It's a brag book. You can put pictures of your great-grandchild in it and bore everyone with them."

"Brag book," she repeats. She opens it to the first page, where I've drawn a manga version of her chasing a crawling baby. "In China, we say bad luck brag about children. It tempt fate to take them away, bring lots bad luck."

"Oh." I grimace, wondering if I've made a colossal mistake, given Bao-mu a *bad* present when all I've wanted to do is make her happy, remember me.

But Bao-mu sighs. "Maybe I not brag enough about my daughter. Ah, Syrah, life sometime so hard." She looks at me intently, willing me to understand. "Just because someone leave you, not mean they not love you."

113

"I know."

But she makes a tsking sound as if she doubts that I know, and then she says in Mandarin, the way she always does when she has something Important to Communicate, *"Wo jiang ni ting."* *I talk so you listen.* Bao-mu scoots over and pats the empty spot beside her. "When Christine little, just ten, the Red Guard come to our house in Shanghai. You know Red Guard? Cultural Revolution in 1966?"

I shake my head because, according to my school's history program, nothing much has happened in America past 1945. With the brief exception of a weeklong sojourn into the Far East, Chinese history is a vast, uncharted territory, as far as I'm concerned.

"Communists took control over China about time when your mommy born. They start Red Guard group. Kids like little soldiers. Some your age, only fourteen, fifteen." Bao-mu shakes her head, still unable to comprehend it. Her voice hardens. "One day, they came and burn all my books, smash pots, vases, everything beautiful. They take all my jewelry. I so stupid. I hid diamond in my shoe, one my husband gave me for engagement ring. The Red Guard separate us in different rooms. They tell him, they know I hide something. They tell him, they kill me if they find unless he tell them. So he tell them about diamond. They beat me, my husband in front of Christine. Then they take him away to labor camp."

Bao-mu smoothes the bedspread between us, one pucker refusing to lay flat, its edge trapped under the suitcase. "Christine denounce me."

"What do you mean, denounce?"

"All time in my village, we have meetings. Everyone have to

come. Some make confessions about themselves, that they cap-italist, they landowner. Christine say I bad, a landowner." Bao-mu shakes her head, her fingers pressing down futilely on the bulge of fabric, but like her memory, it won't be smoothed away. "In front everybody, they give me *ying yang tou*. Shave half my head, other half cut short like man's hair. Very ugly." Her eyes narrow in remembrance.

"And you're still going to help Christine and her daughter."

"They my family." And like Baba's favorite explain-all word, *business,* the way Bao-mu says "family" explains why she's leav-ing me. To Bao-mu, family, not money or honor or face, is every-thing. And I'm not family. Her hand sweeps brusquely through the air to clear the ugly wisps of memory and history away. "Old story. We all have old story."

Bao-mu looks at me expectantly, waiting for me to divulge my secret that I've punched down, tried to bury for the last seven months. The reason why I took off at Whistler, not be-cause I'm an idiot but because I was so upset I became idiotic. There's a big difference even if the results are the same. But that's an old story I still can't draw in my manga-journal, much less confess. Not even to Bao-mu. Or Age.

"You never told me any of this," I say, realizing I only know the bare facts of Bao-mu's life where it intersects with mine. How many journals could I fill with what we don't know about each other?

"Sometime, better if we just forget about," she says finally as if she knows everything about my broken heart. "No, no, that wrong. Learn from first," she corrects herself. "And then forget about."

What I want to know is, where's the step-by-step plan for

forgetting all the things that disfigure you inside, in places where only you can feel the scars? My hands are folded, a good girl at church, but good girls don't knowingly let a boy like Jared do what he did to me.

"Seee-raaaah," Bao-mu says, hanging on to the vowels in my name like she doesn't want to let them go. "Look."

When I do, I see that she's holding a picture of me and her, the day I won the school spelling bee in fifth grade. I don't remember where my parents were that time, only that they weren't there. Bao-mu shakes her head in disbelief that so much time could separate that girl in the photograph from the one she's sitting by now.

"You such smart girl." Slowly, Bao-mu works the photograph out of its frame and places it in the brag book, the one I made for her great-granddaughter. She nods once, satisfied, and only then does she say, "You need make own brag book. You need say, I the best. I deserve the best."

I throw my arms around Bao-mu, the one person who has always believed in me, no matter what. Under my hands, her frail shoulders are as delicate as bird wings. Only then does it strike me hard just how much I'm going to miss her when she flies this coop.

Choking up, I whisper, "I deserved you."

"Aaah," says Bao-mu, trying but not succeeding to sound impatient. I can tell she's pleased.

So I take her hand, swallow my tears, and say, "Let's go eat the soy sauce eggs. You need long life if you're taking care of a baby."

"First," she says, stopping me with a gentle hand, "let me take picture of you."

Holding still, I smile for Bao-mu, as she painstakingly positions the camera, so sleek and small in her old hands I'm afraid that she's going to drop it. And after a long minute, she presses down hard, determined to capture this moment.

Still holding the camera before her eye, Bao-mu nods as though I've just given her my blessing to leave me. And in a funny way, I have.

15

"So I was wondering in the shower this morning . . . ," Mr. Delbene says, rubbing his bald head, as smooth as one of those Magic Eight Balls. There are a billion questions I'd like to ask one of those prophesizing balls, and not one of them has anything to do with what a teacher, specifically Mr. Delbene, wonders about in a shower.

Me, I'd ask: Will I see Bao-mu soon? (Most likely.) Will I get out of being Shanghai'ed by my parents and taken to Hong Kong? (Outlook not so good.) Will RhamiWare sponsor me? (Better not tell you now.) Will Age and I be best friends the way we were Before Natalia? (Ask again later.)

"So I was wondering," says Mr. Delbene, pacing, his mismatched feet in blue and orange socks today, "will I hear a scintillating idea today, one that revolutionizes high school journalism? Innovates the way students get news? Anyone? Anyone?"

No one's more surprised than I am when, after a couple minutes of this soliloquy, I blurt out, "We should take advantage of technology. Kids our age get our news online."

"What do you mean?" demands George, editor-in-chief, varsity lacrosse captain, and early admittance to Yale. Obviously, this is one boy whose brag book gloats ad nauseam about all his accomplishments. Now, as if I've offended his family's three generations of news coverage, both in print and on air, he crosses his arms and says defensively, "I read the newspaper. So what are you talking about?"

A couple of months ago, at a charity auction for something or other, I sat next to a big time publisher who moaned and groaned about kids in my age demographic not reading newspapers anymore. I don't want to sound like I'm bragging, so I edit myself down to an innocuous, "The *LA Times* did an internal study on its readership."

"So what? Just publish online?" George shakes his head, and then in a patronizing tone he says, "Good thinking, but people like print."

Instead of backing down, I look around the class and ask, "What's the harm in us blogging about school events, basketball games, the musical even, and giving real-time coverage and commentary? I bet we could sell online advertising to defray our costs."

Silence makes me want to crawl right into my manga-journal. I clench and unclench my pencil nervously, until I realize Mr. Delbene's considering my ideas, head cocked, interested. Most people only care what I think because of who my dad is. Their logic goes like this: Win Syrah over and she'll tell Mr. Cheng, who'll have one of his minions do the research, and voilà! Instant cash infusion.

"No one's going online to look at what a blogger has to say about our football games," says George with a smirk.

That's the thing with opinions. As long as you parrot what people want to hear, you're a Wise Woman. Say something they don't, and suddenly you're the Village Idiot.

"No, Syrah's got a point. We've got to think outside the box," chimes in Lillian unexpectedly for a toe-the-line kind of staffer. Then again, maybe she sees that the writing on this wall is so clear, it's graffiti: the newspaper she's inheriting next year is sliding fast into mass oblivion. She says, "At my old school, we did crazy things, like run student obits for the graduation edition."

"Right, obits." George mocks her in that same overtly condescending tone I hear from Wayne. Deliberately, he swings one leg onto his desk and leans back in his chair.

I bristle. Considering George is writing our newspaper's obituary with an editorial calendar of boring, boring, and more boring, he doesn't deserve to be Mr. High-and-Mighty, not even if his family owns a couple of newspapers in the Northwest. He's just like Wayne, who, when it comes down to it, inherited his business, the Cheng investment arm, too.

That realization makes me straighten in my chair, throw out my usual go-with-everyone-else's-flow, and build on Lillian's idea. "Senior tombstones could be a lot of fun for our graduation issue," I say.

"Journalism is to communicate news." George folds his arms across his chest. "Not to entertain."

"Real newspapers have gossip columns," I remind him.

"So we print gossip?" he says, all skeptical.

"No, I'm saying newspapers aren't just for hard news."

"And no one's reading the news we're communicating," says Lillian.

"So, what?" George slides his feet off his desk to thump onto the floor, a sound of disbelief. "We write obits?"

It's tempting to compose his: *High school editor-in-chief was Chengulated in front of entire journalism class for being a stubborn, pompous, know-it-all.*

"The next thing you'll be suggesting is that we have comic strips," he says, and slaps himself on the forehead. "Oh, wait, we already have those."

"No," I say, "how about a manga-column?"

"A manga-what?" asks George, a crescent of a mocking smile forming.

Lillian looks approvingly at me. "That could be very cool. And Syrah's a great manga artist."

George is back to shaking his head. "What could she possibly manga about?"

When Chelsea angles her body from her seat in the front, I groan to myself. As everyone knows, just because her dad is some old-money, big-time real estate developer, she thinks everyone should hear her talk about him. Newsflash: Mr. Dillinger inherited his job from his dad, who got it from his father. So it's not like Chelsea's dad earned his position and power with his brains or work ethic or philosophy the way Baba did.

No matter, Chelsea clenches the back of her seat, a pulpit to grandstand with her Heavenly Father oration. "Well, the other night, my father was honored at the Juvenile Diabetes auction, and we bought a couple of tables."

"So?" says George, which I'm sure is the sentiment echoing in everyone's heads.

"So, focusing on more kids at our school means they'll read the article about themselves. And so will their friends," Chelsea says.

"And their enemies," says the resident goth in class, his black lips spreading into a grim grin.

As hard as it is to admit, Chelsea is onto something. My neurons can hardly believe it. The way George leans back in his chair again, his reigning monarch pose, makes me want to pluck him off his family throne.

"Okay, so tell me, who?" George smiles smugly, like he knows the answer. "Who's doing anything special that we haven't covered already?"

True, the usual suspects have been featured extensively, not only in our newspaper, but in the *Seattle Times*. James, the concert pianist who won sonata competitions against teenagers when he was just eight. Becky, the future Nobel prize–winning scientist who scored a summer internship with the Hutch, the cancer research center on Lake Union.

Lillian says, "People's community service projects. Some people are doing amazing things."

"Some people, meaning you," snickers Chelsea, morphing from girl-with-no-brains back to girl-with-no-heart in 0.3 seconds. "Great, we can all write stories about how Lillian is saving the world."

"I've already done it," I say, my voice so emphatic that it shuts Chelsea up. "I've covered Lillian."

Lillian blinks at me in surprise. So does Mr. Delbene, who finally wakes from his trance and strides over to my desk to read the manga entry in my journal of the Groundhog Day party, starting with Lillian commanding a troupe of socialites. Imminent sickness fills my gut, and I stare down at my hands balled up on my lap. But when Mr. Delbene starts laughing, I glance up sharply at him, and he's looking at me differently. With respect.

"Political cartoon meets social commentary," Mr. Delbene says just as freedom rings, and the class becomes a flurry of movement out the door.

I bend down for my backpack and note that two mismatched socks in Birkenstocks are not moving out of my way. Years of dodging unwanted conversations with older men have me perfectly attuned to this danger. Let me guess; I'm about to be bombarded with a "brilliant idea" about how I really ought to manga-column about my father instead of Lillian. Look, if Baba doesn't grant any personal interviews, not with Katie Couric or Diane Sawyer, then he sure as hell won't divulge confidences to me.

"Syrah," says Mr. Delbene as he eases his potbelly into the desk across from mine. "Just like your dad wrote in his book, right? 'The best ideas are born out of crises.'"

"I haven't gotten to that part yet," I say, shrugging into my jacket quickly.

"Really? It's in the introduction."

He looks at me like he's waiting for my aha moment of recognition so the two of us can share an impromptu Ethan Cheng fan club lovefest. Hate to disappoint, but I continue to look blank. Mr. Delbene shrugs. "Anyway, all I wanted to say was good thinking out of the box today. Your ideas just might turn our paper around."

"Really?"

"Sure. Get your class to think, motivate them to act, shake their world up. You'll be surprised at the power you could wield."

"Because my dad's Ethan Cheng?"

"No," he says, surprised. "Because political cartoonists

communicate more than even essayists. I don't have to tell you what a picture is worth, do I?" Mr. Delbene holds his breath and with his hands clenched on the edge of the desk, he wriggles himself out from behind it. "So think about the name for your column. The Syrah Cheng Way, maybe?"

On my way to English, I think about that. The Syrah Cheng Way. How can an outsider see me as a rightful Cheng the way my siblings don't? The way I haven't? Syrah Cheng, The Turnaround Queen. As I get sucked into the milling crowd, I wonder if maybe the rush I'm feeling from leading, not just following, from improving a newspaper, not just proving myself, is what addicts Baba to business.

At lunch, George waves me over to his table to "review" my ideas when Chelsea and her Six-Pack descend. Setting her tray down, Chelsea says, "So, Syrah, I heard you aren't going to Wicked in Whistler."

I shrug, noncommittally.

Chelsea leans in for The Ask. "If you're not using your VIP tickets, can I have them?"

Suddenly, I hear Bao-mu: *you too much good girl.* This time, I'm not going to give up what I want, not these tickets. With a deliberate look at my watch, I stand up the way I've seen my mother do so many times when she's late, abruptly and with an air of importance. "I just remembered something I forgot to do," I tell them, grabbing the remains of my lunch.

It's one of those rare sunny days in February, warm enough to sit outside, which is where I should have headed in the first place instead of The Six-Pack hunting grounds inside the cafeteria. A couple of kids are in the meditation garden, only they seem to be meditating on physical rather than spiritual matters. I sidestep the couple who are going at it — all "I'm going to miss you so much over winter break, Pookie" whenever they come up for air.

Since Age hasn't returned my calls this morning or last night, I know a different strategy is in order, but what? Sitting on a stone bench in the corner, facing the sun, I picture Age at lunch with the crew, probably at some Vietnamese phò noodle dive near their school where the portions are enormous and the price is right. Smiling, I dial Mobey's phone and ask to talk to Age.

"Oh, ummm, sure," says Mobey uncomfortably. In the moment between my request and Age's answer, I hear unintelligible boy-talk, then Age's awkward, "Hey."

This is no time for small talk or boy-talk — is it the same thing? — and I aim straight for a killer headline: "How do Wicked at Whistler tickets sound to you?"

Just as I'd hoped, my suggestion shocks Age into normalcy. "You're crazy. What about your parents?"

"They can't take me. Business. Look, they won't care if we go together."

"That would be negative."

Age is right. My parents would ship me to Hong Kong faster than Mama can say "charge it" if they found me with Age, a boy with no name, no money, no prospects.

"I mean, they won't know," I revise quickly, realizing that negotiating is no different from riding the backcountry, both are

125

adventures into the Great Unknown. While you may know where you want to end up, you have no control over the obstacles you hit until they spring on you. Nimbly, I alter my course: "You could drive us to Whistler. Those VIP tickets are going to go to waste if you don't."

"So all I am is your chauffeur?"

"No —"

"Because that's what this sounds like. I'm your backup plan. Again."

"How can you say that?" I'd ask where this is coming from, but I know. Seven letters, begins with N, wears pink, lots of pink, and has signed Age up for the new zero-minute cell phone program that's all the rage among jealous girlfriends. Obviously, Natalia can't stand the thought that, omigod, her boyfriend has a friend of the opposite sex, and is doing her best to poison our relationship.

Age is so silent, I can hear the sound of cars driving by, which means that he's taken our first real argument outside the restaurant. Clearing his throat, Age says, his voice deeper now, "Look, even if I wanted to, I can't drive you to Whistler. For one, I've got to work, and then there are my brothers. . . ."

The couple across the garden from me has rolled into my line of vision, now meditating fully stretched out on top of each other. I can't stop myself: "And then there's Natalia."

"Yeah, and then there's Natalia."

I can imagine Age, in front of the restaurant, one hand shoved into his jeans pocket while he's kicking all the random pinecones and rocks out of the path. On the bench where I'm sitting, I tuck my knees up to my chin like I'll be able to dodge all the detritus heading my way.

"Look," Age says heavily, "the only way things are going to work out with me and Natalia this time is if you and I —"

"Okay," I interrupt. "I get it. She can't handle that we're friends."

"Look at it from her perspective. You've got everything. There are nothing but open doors for you."

"What?" The word explodes out of me.

But before my disbelief can gather momentum and build to anger, Age cuts me off neatly: "If you want something badly enough, you'll find the way, Syrah. You've got the means to do whatever, whenever."

"Right." I think about how there's no one on the staff back home who I can trust enough to drive me to Whistler without tattling to my parents.

"For all your talk about being locked inside The House of Cheng, have you ever thought that you're the one locking everybody else out?"

"That's so not true."

"Oh, yeah, so when were you going to tell me about Hong Kong? It was in Friday's paper, Syrah. All I'm saying is —" He breaks off and sighs. "All I'm saying is, I'm tired of never being your front-door friend. That's all I'm saying."

16

After school a few days later, I dump my backpack in the mudroom, nod at one of the groundskeepers through the bank of windows, and try to ignore the feeling that I've misplaced something. Say, my entire heart. And now, without Bao-mu bustling about, clucking over my day, force-feeding me some Chinese dish that she whipped up (never mind that Lena prepares a low-fat, low-carb, low-calorie snack for me per Mama's instructions), I can't get rid of Age's words still ringing in my head with the perfect pitch of truth.

I rush upstairs to finish packing Bao-mu's suite, but when I get there, her sitting room is empty. Everything, and I mean, everything, is gone — furniture, artwork, pictures. I stride into her bedroom. Even the macaroni necklace I made for her in preschool, which she displayed next to her bed, is gone. Fifteen years of being with our family, with me, vanish as though she was never here.

Packing up for Bao-mu, the one thing I could do for her, wanted to do, is no longer necessary. Disappointed and feeling about as useful as the one stray dust bunny on the hardwood floor where her sofa used to be, I shuffle out of the suite, my footsteps loud with nothing to muffle the sound. Down the hall, I spot a note hanging like a public notice in the middle of my door. Great, maybe Mama's announcing that I'm about to be evacuated without warning, too.

Mama's spiky handwriting reads: *Syrah: The Fujimoros canceled tonight. We need you to fill the table. See you after my pedicure. Mama.*

When I rip off the note, I see the invitation to a black-tie event paper-clipped underneath. My parents have been gone since the family meeting on Saturday, virtually an entire week, and seeing me ranks lower than toenails on Mama's to-do list.

I fling open my bedroom door and slam it closed. In the middle of my room, I scream, "I don't want to go!"

No one hears me, not the house manager nor Mama's personal assistant, who are no doubt in a shopping-organizing-errand-running tizzy now that The Empress is back home.

The last thing I want to do tonight is truss myself in a girdle, hobble around in heels, and smile until my cheeks go into spasms. I kick my antique bed, the one that makes me feel caged with its carved canopy and three walls, immediately feeling guilty. Besides, now my toes throb inside my scuffed-up sneakers, the ones Mama hates because they make me look like a poor waif.

Funny, isn't it, because a waif is a hungry-thin girl, not a hungry-fat one like me.

If I can't be thin, I can at least feel thinner. That is The Syrah Cheng Way, after all. So after I check my messages — no Rhami-Ware, and naturally, no Age, I run to Mama's pavilion, not her office on the first floor, but her workout studio on the second. Mirrors span the entire light-filled space. Why, may I ask, would anyone want a 360-degree view of their butt, even if Mama has the cutest one on the Pacific Rim? Her scientifically calibrated scale, the one she has serviced once a quarter, dominates the front corner of the studio. I avoid it since according to my scale this morning, I've regained one of the two pounds I've lost in the last week. On the opposite side of the room is Mama's Reformer, the medieval-looking Pilates device she uses to stretch herself into a lean, mean shopping machine.

For forty-five minutes, I run on the treadmill. The first four miles are easy enough, mostly because I keep thinking about Bao-mu's empty room and how much I wish she were here so I could talk to her about Age. As I approach mile five, the front of my knee starts aching.

So I hop off the treadmill and lunge down the room, gripping fifteen-pound weights in my hands. My knee wobbles, my balance off. What I wouldn't give for that false sense of security of a custom brace. As I work hard at keeping my abs tight, chest upright the way my physical therapist taught me, I make three circuits around the room when I wonder if that's what Age was getting at. That he was my crutch, only good enough to squire me when I needed him. But that's not true. Or is it?

On my sixth circuit around the room, my legs can't take a single squat more and I don't want to face the fact that I never ask Age over when my parents are around. As much as I tell myself it's because I don't want Mama to make some derogatory remark about him or Baba to interrogate him about his future plans, I wonder if it's because I don't have the guts to stand up for Age. I pit-stop at the water cooler. As I inhale cup number three as if that will wash away my guilt, I spot a floral notebook on the floor.

Partly out of curiosity and mostly out of procrastination because who, truly, likes doing lunges, I open the planner.

Breakfast: green tea, multivitamins
Lunch: grilled chicken breast on spinach (no dressing)
Dinner: edamame

There's no doubt whose this is. Like a sales ledger, Mama has tracked her daily workouts in red ink: one hour treadmill (600 cal.), half hour weights (300 cal.), forty-five minutes Pilates (300 cal.).

This is no journal to pour out thoughts, make sense of feelings, or, in my case, rewrite history. It's a personal profit-and-loss statement where being calorie-poor and exercise-rich is the goal. Sickened because I now have physical evidence that what I eat at breakfast is more than Mama's entire caloric input for a day, I lunge away from her journal, adding bicep curls to intensify my workout. That's got to be worth another ten calories.

Halfway across the room, I can't help it. *Don't do it! Don't do it!* I tell myself, even as I stop to examine my reflection. My right thigh, the one used to harvest hamstring muscle for a new knee ligament, is still thinner than my left. Instead of bulking it up, I wonder how I can lose the fat on my good leg, make it atrophy, too. I turn to my side and press at the bulge of my stomach, wishing that it were as flat as Mama's. That greenish-yellow bruise still flowering on my shoulder? It's the least of my worries.

I add another fifteen minutes on the elliptical machine, pumping my arms hard, watching my calories add up on the digital board. But no matter how hard and long I go, I can't run away from Age's words and the image of him sneaking into my *hsuan,* never using the front door.

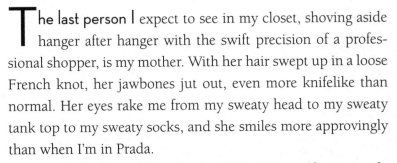

17

The last person I expect to see in my closet, shoving aside hanger after hanger with the swift precision of a professional shopper, is my mother. With her hair swept up in a loose French knot, her jawbones jut out, even more knifelike than normal. Her eyes rake me from my sweaty head to my sweaty tank top to my sweaty socks, and she smiles more approvingly than when I'm in Prada.

"Hi, Mama. When did you get back?" I ask her, self-consciously tucking a wet tendril behind my ear.

There's no answering "good to see you, Syrah." No "D.C. was lonely without you." And definitely no hug.

Instead, she cups my face and inspects one side after the other like I'm a Tang horse she's evaluating before acquiring for her collection. "You lost a little weight. Brilliant. We got back a couple of hours ago." She drops her hands off me to examine her forehead critically in the mirror, her fingers reading imaginary wrinkles like braille. "Can't you tell? I look horrid."

"You look great, Mama."

And she does. Effortlessly elegant and always put-together, four-hour flight or not, Mama is impeccable, fashionable, and breakably thin. The stats in her notebook blink in my head, a scorecard where I am always the loser: She's three inches taller and ten pounds lighter than I am. As I turn away from my reflection, I catch sight of my bruised shoulder. Casually, while Mama returns to her futile search for my perfect outfit, I hug my arms around myself, hands cupped over my shoulders like epaulets on a jacket.

Mama pushes aside the last hanger and turns to me, frowning. "Honestly, Syrah, where are all your nice things?"

"Right here," I say, considering my closet packed with clothes from designers whose names I mix up or mangle. I point to one of the short black dresses. "What's wrong with this one?"

"You wore that to the company party two years ago."

"I did?"

"Yes." Mama looks impatiently at me, fashion amnesiac that I am. "People will think we're too cheap to buy you new clothes." Her lips thin to the point of disappearing. As if wearing an outfit twice would really hurt the all-important Cheng Family Honor. She sighs, pressing newly manicured fingertips to her temples. "I knew I should have picked you up something from San Francisco, but I just didn't have time."

"San Francisco? I thought you were in D.C."

"We made a quick stop in California this morning." Crossing her arms, Mama stares at me. "You won't fit into anything of mine."

Of course I won't. A strand of my hair wouldn't fit into Mama's size negative four clothes.

Her eyes settle on my hands, still clutching my shoulders.

134

Mama says, "You didn't get a tattoo while we were in D.C., did you?"

If only the bruise were a tattoo, and not evidence of my disobedience.

Mama pries my fingers off my shoulder and sucks in her breath when she sees the bruise, big as a peony, her favorite flower, the one that represents beauty and wealth.

"How could you do this to me? Tonight of all nights?" she says, her voice growing louder. "What happened?"

I shrug.

"You went snowboarding, didn't you? After we told you not to anymore." And before I can stop her, Mama summons Baba as if my bruise is a matter of national security, "Ethan!"

In no time, it's we three Chengs in my closet.

Baba demands, "What's wrong?"

"Ethan, Syrah has been snowboarding again," Mama says.

"I told you snowboarding is dangerous," Baba says impatiently, like he's talking to a dog who won't obey simple commands: sit, stay, shut up. So begins his instant recall of every scary stat about snowboarding: "Snowboarders get in more accidents than any other participant in winter sports. Those accidents are more serious than other sports. Last week, a sixteen-year-old died in Utah going off a cliff. That's the ninth death this season alone."

Just this once, couldn't Baba have an Alzheimer moment? Nothing permanent. Just a temporary glitch in his perfect recall brain.

But data, facts, and numbers are what Baba built his billions on.

"We warned you before your surgery," he says.

"But —"

"No more snowboarding," he says, his voice harder.

Ever his backup chorus, Mama chimes in, "We don't want to see you hurt."

Something in me snaps. Maybe it's the latent shock and hurt from seeing Bao-mu's room emptied out or hearing the truth about what Age thinks of me, but I mutter, "No, it's just that you don't want to see me at all."

Mama gasps like her ears have never heard such insolence. They haven't, not from me, anyway, the good girl who tries to be perfect to get into everybody's good graces. Baba's eyes narrow, because I dared to talk back, dared to show the real me.

As if I'm just one more disposable employee, Baba says harshly, "What will it take for you to learn? Another avalanche? Do you want to be paralyzed for the rest of your life? Die?"

"No, I just —"

Baba takes a step closer to me, his fists curled like he's barely containing himself from punching some sense into my snow-addled brain.

"Are you so stupid that you would risk your life?" Baba demands, his eyes cold, forgetting that I'm his youngest daughter, the one Grace and Wayne say he spoils.

My resolve withers under this verbal attack. I gulp, the "sorry, sorry" on my lips. God, no wonder Grace and Wayne talk about *surviving* The Ethan Cheng Way, like their childhoods were spent in the war years. I shake my head, unable to stop my tears.

"For what? For fun?" Baba spits out the word as if it's a disgrace to say. His hand makes a sharp, slashing motion, a guillotine for my dreams. "I didn't work this hard to support a paraplegic daughter for life. You will not snowboard again. Do you understand me?"

Frozen in place, I nod, acquiescing the way I've seen Wayne and Grace do under the force of Ethan Cheng's will.

"Good." Baba shifts his eyes to Mama. The snowboard discussion closes, and Baba, all business again, informs Mama calmly, as if nothing has happened, no lambasting, no lectures, "We need to get ready. The dinner starts in an hour."

"Wear this," says Mama, yanking a red dress with long sleeves out of the closet, one I've never worn before because every time I try it on, I feel like my hips balloon wider than they are. As obvious as I feel in that loud dress, I might as well wear a neon sign on my back, one that flashes CASH COW! CASH COW!

United arm in arm against me, Mama and Baba leave, and I follow them to my door, dress in my hand. While they disappear down the stairs to their wing, I gaze not at their retreating backs but at Bao-mu's empty room.

No, you just don't want to see me at all. What I said is the truth, I think, as I look at myself in the mirror. I haven't wanted to see me at all, either.

In the six minutes before our departure time, I check my e-mail inbox, willing Age to instant-message me, but find another message instead. The one from the RhamiWare rep. My hand trembles as I click on the e-mail that holds the key to my snowboarding dreams.

Dear Syrah,
It was good to hear from you. I enjoyed looking at your video résumé and you definitely have a lot of talent. But after your unfortunate incident a few months ago, I'm afraid that my

management believes that you would be more of a liability than an asset at this point in our marketing strategy. Of course, times may change and we can revisit this.
Best,
Ralph

However cleverly packaged, thanks to chapter six of *The Ethan Cheng Way*, I can spot a yes-but-no rejection when I get one. *Yes*, I'm good. *But* I'm not good enough to escape my past or coast on my last name. So, *no*, there will be no sponsorship now or in the future for as long as I shall live. The guardians of this golden opportunity have slammed the gate shut, padlocked it, and relegated me to stand wistfully on the other side with the rest of the pro snowboarder wannabes begging: please let me into your exclusive club.

God, isn't there a tiny little alcove in the world where I'm good enough as is? Angrily, I delete the message just as Baba's voice intones insistently over the intercom: "Syrah, we're leaving. Now." Instead of rolling up in a ball on my bed the way I want, I power off my computer and head downstairs.

18

Middle-aged men in tuxedos and women in black cocktail dresses swarm the Spanish Ballroom in the Fairmont Olympic like well-coiffed socially conscious ants. You can guess who the Queen is. Across the room, Mama glimmers in her gold-dusted dress and large jade pendant. Her peck-in-the-air ritual with her friends is just beginning.

As an old guy raves to Baba about an epiphany he had reading *The Ethan Cheng Way,* my second-guessing game begins. Maybe I shouldn't have e-mailed the rep without putting together an entire plan. Maybe I should have worked my video over a couple more times. It's easier to beat myself up than consider the possibility that maybe my riding just wasn't good enough even when my knee was perfect.

"Right, Syrah?" I hear Baba ask.

I blink, give the requisite "hmm, wow, amazing" answer, and just as I tune back into my worries, a new one emerges on the horizon, an old guy who leers down at me, his blue eyes gleaming under a silver ridge of eyebrows. I can't remember which

"O" he is: chief executive officer, chief operating officer, chief financial officer. Whoever he is, Chief Overaged Ogler says, "You remember me, right? Bill Radcliffe? You're growing up before my very eyes."

I don't think Mr. Radcliffe is referring to my munchkin height. Not when — for real — he's staring at my chest. However much I want to carve around the lech like he's nothing but an ancient tree, my job duties have been ingrained into me since Baba's company went public when I was ten. Life, according to my parents, is one big networking opportunity. So I smile prettily at Mr. Viagra, who takes it as an invitation, because the old guy oozes, bending over me with dried-out, puckered-up lips: "Good to see you, sweet Syrah."

Oh. My. God. He's going to kiss me. He's got to be at least twenty-five years older than I am, making him old enough to be my . . . husband. I want to tell him, just because there's a thirty-one year age gap between my parents doesn't mean I'm shopping for one of those September-May relationships myself.

Quickly, I murmur to Baba, "Excuse me, I see Mama waving to me," and make a fast getaway.

Like always at these events, I comprise the entire under-ancient crowd, and have to swerve around conversations like "Have you seen the new BMW?" and "We just upgraded to a sixty-foot yacht." A waiter offers me a coconut shrimp skewer, but in this sea of taut tummies, I dare not go down the slippery slope of just one taste. Especially when the one with the tautest tummy beckons me to her conversation.

"And here's Syrah," says Mama, smiling at me. "We were just talking about everyone's winter break plans."

Right, "just talking." When it comes down to it, this crowd's "just talking" is nothing more than Black-Tie Boarder Cross, the down-and-dirty event played out in the ballroom.

Ladies, on your marks, get set . . .

The first woman whose green eyes glitter competitively bolts out of the starting gate, saying, "I can't believe winter break is in a week. I can't wait to get to Aspen. So where are you all going?"

A pallid woman with seaweed-straight hair jockeys into the front position. "I can tell you where we're not going this year. The Virgin Islands."

The competition roars, "No! But you always go there."

Pulling ahead into the lead, the pale woman shakes her head. "I know. I was just saying to James on our way here, remember how we used to spend a month in the islands every year before the kids? But now, the kids are so busy, it's just not worth going all that way for seven days. So we'll go to the Big Island instead. The Four Seasons, the only place worth staying."

A new competitor lays her sapphire-encrusted hand on the pale woman's arm, cutting her off neatly. "Seven days or seven weeks, it's such a chore getting everything packed. Especially when you're skiing and going around the world to Switzerland. There's all that equipment to haul."

I want to scream, not because she's going to Switzerland to ride, but because I sent my video to RhamiWare. Stupid, stupid, stupid. It wasn't ready; it wasn't perfect. I wasn't good enough.

Out of nowhere, Mama, the reigning champion, darts to the forefront. "I hate to admit it, especially with Syrah standing here, but I'm a little relieved that we're going to Hong Kong instead of Whistler this year."

Ms. Switzerland is confident of her lead and murmurs, "Hong Kong?"

Smiling modestly, Mama nods. "Nothing exciting." And then, like the all-time champion she is, she pulls even farther ahead with a deft move. "But when world leaders personally ask your husband to attend, well, duty calls."

The pale woman grows paler, sensing she can't make up this distance. Faintly, she repeats, "World leaders?"

Mama now leads so far ahead of the pack, there's no chance of anyone recovering. "Oh, you know, the regulars. Ethan wasn't planning on attending the World Economic Summit. He's been traveling so much lately, you know, wrapping up business before his retirement. But what can we do, right?"

The once and forever champion of the my-husband-is-more-powerful-than-yours competition leads everyone into the ballroom for dinner, burning more brightly than all the candles on the gold-draped tables. As I follow Mama's ego-bruised competitors, I know I don't want to be a woman who derives her self-importance from her man. Or her father. However amazing these men are, I want to be amazing, too.

Salad is being served when Grace slides into the empty chair next to mine. Her favorite accessory, Mochi, glitters like a miniature fireworks show, wearing a collar that coordinates with Grace's bracelet.

A waiter armed with wine bottles advances and asks Grace, "Syrah or chardonnay tonight?"

One guess which Grace chooses.

The ballroom lights dim, and a spotlight illuminates the executive director for the Evergreen Children's Fund; a middle-aged woman whose bouffant is leftover from a couple of decades ago smiles broadly from the podium on the stage.

Sighing, Grace leans back in her seat, removing Mochi from her bag and propping him over her shoulder. At least she has something to distract her from the usual blah blah blah, thanks for your generous support, blah blah blah, we've made huge strides, blah blah blah, we need more of your money now. It's almost enough for me to consider adopting a yippy dog of my own. Mochi bares his little teeth at me. Almost.

As predicted, the executive director sticks to the standard formula. "For the last ten years, I've had the privilege of working with Ethan and Betty Cheng. They've been passionate supporters of the Evergreen Children's Fund."

Really, this does make me wonder whether the snowboarding event I impulsively floated at the family meeting is just the fresh new fundraiser this jaded crowd needs. People may be turned toward the executive director, but those sedated expressions aren't truly paying attention to the photographs of children, flicking one after another in time to soft music on the two large overhead screens. I smooth down my dress and hope that Mama and Baba won't feel the need to drag me onstage with them, where they'll inevitably go after this long introduction.

The executive director continues, "When I first approached the Chengs, I asked if they would consider covering our operating expenses, so that we could designate a full one hundred percent of proceeds to the children we help. At that time, most people didn't understand the power of this unglamorous gift. The Chengs asked, 'How much?'"

The audience applauds, but the executive director holds up

her hand, quieting us, so that we can focus on the photographs of a woman I don't recognize: on the floor reading to children in her lap. Wearing a smock and painting with a group of kids. Laughing as she kicks a ball, hair in an untidy ponytail.

Next to me, Grace gasps at the same time I do. This is Mama, she of the couture-only closet, the woman with the no-unmanicured-hands-in-public grooming rule. Her smiles in these photographs aren't the practiced ones of her professional head shots; they're real, natural, relaxed. And adoring. My emptied-out heart caves in.

"But that doesn't explain how involved Betty has become with our children," drones the executive director. "For the last five years, she's been volunteering once a week at a day care for homeless kids, one of the groups the Evergreen Fund supports, thanks to your generosity."

Another photograph blinks onscreen, Mama playing ring-around-the-rosy. How is it possible that I'm jealous of homeless kids, some who, according to the executive director, have been beaten, others who've watched their own mothers prostitute themselves for cash, all who bring every last belonging with them to this day care because they don't know where they're sleeping that night? I'm so ashamed of myself as picture after picture changes — now duck-duck-goose, now a game of hop-scotch — but I dredge through my memories and come up empty. I don't have a single memory of hands-off, don't-touch, this-is-a-new-outfit Mama visiting me at school.

"So please help me honor two of Seattle's most warm-hearted, hands-on philanthropists, Ethan and Betty Cheng," cries the executive director.

As Mama and Baba rise from our table and approach the dais

for their speech, I clap robotically, stopping when everybody else does.

"As we all know, the true hero is Betty," Baba says, his powerful voice reverberating through the ballroom without a microphone, "a woman who can raise more money with three phone calls than I could in five months of road shows. She has single-handedly increased the Evergreen Fund by four hundred and twenty-three percent since she announced that we had to be involved."

The last photo remains onscreen, Mama kissing a grubby little boy on the cheek, his arms wrapped around her neck like she's the one person he can count on in his shattered world. Her eyes are closed as if more joy, more bliss, more love she can't handle. This unstudied image is the straw that breaks my Qué Syrah Syrah back. I can't let this one go, not with a blithe whatever. Instead, I rear from the table. My jealousy sucks all the oxygen in the ballroom until I'm suffocating. All eyes are on Mama, glittering so brilliantly onstage that she blinds everyone, except for Grace, who looks at me with pity, that ugly half-sister of empathy. For the first time, I know how Grace and Wayne must have felt, shunted aside to make room for me, but it's an uncomfortable thought I don't want to try on when I'm shaking off my own mottled feelings.

Unable to stay with this Mama I don't know but have always longed for, no matter if it's going to cause my parents to lose face, I start to stand up. I don't even know what I'm doing, what I'm intending until Grace grabs me, tugging me back down.

"Don't make a scene," she whispers urgently.

A scene? A scene? Of course, that's all Grace would care about, all the Chengs care about. Protect the family name. Do

145

nothing to besmirch the precious family honor. Forget keeping a stiff upper lip. It's all about saving face, but after these photographs, there's nothing of mine to save.

"Let go of me," I warn Grace in a low voice, shrugging off her hold the same time I do my adoring little sister mask. I stride out of the ballroom, out of the hotel, and into the cold night.

19

I must be sending out girl-on-the-verge vibes, because there's a ten-foot perimeter between me and the valets. Happy to be left in my own safety zone, I stand to the side of a mammoth planter, three times the size of Mama, and catch myself before I dial Age the way I usually do.

I breathe deeply. Inhale, exhale, wishing that I couldn't hear Age's accusation: *I'm just your chauffeur, your back-door friend.*

A couple gets out of their silver Jaguar, and before they can "Syrah Cheng!" me, I turn my back on them. Apparently, I need a remedial course in Denial & Consequences, because I, who complained about social class, was the one who kept a glass partition between me and my chauffeur, Age. A gust of wind blows a few leaves off the planter and into my face. As I swat away the dead leaves, I recognize Chelsea Dillinger's parents as they leave the Fairmont.

While Mr. Dillinger deals with the hyperattentive valets, Mrs. Dillinger hustles to me at a speed that defies her four-inch heels. Like her daughter, she is what Mama would call obese when in reality she's no more than ten pounds overweight, placing her somewhere between ample and voluptuous. Just like Natalia. When I groused to Mobey about how I just didn't understand Age's attraction to Natalia the first time they got together, he sat me down for a crash course in Boys & Other Unsolved Mysteries. According to Dr. Mobey, guys may like to look at skinny girls, but in bed, they want something to hold on to. Needless to say, I held up my hand, not wanting to imagine Age, Natalia, and a bed.

"Syrah, I swear, you and your mother are just looking more and more alike," coos Mrs. Dillinger.

It's such a bold-faced lie that I nearly snort. Yeah, the day Mama and I look more and more alike is the day I check into the hospital as an anorexic after finally waging a successful just-say-no-to-food campaign.

"But then again, your mother is simply ageless," simpers Mrs. Dillinger.

Over her shoulder, I catch a glimpse of myself in the window, and realize that Mrs. Dillinger is right after all. For once, I look like Mama. I look simply Age-less, too.

"Now, what are you doing out here in the cold? A little girl like you, you'll catch your death," says Mrs. Dillinger, all concern but no action. She doesn't volunteer her jacket or her husband's.

"Leaving early, too?" I ask, wondering if I should beg a ride off them.

But as Mrs. Dillinger talks about how she's got so much work to do before they leave for Whistler tomorrow, I know that there's no way I could tolerate a ten-minute drive in the confines of their car.

She and all those women back at that Ode to the Chengs event masquerading as a fundraiser were wrong, griping about the pre-vacation hassles of leaving. Leaving is the easy part. The trick is forgetting all your old baggage. Just go. Isn't that what my parents do? What Jared did?

What I want to do now?

Like Mama, I smile politely, waiting, waiting, waiting for the valets to bring around the Dillinger vehicle, yet another brand-new Hummer. Please. Black-tie functions may be polite skirmishes to establish wealth, power, and standing, but must we armor ourselves for the Fairmont?

As the Hummer rumbles away, I shiver, wishing now that, fashion be damned, I had packed my parka. My itty bitty jewel-encrusted sandals, which cost more than a season's pass at Stevens, couldn't last more than ten city blocks. With nowhere else to turn, I set out of the circular driveway.

"Syrah, wait!"

The wind blows Grace's hair fetchingly as she hurries to me, Mochi a shivering bundle in her arms. Here is the moment she's been waiting for since Bao-mu carried me home from the hospital. My moment of ultimate disgrace.

Instead of gloating, Grace asks quietly, "You ready to go home?"

Embarrassed that she's witnessing this new low in my life, I look toward the Dillingers' Hummer, still stopped at the light. My only other course of action is to return to the ballroom and pretend that everything is okay. That I'm fine with a mother who showers more love and attention on homeless kids than she ever has on me.

Being a model Cheng-ling and a star publicist to boot, Grace doesn't take my "no comment" for an answer. Instead, she strides, relieved to have something to do, all woman-on-a-mission, to the valets and announces, "I need my car."

"Yes, ma'am." The valets practically salute her, one sprinting in the direction I should be walking.

"Don't even think about it. You won't be able to snowboard for two weeks if you try walking home in those," says Grace, guessing that I'm planning to hike home on my own. By the time I turn to stare at her, she has Mochi swaddled in a color-coordinated cashmere wrap.

While we wait for Grace's car, she doesn't push me to talk, nor does she make ephemeral cotton-candy conversation that means nothing and is forgettable the instant it vanishes. Only later, when we're at the gates protecting The House of Cheng and Grace leans out the driver's side window to press the four digit code — 1937, the year of our father's birth — into the small metal keypad on the gate, does she speak. "Do you want me to come in?"

The gate swings open slowly, like it doesn't want to admit us any more than I want to admit that our silence during the drive to The House of Cheng is loud with questions we aren't asking each other. Why is she doing this, driving me home? Did Baba yell at her all the time when she was my age, the way he did tonight in my closet? What does she think of me now?

"So, do you?" she asks again as she slowly drives down the winding driveway.

I keep my eyes out the side window, as inexplicably I think about Baba's yes-but-no chapter. The strategy to use when you need to buy time while you make up your mind. *Yes,* Age has been my best friend and he's dated other girls. *But* I never invited him inside my house, just my heart. So *no,* I can't take his rejection, no matter how much I might deserve it.

Yes, Mama is my biological mother. *But* she mothers these abused and neglected and homeless kids in the way that I've always wanted to be mothered. So *no,* I don't feel like a beloved daughter, a little sister, or a friend. I don't feel anything at all.

As we pull up to the front door, I glance at Grace, surprised that she's looking back at me, not with pity, but with tenderness as if she knows I'm going to yes-but-no her.

Yes, I've always wanted a big sister who would listen when I needed her, who could have dispensed free boyfriend advice that might have saved me from Jared, who would know what to do with girls whose personal anthem is "This closet is your land; this closet is my land. . . ." *But* you and Wayne made it perfectly clear you never wanted me. So *no,* I can't trust your insta-sister act no matter how much I've yearned for this very moment.

It is absolutely ludicrous that now that I have the entrée to Grace that I've always wanted, I feel too raw to talk, too mixed-up to make any sense, too brittle to even try, which is why I yes-but-not-now her.

"Another time," I tell Grace, and mean it. "Really, another time. Thank you, Grace." As I close the passenger door, I worry that I'm shutting more than a car door, but a golden opportunity to have a real sister.

I shouldn't have worried. Grace rolls down the passenger

window a crack, enough for her to say and me to hear, "I told your parents you were feeling sick so I"d drive you home." That's when I know for sure that something, what or how I have no idea, but something has thawed between us. Grace doesn't leave until I'm inside the house.

20

Valentine's Day starts with me nearly colliding with Lillian, who's standing statue-still and transfixed, contemplating the heart-shaped pastries at the end of the salad bar. I'm about to tell Lillian just to choose one already — her perfect-size toothpick figure can take the calories — but that's when I realize she's not ogling the high-fat, high-calorie baked goods, but the ultrathin anorexic girl, staring, staring, staring at those overflowing baskets as if she were Mama at a jewelry store, weighing the worth of every bauble before her. How can jeans in a size I haven't worn since fifth grade possibly look baggy on a girl who's got to be around my age? Her shoulder blades poke out of her sweater more than her nonexistent chest does. Suddenly, her clawlike hand darts out and breaks off a tiny section of a blueberry bran muffin. Skeletal Girl retreats with her stolen crumbs to the grab-and-go refrigerator. As she stands there, eyeing one sandwich after another, she furtively slips a piece of muffin into her mouth, sucking on the crumbs like Baba tasting a rare vintage.

"Who is she?" I ask Lillian.

"Some prospective student who's perfectly healthy," Lillian says in a fierce undertone, glaring at the girl. "I mean, nothing is wrong with her, and she's killing herself by not eating. God, it makes me sick."

I place a hand on Lillian's arm. "You okay?"

"*I'm* fine," she says, studying me like she knows about my own whacked-out relationship with food. I look away guiltily. As if she's proved a point, Lillian nudges me past the salad bar and leads me to the grill, where she surprises me again. "So I've been meaning to tell you, thanks for that manga on the Groundhog Day party. I mean, you could have made me out to be some kind of do-gooder dork."

"Well, I still have a lot of work to do on it," I tell her. "You know, I wasn't planning on publishing it."

After she orders a hamburger, Lillian asks me, "So you want to go to Children's after school today?"

"Valentine's party?"

"Something like that." The way she's looking at me, I know it's a test. Will I or won't I take this small step to friendship? Lillian adds, "But only if you don't already have plans."

My parents do tonight, but I don't. And I don't want to see Mama yet, not when I'm still processing last night's revelation that she is the Mother Teresa of the Northwest homeless.

Without hesitating, I say, "Sure."

"Bring your manga-journal, will you?" she adds with a look of pure relief.

And that's how I find myself back on the giraffe elevator at Children's Hospital, this time thankfully without clowns. Only today, Lillian pushes the button for the third floor. With a shiver, I recall how that little kid, Frank, introduced me to Derek of the *third floor*, as though being a patient on the oncology ward made him someone to revere or fear.

"What are we doing here?" I ask Lillian.

"My sister's a patient," she tells me.

"She is?" Again, I hear the inflection in Frank's little voice: *third floor.*

"When all the kids brought back the manga drawings you drew of them, Amanda promised she'd actually eat every day for a week if she got one."

The elevator door opens, and down the hall is a large sign that reads SCCA, Seattle Cancer Care Alliance.

"It's all right," Lillian says, following my gaze to the tall STOP sign that warns against entering the oncology ward if you're sick or have diarrhea, but it doesn't mention anything about the anxiety attack I'm experiencing. "If you don't want to go in . . ."

Don't want to go in? Try wanting to sprint out of here, but I clamp down on my urge to flee and with a smile, I say, "Are you kidding? My fan awaits."

"No cell phones," Lillian says softly.

After we both switch off our phones, Lillian hands me an inpatient visitor badge, and I sign my name on the pink sheet, swearing that I don't have a sore throat, runny nose, cough, fever, chills, or general aches.

"Ready?" she asks, but doesn't wait for my answer, as if I've passed the buddy test, one that jettisons me from acquaintance to friend she can count on.

A bald-headed boy with puffy cheeks zooms down the hall on a bike, narrowly missing a head-on collision with me and Lillian. His father gives us a weak apologetic smile and reprimands his kid halfheartedly, "Hey, speed racer, watch out for the girls!"

"Are they allowed to ride bikes in here?" I ask Lillian quietly.

"Oh, yeah, definitely." She points to the fleet of plastic cars and scooters around the corner. "And those, too."

Rooms line the hall, most with their shades pulled. Through one set of open windows, I see some parents sitting beside a crib. In another, a girl is lying on her back, TV on but she's staring up at her ceiling. A large Seattle Mariners banner stretches across another door, its windows plastered with pennants and a manga of a kid in a baseball uniform.

"Hey, Derek," I call through the open door.

"Syrah!" Derek waves shyly at me from his bed. At my name, his mom's head lifts, and I wonder as she rushes to the threshold where I'm standing whether she's going to "Syrah Cheng!" me, but instead she says quietly, "Your drawing changed his attitude." Her hazel eyes shine. "Your parents must be so proud of you."

"Mom!" comes the anguished, embarrassed cry from the bed.

I smile back at his mom and then look over her shoulder to Derek. "You going to be around in a bit?"

"I'm not going anywhere," he says, chin thrust out, denying that anything could possibly cheer him up. But when I tell him, "Cool, I'll catch you later," his droll "yeah, sure" belies the hint of a smile.

"Amanda's over this way," says Lillian as we continue around a corner, past a nurses' station littered with medical charts.

In my mind, I've pictured Amanda a couple of years younger

than we are, so I'm not prepared for the little girl, a mini-Lillian, on the poster board tacked to her window. In the photograph, Mrs. Fujimoro and Lillian encircle Amanda protectively, her thick brown hair pulled into a high ponytail, and her cheeks so rounded, she could be stashing her entire Halloween haul in them.

"How old is she?" I ask, studying the portrait of childhood plumpness grinning at me from the center photograph.

"Three now. She was diagnosed with leukemia when she was just eighteen months old." Lillian squirts more cleanser into her hand from the vial attached to the wall, rubbing quickly. "We thought she had this beat until about a week ago. She came down with a fever, and then I saw the bruises on her arms."

A week ago. A week ago, I was whining about having to go to Baba's birthday party instead of snowboarding and feeling sorry for myself because of my busted-up knee. Now, even the rejection from RhamiWare seems so trivial compared to this.

Tossing back her hair, Lillian grins widely, as if that will mask her sadness, but the fake smile only heightens it. "Why don't you wait out here for a second? She's a little shy with strangers." She straightens, girding for battle before pushing through the door into the dim room, and part of me wants to yank Lillian back from visiting adulthood way too soon.

Immediately, Amanda spins around on the bed, hands out-stretched. Mrs. Fujimoro doesn't stir, an unmoving lump on the pull-out sofa bed by the drawn windows.

Feeling like an intruder, I focus on the poster board. Amanda's World. Every brushstroke of her name painted on the collage is capped with a large happy dot. Snapshots from Christmas, birthday parties, Disneyland decorate the board. All the normal activities of a family. Even mine. Compared to this third floor, Hong Kong doesn't seem like such an awful place to be exiled.

A nurse wearing scrubs decorated with Disney characters pumps cleanser into her chapped hands as she stands beside me, both of us watching Amanda talk earnestly with Lillian, their heads together so they don't wake up their mom.

"Amazing people," says the nurse. "Not many families would go to the lengths that the Fujimoros have. Picking up and moving. The pregnancy."

I nod as if I know what she's talking about.

"Now, a lot of people might not agree with what they're doing, but I say, what wouldn't you do for your own kid, right? We're all praying that the baby will be a great tissue match."

According to The Ethan Cheng Way, if you want information, you have to ask. "What do you mean?"

"Unless that little girl finds a bone marrow match, most likely from another biracial person . . ." the nurse's voice trails off but her meaning is obvious even to a third floor neophyte like me. "It's really too bad that most of the volunteers on the bone marrow registry are Caucasian. Autologous transplants are just not as effective." With one hand on the door, the nurse says, "Now, let's see if Lillian can sweet-talk her into taking a couple of bites."

I stare at Mrs. Fujimoro's large belly as the nurse's information sinks in. The real reason for Mrs. Fujimoro's pregnancy is a last-ditch effort to save her daughter. An awful niggling thought sneaks into my head; under no circumstances can I imagine Mama willingly gaining thirty pounds for me.

Lillian peeks her head out of the room and says, "Amanda would really love a picture of herself as a snowboard girl."

"Really?" I ask, surprised.

"Yeah, who knew? It must be all the ESPN my dad's been watching. Come on in."

Reluctantly, I follow Lillian inside Amanda's room where Mrs. Fujimoro is awkwardly easing herself into a sitting position, patting her hair back into place self-consciously when she spies me. Looking away to give her some semblance of privacy, I focus on Amanda, who's grinning at me from her bed, bouncing up and down, unmindful of her IV.

No sooner do I park myself in one of the chairs beside her bed than Amanda begins to art direct me. "Pigtails!" she demands.

"Amanda," reprimands Lillian.

So much for shyness with strangers. Oddly, I feel pleased and smile back at Amanda.

"With pom-poms." Amanda looks at me so steadily, there is no question that she might be bald now, but in no time, she'll be sporting short, stubby, and pom-pommed pigtails.

"All the cool snowboard girls are rocking helmets with speakers in them," I tell her. "So what's on your helmet?"

"A hummingbird. Red and green," she says decisively. "And I want a red snowsuit. Not pink. And goggles. Definitely goggles."

"How old are you?" I ask, laughing as I begin to draw her on top of a mountain.

"Big enough to snowboard," says Amanda.

Mrs. Fujimoro smiles tremulously at her. "Maybe next year."

The nurse's words — *unless that little girl finds a match* — hang in my head, dark clouds portending a storm. I press down hard on my journal, as if the heavy lines will make my image come true: Amanda, a fearless grom with luscious pigtails, the picture of health and serious attitude, soaring sky-high over Bold Mountain.

When I hand the finished page to her, I say, "Now what are you going to eat?"

"Everything," Amanda breathes and holds the manga in her chubby little hands like it's the ultimate pass to Paradise, one I'd give to her for free if I could.

As Amanda wanes between bites number three and number four, I ask her, "Do you want to see me as a snowboard girl?"

She nods eagerly.

"Another bite then," negotiates Lillian, smiling her thanks to me.

As Lillian shovels another spoonful into Amanda's mouth, I open my manga-journal to Shiraz.

"That doesn't look like you," says Amanda, frowning.

"What do you mean?" I flatten the page with my palm, but as I do, I study my manga alter ego under the bars of my fingers, and suddenly see Shiraz with absolute clarity. She's a stick figure in a parka. A stick figure with an ample chest, if I have to be totally honest. Boobs on a board, that's how I've drawn Shiraz. Suddenly I remember how once, after I had moaned to Age about how fat I was, he said, "You're compact, Syrah. You're the prototype for the perfect snowboarding body."

"You're right," I tell Amanda softly. "That doesn't look like me at all."

o   o   o

160

Later, near the main entry of the Children's Hospital, Lillian points at the statue of a mother elephant, her trunk wrapped protectively around her baby. "Guess what Amanda's favorite part is."

I tap the mother's trunk, which ends in a pale pink heart. "This?"

"Nope, their toes."

"Are you kidding?" I have to laugh, because both mother and child have red toenails, as if they made a pit stop at Spa Safari for a pedicure before hoofing it over to the hospital. "Your sister is something else."

"I know."

"You know, *you* should write about your Groundhog Day party, what it means to make a difference. That'd make a great column."

"Nah, I'd be a one-sentence story: girl with sick sister throws party. Big whoopee."

"Better a great one-sentence life than a boring book-length journal. At least, for me," I tell her as we walk outside past the purple hippo crouched in front of the fountain shaped like a watering hole. It's already dark. I check my watch, surprised that it's eight. After drawing Amanda and then visiting Derek, a couple of other kids wanted manga-portraits, too. So did a few siblings. And two nurses.

In silence we walk to the parking garage, and I finally ask the question that's been bugging me since I met Amanda. "How come you don't talk about your sister? I had no idea she was sick."

It could be that Lillian is ignoring me, she's walking fast enough to outdistance my question. But her first "oh" after my question had sounded more surprised that someone would ask, than offended. Not until we're safe inside the minivan does Lillian answer, "Probably for the same reason that you never talk about your dad. You never mention him or your airplane or your gazillion cars. There aren't that many people who don't get all freaked out that my little sister may be dying."

Who would have known that it would be Lillian Fujimoro, the star of Viewridge, who would understand me so perfectly? "Yeah" is all I say.

It must be all I need to say, because as Lillian drives out of the garage and we approach the traffic light that changes from red to green, she asks, "How does pizza sound? Pagliacci makes a mean pepperoni."

I sink all the way back in my seat happily and tell her, "Pep-peroni sounds perfect."

21

After dinner, when Lillian pulls down the driveway to my house, I'm in such a food coma, I can barely move. What's weird is that I don't feel (too) guilty about my two slices of pizza, and I haven't calculated how much time I'll need to spend on the treadmill tomorrow morning to ward off the ill effects of cheese, pepperoni, and grease on my belly pooch. After seeing Amanda and that anorexic girl at my school and my Shiraz alter ego, Lillian has it right. It's just so stupid to obsess about weight and calories when my body is perfectly healthy, even my knee.

"Okay," says Lillian, turning her head to me.

"Okay, what?" I ask.

"Okay, here's the deal. Since you did your manga on me, I get to do a feature on you."

"But I'm not doing anything. . . ." My voice trails off as an inkling of an idea starts to form. Amanda, snowboarding, charity benefit, bone marrow transplants. But the sight of Baba's BMW haphazardly parked in front of the house instead of inside the garage stops my brainstorming. It's not yet ten, way too early for them to return home from their Valentine's dinner.

Instead of a "Syrah, where were you after school?" or a "Syrah, how dare you leave an event early," when I walk inside the house, I hear a keening wail, so pained, my instant thought is that Baba has died. God, did he have a heart attack? Immediately, I rush, mouth dry and heart pounding, toward the anguished sound, coming from my parents' wing. The crying turns into a single-note shriek. I stop in the hallway, scared now that an intruder has breeched our state-of-the-art security system and attacked my parents on their way in. No wonder Baba's car was parked so carelessly. My heart thuds as another ragged cry tears through the house. Why hadn't my parents taken that retired FBI agent's advice and employed a couple of bodyguards to roam the grounds, twenty-four seven?

I'm fumbling with my cell phone, ready to dial 911, when I hear Mama wailing over and over, first in Cantonese, then in her British English made unrefined in its raggedness, "My Mama is dead, Mama is dead."

I don't understand and hasten to my parents' bedroom, where the crying is coming from. My grandmother, Weipou, has already passed away, dead when I turned seven. I have a vague recollection of standing in front of her coffin, too scared to look in, so I closed my eyes. The lit incense in my hand made me want to gag, its smell so pungent, but I kowtowed three times the way my Hong Kong cousins did, while needing to go to the bathroom desperately. Mama tch-ed at me and made me wait so long that I wet my pants. "Shameful," I overheard a guest muttering, and I wanted to drown in the tiny pool under my billowing white dress.

Then, on the day Weipou's coffin was carried to the cemetery, her friends grumbled that for as few tears that were shed by the family, we should have hired professional mourners to rip their hair out and weep the way they did in olden days, as a sign of respect.

Whoever this unknown Mama is needs no professional mourners, not the way my mother is crying inconsolably. Before tonight, I've never heard her so much as sniffle.

Baba murmurs something so softly that I don't catch the words, only his soothing tones.

Mama, sounding broken, asks, "How could she have died three days ago and I didn't know? No one told me."

When I peer inside their bedroom, I see them sitting on the edge of their bed, their backs to me, Baba holding Mama, rocking her as if she were one of the Evergreen Fund's beneficiaries, a homeless child he's sworn to protect and cherish. Both are so attuned to her grief that neither notices me.

Feeling every bit the outsider, I draw back. Reality is, I'm uncomfortable viewing this breakdown in the understood Cheng code of conduct: always be in control, dispassionate, analytical.

So I leave them and climb the stairs to my bedroom with my arms around myself. I want to call Age, but know I can't. Something tells me that Grace would talk, if only I called, but I don't want her to know how vulnerable Mama is now. And it's too late to phone Bao-mu.

So I lie down on my bed and try to remember. My few disjointed memories of Weipou are concentrated into a couple of sharp images that smolder with unease. Like how Mama put Weipou in the best room of our old house, but my grandmother's miss-nothing eyes narrowed accusingly, as if Mama was showing off how much we-who-deserved-so-much-less had. How she covered her ears whenever I spoke in Cantonese, as if I were an out-of-tune piano. How she commanded Mama to forbid Bao-mu from speaking Mandarin with me, since it was obviously ruining my speech. And I remember shopping with Mama before our yearly trips to visit Weipou, filling up suitcases with cigarettes, lotions — anything that would be expensive to purchase in Hong Kong. Once we got to her mother's house, Mama would lay out these gifts like peace offerings or a tribute that Weipou inspected and deemed never good enough.

22

The next morning, Mama's overstuffed luggage is lined up by the front door, like the two obese suitcases can't wait to clear out of our Nonfat Farm. Personally, I can't either. I am swarming with so many questions, I go hunting for Mama and answers, armed with my decision that I'm attending the mystery mother's funeral with her.

The first place Mama hits as soon as she wakes up is her workout room. But she's not running, running, running as if wife number three were on a treadmill behind her. There's no trace of Mama in her office or in Baba's pavilion, where the only sign of life is the stock ticker scrolling on his computer screen. Outside, the courtyards are damp, the sky a soggy gray backdrop that makes the evergreen trees appear even greener. And that's how I figure out where Mama has gone.

Wrapping my arms around myself, I pick my way through the worms squiggling along the cobbled path. After what seems like an inordinately long time, I pass the public reception hall to finally reach Mama's greenhouse. The glass door is always kept partially open in the winter so that her beloved bonsai get enough fresh air to prevent a blight of mold, but are protected from cold death. Through that cracked open door, I see Mama, her back to me, as she bends over to tend her stunted trees.

"Good morning, Syrah," Mama says without turning around when I enter. "How was your Valentine's Day?" The way she's talking, she could be the perky star of a cereal commercial, not the woman whose late night weeping I can still hear, it was that raw.

Just like the first Chinese *penjing* gardeners must have done and Japanese bonsai ones later copied, Mama coils a copper wire around a tree, training its branch to bend as if it's been windblown by nature. She skips over my non-answer and asks, "All set for school?"

Wind rattles the greenhouse, but Mama doesn't notice. I shiver. If Bao-mu were here, she'd say it was the ghost of the woman Mama was mourning last night. In my haste to know who this woman is, I clumsily ask, "Is everything okay?"

"Of course." Mama snips off the extra length of wire, not noticing that it drops, unneeded and discarded, by her feet. Calmly, Mama clips another long length of wire and begins painstakingly to cinch the copper corset around a different branch. It's all I can do to stop myself from flinging in front of the besieged, belittled tree, like I'm the charter member of the Bonsai Liberation Front.

"Mrs. Fujimoro mentioned that you were working with her daughter on some project at the hospital," says Mama, sounding as surprised as I was that she is so involved in the Evergreen Fund.

Our knowledge of each other is as limited as these bonsai,

cut back before they can sprout overlarge. What I know of Mama — and my whole family — is the idealized version that she presents to the world. No different from me, my public persona pruned of all the messy bits in my history.

"Did you finish?" Mama asks, all the while her busy hands bend the branch gently down.

At first I think that Mama is asking whether I've finished pruning myself to perfection. I haven't. But then I recognize her diversionary tactic for what it is: a Mama-made obstacle course of conversational distractions. Swallowing hard, I commit to my own route, no matter how unpredictable and frightening it is. Softly, I say, "I'm going with you."

"Now, why would you want to go to Hong Kong?"

"Hong Kong?" For a fleeting moment, I wonder if that's where the funeral is going to be held.

"Yes, it's the World Economic Summit. Where else would I be going?"

I think to myself, *Like, to a memorial service maybe?*

As if Mama hears my question, her hand trembles, and she sets the pliers down between two Japanese larches, displayed on the tiered bench in different pots. Twins separated at birth, one grows tall and straight, the other twisted as though it has weathered nothing but storms.

Instead of answering, Mama handles a conical spruce, the size of my hand. "Do you think this pot is too big?"

"Maybe," I say, drawing closer to Mama so that we're standing side-by-side in front of the bonsai and its teardrop-shaped pot. I will her to tell me what's wrong. "What do you think?"

"Hmm," she says thoughtfully, like it's the most important question in the world, not the one that she's dodging, the one

I'm trying to ask: who was the woman you were crying over last night? The mother I'm crying over now muses, "Perhaps something shallower. I'll have to look for one in Hong Kong."

I summon up my courage and say softly, "But I heard you crying last night."

Mama shies away from me. We might as well be two negatively charged magnets; all the questions I'm trying to ask repel her. From the rack of tools on the far wall, she removes a pair of shears and clips a twig sticking up on a silver birch. Admiring the clean-cut effect, Mama wonders aloud, "Maybe this one should be brought inside."

Inside our house is where all "perfect" bonsai go to be displayed once they've been pruned and trained, bound in wire for months at a time until they attain the exact appearance Mama has intended for them. The process of perfection can take years. Even generations.

"How long will you be gone?" I ask.

"Ten days, just as planned. You know that, Syrah," says Mama, a touch reproachfully, as she snips a leaf off a gnarled hornbeam, which cascades over its pot as if storm gales have pummeled it into submission. "I left our itinerary in your inbox as usual."

How is it that my family made its fortune in telecommunications, yet there's so much static between us, our words and meaning are all garbled?

Mama steps to the next bonsai and adjusts the miniaturized pine tree to display it at a more appealing angle. "You better get going or you'll be late for school. You'll need to take the school van this morning, but I'll arrange for someone to pick you up, OK?"

"I don't mind taking the van home."

Mama casts me a sidelong look, her smile beautiful and practiced and lacking all the warmth in that photo montage with those homeless kids. "Of course you should have a private driver. You'll get home faster. And then Baba and I will be home before you know it." She turns her back on me, already gone.

As I leave the greenhouse, I can't help stopping at the door in case Mama is sending me a sign that she wants to talk, mother to daughter. But her placid face betrays nothing. Instead, she stands motionless in the middle of her bonsai forest. I have to wonder whether I've imagined it all, her uncontrollable weeping for a mother she didn't have. Maybe it was just a dream.

If Bao-mu is right and ghosts live in trees, then the ones in the greenhouse are so stunted, they can't possibly roam free to haunt me. Or Mama. We have nothing to worry about. So I exhale slowly, ready to follow the wisps of my breath down the garden path to the warmth of our home. Just as I relax the vigil I hadn't known I was practicing, slowly, deliberately, Mama starts to whittle away at her perfect bonsai, the silver birch she had deemed good enough to bring inside our house. She attacks it, a branch-by-branch diet, her shears stripping it at a steady clip-clipping rhythm: mis-take, mis-take. And I wonder, as she cripples the bonsai beyond repair, whether Mama hears the same mis-take chant as I do. Or a different one. Whatever it is, Mama doesn't stop, doesn't miss a single beat until the tree is diminished to a mere twig.

23

All I can think about on the drive to school is how I need to figure out who my Jane Doe grandmother is, the one who's been a skeleton in Mama's couture-crammed closet. I hunch over my journal using my unzipped jacket and up-drawn knees as a makeshift study carrel so that none of the other kids in this privately chartered van for my neighborhood can see what I'm writing. As soon as the van stops at a light, I scribble the question I can't stop thinking about, not how the hell am I getting to Wicked in Whistler, but how the hell am I going to find this lost family of mine? I don't even know where to begin to look.

The van bumps through a pothole, making my writing as unintelligible as any logical answer for this pruned back branch in my family tree. Besides, Chelsea's musky perfume from the seat ahead of me is making me too woozy to think straight.

"Omigod, can you believe it?" Chelsea shrieks into her cell phone studded with pink crystals. "My parents want to drive to

Whistler instead of fly!" Like always, the boom of Chelsea's voice turns her secret confessions into public professions.

Geez, if only it were so easy to call Age and dump out my woes. But Age and I are still on the don't-call-me-I-won't-call-you cell phone plan.

"Yeah, so we'll be heading to Whistler today with the masses," whines Chelsea. She chooses that moment to unscrew the cap of her oversized water bottle. The stench of what must be a science experiment gone terribly wrong is released, momentarily camouflaging her perfume.

"What is that?" kids demand, everybody twisting around, looking for the odorous culprit that Chelsea swirls like a glass of fine wine that only needs to breathe properly before it's enjoyed. My nose wrinkles at the smell, which I now identify as a cross between spoiled milk and old tofu.

"What? It's Syrah's mom's detox diet," Chelsea says.

I abandon my feeble attempt to manga-journal. "Excuse me?"

Recapping the bottle, Chelsea gives it a good, hard shake, as if that'll make her mystery cocktail easier to swallow. "Aren't you on it, too?"

"No."

Another whiff of the Mama-Chelsea brew blows my way. God, what I need to do is detox my life, whittle away my mixed-up emotions until all that's left is clear focus. If I want to find this long lost grandmother, I can't randomly grab what I want. I need a plan.

Leaning back in my seat, I close my eyes and visualize my goal just the way I used to visualize the snowboarding tricks I was trying to learn, deconstructing the steps. I want to know who this mystery mother is, and more than that, why she wrings out more emotion from Mama than she's shown me my entire life. I can't talk to Mama, the Wonder Woman of deflecting personal questions. Besides, she'll be on their private plane, co-ordinates Hong Kong, in an hour. Other than Age, who is in-communicado, the only person I truly trust is Bao-mu. Bao-mu will know what's going on. When the van pulls into Viewridge, I'm ready, trading my manga-journal for my cell phone.

Viewridge is a cross between country club and Ivy League college, ten acres of East Coast–style brick buildings, weath-ered to look three hundred years old instead of thirty. Like any good country club, all digital devices are banned on the prem-ises. Still, when the head of our school, Dr. Vandermeer, spots me on the bench with my contraband phone, I lift my shoul-ders apologetically and murmur, "My father." That does the trick. All Dr. Vandermeer does is nod as if I'm on a very impor-tant business call that could make or break a healthy contribu-tion to the school capital campaign.

The wind picks up, racing along the stairs to whip open the flaps of my jacket. The edge of the zipper hits me painfully on my cheek. The phone rings and rings. Did Bao-mu forget to turn on her phone? Another blast of wind penetrates through my sweater to my skin. With the phone tucked between my chin and my shoulder, I double my jacket around myself, ki-mono style.

Suddenly, I hear Bao-mu demand, "Who this?"

"Bao-mu, it's —"

"What wrong? Something wrong with your knee? Your arm?"

In the background, I hear a woman grousing, "Is it that girl?

174

You don't work for her anymore." Three guesses who that woman is. Could it be Christine, her medical doctor daughter who's always too busy to be nice?

"No, no, I'm fine." I hunch against the wind. Students jostle past me, but I ignore them. My automatic response of "How are you?" gets drowned out by the first bell. I ask instead, "Where are you?"

"Hospital still. *Aiya!* Pat baby, not too soft. He not silk you snag by accident," Bao-mu says, either not bothering or not knowing to cover the mouthpiece, as she orders her daughter and granddaughter around in a way I miss. "Not too hard! Not too hard! Like that. See, he stop crying. So easy." She makes a frustrated sound for being surrounded by incompetence. "Syrah, what you need?"

The wind wraps my hair around my face, covering my mouth. Is it a warning? Not to divulge too much of myself, even to Bao-mu? To protect the Cheng family honor and up-hold a pretense that all is perfect? I pull my hair off my lips and hold it back in one fist. Then, I get to the point the way I can with Bao-mu, no fluffy chitchat required to ease the way to a hard topic. "Mama was crying last night. She kept saying that her Mama is dead, but that doesn't make sense, does it? Didn't Weipou die when I was little?"

Bao-mu sighs, her long breath communicating as much grief as Mama's crying. She murmurs, "Her mama dead?" When Bao-mu makes her exasperated "aaahh" sound, at first I think she's about to put me off. But she doesn't. She tells the women on her side, "I need talk couple minutes. You be okay."

I can imagine Christine protesting, hands on her hips, that her mother is no longer a servant, how she aches to wrench the phone away and tell me off the way she did the one time I met her and called Bao-mu my *po-po*: "She's not your grandmother; she's your nanny." And how I wanted to cry because all I wanted was one person to call my own.

"Bao-mu, you have to tell me, please." The tears welling in my eyes have nothing to do with being wind-lashed. "You don't work for us anymore."

There's a moment of silence when I don't hear anything, not the wind, not Bao-mu. And then Bao-mu says slowly, like she's making a deal with herself, "No. I not work for your mama anymore."

"So you'll tell me?"

The way Bao-mu says, *"Wo jiang, ni ting,"* she could be patting the empty space beside her, clearing time for me.

"Your mama, she given away when baby," says Bao-mu simply.

"She was?" My voice is so sharp, kids bounding up the steps look at me curiously. I turn away from them and lower my voice. "Mama was adopted?"

"Something like that. Your po-po — your *real* grandmother — have hard time in Cultural Revolution. Your *gonggong* was famous calligrapher, always writing, just like you. When Red Guard find some papers your grandpa tried bury in backyard, they kick him so hard, he not wake up. Coma."

According to the sanitized version of Mama's life, it was one Great Leap from her wealthy family in Hong Kong to London boarding school when she was twelve. Her happily-ever-after came when she was attending university in Cambridge, and Baba was guest-lecturing. I clench the phone tightly to my ear, afraid to miss a single word that could unlock the mystery of my mother.

"He die three day later. Red Guard going take away your po-po. Put her in labor camp," Bao-mu continues. "She have five kids, no food. When I leave for Hong Kong, your po-po beg me take Betty. Betty just baby, easy to bring on train, not need buy another ticket. She tell me, give Betty to her rich brother in Hong Kong." Bao-mu's voice drops, her dislike palpable: "And his wife."

His wife. My Weipou — the grandmother with the lips pursed permanently into a never-good-enough line — whose funeral I attended a long, long time ago.

As soon as one question forms on my lips, another ten queue in my brain. Did Mama ever reunite with her real mother or her siblings, and if she did, why didn't I ever meet them? And where is everyone now? And how come Bao-mu never told me?

A baby wails in the background, and I know that my time with Bao-mu is about to end. Quickly, I ask the most important question, the one that might answer why Mama wanted to leave this morning: "So Po-Po's been in Hong Kong all this time?"

"No, no, she left when Hong Kong given back to China. She move to Vancouver," says Bao-mu.

"Vancouver? When?"

"1997."

Vancouver, British Columbia. Three short hours up north, my grandmother, my real grandmother, was there for over ten years, and I never knew. Across the campus, the tops of the tall fir trees arch in the wind, these giant, unbound cousins of bonsai. I wonder if Mama knew.

177

"Bao-mu," I say suddenly, as the thought occurs to me, "how do you know?"

"*Aiya!*" exclaims Bao-mu, so loudly I ease the phone off my ear. "Let me do before you drown baby. Two women, one man, and still cannot give baby bath?" Bao-mu returns to our conversation. "I talk you later."

"Bye, Bao-mu," I say, but the line is already disconnected.

After the final bell rings, I stay outside, wishing the wind could strip the candy coating off Mama's history as easily as it does the deadwood from the trees. Leaves and twigs circle around my feet. Across the field, a fir tree releases a branch as if it's been lopped off by giant shears.

A car pulls into the bus circle. As soon as Lillian closes the passenger door, she races for the stairs at the same time her mother speeds out of the parking lot. If I hadn't moved out of her way, Lillian would have crashed into me in her rush to get up the stairs, into class, and back to her good-girl-always-on-top-of-everything public persona.

"Syrah! Oh, sorry," she says, surprise erasing the hurt on her face before turning into worry. "The bell didn't ring, did it?" she asks hopefully, despite all evidence otherwise — no cars or kids.

I nod.

"Oh." By the second step, a veneer of calm covers her anxiety. I know that placid mask. It's my signature look. Even though Lillian and I spent all yesterday afternoon at Children's, hung out with her sick little sister, ate dinner together, there's a discomfort between us, bred from becoming too intimate too fast with each other. We both feel vulnerable from over-exposure.

"Well," Lillian asks, "aren't you going inside?"

Choose your partners wisely; that's what Baba advises. Hire people who are smarter than you are. Unquestionably, Lillian Fujimoro has more brain cells than most of my class combined, including me. And there's no better investigative reporter.

"Hey, Lillian," I call, mounting the staircase until I share the same step as her.

"Yeah?"

I find myself saying the three words that are hardest for a true Cheng to admit because it means making myself vulnerable, losing precious control, conceding imperfection: "I need help."

"You do?"

I nod.

"What do you need?"

"How would you find someone who just died in Vancouver?"

"Check the obits," she says with no hesitation, as if she does just that all the time.

"Obits."

"Who are you looking for?"

I'm about to lie, *no one,* until I recognize the concern, not curiosity, in Lillian's dark eyes. So I tell her, "My grandmother."

"Oh, I'm sorry."

"Me, too." I wait for Lillian's follow-up questions, the ones that tease out the best information from her interviews and turn up in her incisive, fact-filled, tell-all articles. But she doesn't pry, doesn't ask a single question, such as why on Earth don't I already know where my grandmother is?

Instead, Lillian looks as though she understands that some

topics are off-limits, even if the subject of my mystery grandmother tempts like forbidden fruit in my walled-off Garden of Ethan.

"Do you want me to show you how?" she asks.

Yes, I want to know where my real po-po is. *But* what tenfold bonus will you want from me in return? So, *no . . .*

I stop at my automatic no and take a deep breath. Today may have been pruning day for Mama, but it's the start of harvesting season for me. Slowly, I open the rusty gates of trust.

"Yes," I tell Lillian. "I'd love it if you could."

24

This early in the school day, the library is a ghost town, and Mrs. Hodgkins, the librarian, is the lone, frizzy-haired tumbleweed knocking around the bookshelves. I fully expect her to kick us out because Lillian and I are supposed to be in our homerooms, along with the other two hundred and twelve high schoolers. But the beauty of Baba's advice to choose the right partner becomes eminently clear when Mrs. Hodgkins sets eyes on Lillian and becomes a one-woman welcome wagon.

"Lillian, I've got something for you." She bustles to her desk, dirndl skirt billowing behind her, and ducks down so all that's visible are her short red curls, tied back with a long scarf. Mrs. Hodgkins hands a small scrap of paper to Lillian. "I hope it's what you were looking for."

While Lillian studies the note, Mrs. Hodgkins studies her, sympathy softening her thin face.

"Thank you," says Lillian, clutching the paper so tightly it could be the Pulitzer Prize.

Mrs. Hodgkins brushes off her gratitude. "Okay, girls, just holler if you need any help." But she smiles, pleased, automatically lifting her hand to hide her oversized teeth and wide swath of gums that's earned her the nickname Horsekins.

"How'd you do that?" I whisper as Lillian and I head to the bank of computers occupying the far end of the room.

"I'm in here a lot." Lillian hesitates. Her face is so guarded she reminds me of me. "Independent research."

But I'm not like her pseudo-friends, The Six-Pack, who mock her go-the-extra-credit-mile mentality to both her face and her back. Especially when I suspect that her independent research circles around the survival of a tiny snowboard tot.

"Let's get you started," says Lillian. "Then I've got stuff to look up."

I slide in front of a computer, expecting Lillian to take the terminal next to mine. But she's eyeing the computer one over, like the grass is evergreen thataway.

"I don't have any communicable diseases," I say. "Not even rich girl-itis."

Which must have been the right thing to say, because Lillian laughs and settles in the chair beside me instead of giving me, an untouchable social leper, space.

"So I was thinking I would just Google 'Vancouver newspapers' first," I say.

"Good idea. See, you didn't need me at all."

"But I'm glad you're here." I smile shyly at her before we both belly up to our keyboards and begin our separate searches.

The Google homepage is no longer decorated with hearts the

way it was yesterday for Valentine's Day. My mind meanders briefly to Age and Natalia, and I force myself to eyeball the list of newspapers in British Columbia.

Lillian glances over and says, "Go with the *Sun*."

"Thanks." When the newspaper's homepage appears, I type "obituaries" in the search box and get a listing of "remembrances" for thirty-six people who've died in the last week. What happens to the people whose families don't pony up the money for their "remembrances"? Are they forgotten?

I guess that Mama's maiden name, Huang, is the surname of her adoptive parents, her uncle and his wife, but there's not a single Huang listed among the Clarks and Davidsons and Featherstones. I keep scrolling until I hit on a Chinese name, Kwan.

Holding my breath, I click on it, only to find Sarah Kwan, a woman in her thirties who has "lost a courageous battle with breast cancer."

I sigh at the same time that Lillian does.

"No luck?" I ask her.

She shakes her head. "You?"

"There was only one woman with a Chinese name. I guess she could've remarried a guy who's not Asian."

"Or, if she just passed away, she might not be listed yet." I must look despondent at that because Lillian quickly adds, "Or she married a white guy like you said."

But the real reason I didn't find my grandmother is because I rushed. On my trip back up the list, there it is, another Chinese surname. Nervous, I hold my breath the way I did before I flew off cliffs, and then click.

Evelyn LEONG

Evelyn (Evie) Mar Leong was born July 5, 1931 in Shanghai, China. She was preceded in death by her husband of fifteen years, Pei-Ran Leong.

In 1951, Evie met and married the love of her life, a noted Chinese poet and political dissident, whom she lost shortly after the birth of their youngest daughter. Evie moved her family to Hong Kong in 1975.

Just prior to 1997, Evie followed her children who had already emigrated to Canada and America, settling in Vancouver with her eldest daughter.

After that brief scan, I scroll to the bottom of the obituary.

She is survived by her children and their spouses: Marnie and Norman Chu of Richmond, British Columbia; Patrick and Susanne Leong of Vancouver, British Columbia; Yvonne and Gregor Crowley of Hong Kong; James and Kay Leong of Sunnyvale, CA; Elsie and John Holley of New York, NY; and Betty and Ethan Cheng of Seattle, WA. She is also survived by her beloved grandchildren: Kyle, Stanley, Roper and Jocelyn Chu, Jordan and Justin Leong; Matthew Crowley, and Syrah Cheng.

My name that I've hated — Syrah for fitting not the girl I am but the wine my father loves and Cheng for eclipsing the rest of my name — is right there in the obituary, looking like it belongs with all the other beloved grandchildren.

"Did you find her?" Lillian asks.

"Yeah." I scroll up to where I left off. "I found her."

All through her life, Evie could be found drawing, but felt most at home in the mountains. She was loved by all who knew her for her sense of humor and kind heart.

Except for me. I didn't know her or her sense of humor or her kind heart. And I don't know all these aunts, uncles, cousins. Some of them live not even a half-day's drive away. How could my parents have kept me from my grandmother and the rest of my family? Why didn't they tell me about them?

As the remembrance of my grandmother prints out, I ache to call Age and tell him what I've discovered: more than just my grandmother, but an entire family I didn't realize I had, a clan that claimed me sight unseen, at least in this notice.

For what feels like the fiftieth time this morning, I check my phone, but Age hasn't left a message.

Next to me, Lillian sniffles, as she stares bleakly at her computer screen.

"Hey," I say, putting my hand tentatively on her arm. "You okay?"

"It's not fair," she snaps, shrugs off my touch, and grabs her backpack before darting out of the library.

"Wait!"

"Lillian?" asks Mrs. Hodgkins, getting out of her chair. But Lillian, perennial good girl, doesn't stop for me or this authority figure.

"What happened?" Mrs. Hodgkins speed-walks my way so fast her earrings swing like twin wrecking balls.

"I don't know," I tell her, bewildered, and we both stare at the article on the computer screen from a medical journal, written in gobbledygook about autologous transplants. And I spot Dr. Martin's byline. Slimy Dr. Martin.

"You'd think that there's something we could do to help, wouldn't you?" murmurs Mrs. Hodgkins.

That question ripples down my spine, the same chill I get when I watch a snowboarder nail an extraordinary jump. Like I've witnessed Truth in motion.

As I thrust my grandmother's obituary into my backpack, I think about how I've never been a girly girl, the kind who knows how to do her face to match her every mood (sweet, sultry and all the looks in-between) or who religiously subscribes to fashion magazines as if they were life insurance policies for high school survival.

True, maybe *yo no hablo girly girl*. But all I have to do is think about Age and know that I want to speak True Friend fluently. The halls outside are crowded with kids as everyone heads for first period. Me, I go back to the front steps for my second clandestine phone call, this time leaving a message for Dr. Martin. And when I return inside the school, I don't go to math, but back to the library.

"Mrs. Hodgkins," I say, stopping in front of the nonfiction section where she's shelving books about the underground railroad. "Do you happen to have a copy of my dad's book?" At her furrowed eyebrows, I straighten to my full height the way Baomu does when she's about to fight for what she wants. "I think I know a way that I can help Lillian."

For once, Mrs. Hodgkins doesn't mask her toothy smile behind her hand. She beams, beautifully. "I had no doubt that you would. Come." She leads me to another stack and removes

Baba's book, autographed for the school. "I'll let Mrs. Prefontaine know that you're doing some independent research."

"Thanks," I say, and settle down at a table and prepare to work on my first business plan for Ride for Her Life, a snowboarding event to raise awareness for Amanda's plight.

25

The last thing I expect while queuing for the van at the end of the day is a ball of furless dog to explode at me, yipping like I'm trespassing at my own school.

"Mochi, down!" I say, firmly.

Naturally, quasi-guard dog doesn't listen. All eight pounds of him start to leap onto my legs, less attack than annoyance. A couple of kids snicker as they walk by us. One girl actually starts to kneel with an "awww, how cute," until Mochi growls at her.

"Grace, call him off!" I plead, knowing that wherever Mochi goes, Grace is soon to follow.

Luckily, I'm right. Just as I think I'm going to have to retreat all the way back inside the school, Grace walks lazily toward me in her expensively cut pantsuit, snapping her cell phone shut.

"So the prodigal daughter needs help." Her words may have their regular bite, but her tone delivers none of its usual sting. It's like hearing Mama speak Mandarin with her Cantonese intonation, right words, wrong accent.

"What are you doing here?" I ask. Directed at any other person, the question would be rude, but given Grace's rare, unwilling appearances at The House of Cheng, much less at my school, it's a valid one.

"Your mom called me in a panic. Halfway to Hong Kong, she realized that she had forgotten to arrange a driver to pick you up from school. Apparently, I'm first on your emergency list."

The slightest breeze could have toppled me at that moment. I'm even more surprised by Grace responding to Mama's SOS call than I was with her driving me home after the Evergreen Fund debacle the other night.

Grace glances around the school campus, swinging her car keys around one finger. "So this is Viewridge. Very posh."

Here we go, I think to myself as I huff toward her car, *the guilt treatment.* Yes, I get to go to a private school while she and Wayne were consigned to public. Behind me, I feel Grace's eyes cataloguing my butt, the muffin lid of fat hanging over my waistband, the way my bra cuts into my back blubber. I look back at her where she, sure enough, is studying me from five steps behind.

"What?" I demand.

"I'm trying, Syrah," she says softly.

I draw in my breath, sharp, but tell myself that I must have misheard. For sure I've stepped into some new, weird, alternate universe.

The thing is, I know that Grace is trying. She rescued me the night St. Mama picked up her humanitarian award at that Evergreen Fund dinner, and she's here right now. But patterns are hard to break, and hurt is hard to forget. So while part of me wants to talk to her about my grandmother I didn't know I had, or how conflicted I feel about Age and snowboarding, the safer route is to stay quiet. And that is what I do on the ride home.

As soon as we reach the house, I head upstairs to my bedroom and dig through my backpack, scrounging around the scary, crumb-filled bottom for the remains of my manga-journal. Tucked inside, I find the obituary for Evie Leong, long-lost grandmother. It's weird how holding that paper reminds me that there's more to life than being paid to snowboard. Like discovering a family. And helping homeless kids. Or finding a cure for a sick one.

I take the obituary, my thinned-down journal, and my laptop to bed. After I draw the silk curtains, I nestle against my pillows. It's tempting to read the obituary, savor every word in this short story I don't want to end. But The Ethan Cheng Way is to do all your work first and reward yourself afterward. So I set aside the remembrance and open the PowerPoint presentation I worked on at school and start to refine.

After a few hours, I still don't know if this plan has any merit, much less makes any sense. The details are overwhelming me: how much is this snowboard event going to cost to throw? And how on Earth do you go about constructing a rail? Sheesh, the crew and I used to haul truckloads of snow from the mountains late at night, and dump it by stair rails at random buildings we had scoped out earlier to ride.

As I look at all these questions on the last slide, I can hear Wayne deriding my plan: you didn't think about X, Y, and Z? You stupid girl, you really think you can pull this off?

Ask Grace for help.

I try to ignore the voice that sounds suspiciously like Bao-mu's and cover my head with a pillow. But the words bore inside me, discordant as Chinese drummers: *Ask. Grace. For. Help.*

Since the pillow is utterly useless, I swat it off my face and see the canopy carved with coiled dragons, their fanged mouths biting their tails. How can a creature bent on devouring itself possibly be the sign of the emperor?

Using my fingertips as though I'm blind, I trace the raised *fu* and *shou* characters on the posts, the ones that are supposed to bring good luck and long life to me for as long as I sleep within the walls of this alcove bed. As my finger starts to make its third circuit around the character for long life, I think about Lillian's little sister and all the other kids at Children's who are stuck in their hospital rooms with their parents crashed on the pull-out chairs and convertible sofas. My alcove bed is no prison. I can leave any time I want.

So I get up and call for help. As I wait for Grace's voicemail to pick up, I hear a trilling ring tone downstairs that's not mine or Mama's or Baba's.

"Grace?" I ask.

"Syrah, I'm right downstairs," she answers.

"You are?"

"Yes." Grace sighs and hangs up.

Pumped up with adrenaline and surprise, I grab my computer and take the stairs down to the living room so fast I nearly collide into Mama's perfect pine bonsai, one of the Three Friends of Winter. The gnarled tree looks lonely without its two other buddies, sitting by itself on a pedestal.

Looking up from the papers in her lap, Grace nods at me. It strikes me how much she reminds me of Baba, head down and focused. With her glasses perched on her nose, Grace looks older than thirty-eight, and she's tinier than usual, even skinnier than Mama now. Being inches taller, the effect is taffy stretched to transparency.

"What are you still doing here?" I ask softly.

Mochi stirs in his spot by Grace's hip. She automatically places a hand on him, calming him. In bemusement, she answers, "I'm not entirely sure."

Drawing closer until only the low platform table separates us, I admit, "I'm glad you're here. The house creeps me out when I'm by myself." I swear, this is the longest civil conversation we've ever had. Who cares if it's treading the shallow waters of small talk? I don't dare sit down, make myself at home, a signal that I want us to have a nice, long chat. That would just be an invitation for Grace to rub in how much she doesn't really want to be with me. "What are you working on?"

"Oh, this?" Grace takes off her glasses and sighs. "Rude Q and A for a client."

"What's that?"

"Before my clients meet with the press, I script all the possible hard questions they might face, and the answers they should give." Grace hands the Rude Q and A to me.

"No kidding." I scan the document, covered with questions like *How many people have injured themselves using your equipment?* Beneath each is an answer that masterfully turns every possible negative connotation into a golden opportunity, the Midas Touch of words: *I shudder to think how many people have injured themselves by* not *using this equipment, which has been methodically designed by the best mechanical engineers in the world and tested by top physiologists.* "So they, what, memorize all of this?"

"Most of them do." Grace lifts another copy of the document from her lap and shakes it impatiently. "But this client likes to shoot from his hip."

"I hope he has a good hip."

Grace grins at me, and suddenly I know why Mama works so hard to get a genuine smile from her. For a moment, I feel like I've been admitted into the Cheng inner circle.

"As a matter of fact," says Grace, "he does not have a good hip at all. More like a fat ass."

"Grace!" I say, and stare at my half-sister, the one who's always so buttoned up and perfectly restrained. The words "fat ass" I just don't see figuring in any politically correct answer Grace would ever give — even now, to me — however rude the question may be.

Grace's eyes gleam. "Ironic, isn't it, that he's made his fortune building rehab equipment, which he now wants to take mainstream?" She pats the empty spot next to Mochi, a gesture that reminds me painfully of Bao-mu. It's almost as if Bao-mu is behind me, pushing me in the small of my back to Grace. Leery, I perch on the edge, computer in my lap, ready to leave at her first insult. But then I see a photograph of what looks like a ball sliced in half.

"Hey, I had to use this torture device for my knee."

"So did these people. Meet some of his poster children." Grace shuffles the photographs she's been holding and hands me one of an old man in running shorts, his race bib pinned to his singlet. "Hip-replacement surgery, and then he ran his twentieth marathon." She shows me another photograph, this one a woman with a pixie cut. "She finished the Danskin triathlon a year post-op after her mastectomy."

193

Under the shelter of my computer, my hand unconsciously rubs my knee, feeling the ridgelines of the scars that have yet to smooth over. Dr. Bradford had warned me to expect keloids since Asians, like African-Americans, tend to develop scar tissue that heals thick and dark over incisions. The thing is, as I flip through the photographs and listen to Grace's one-sentence diagnoses of each of the athletes, I feel like I know these people who've been scarred and battered from accidents and surgeries and life.

"They're survivors," I say, interrupting Grace even though I know this will shut down our first bona fide conversation faster than a windstorm does a ski lift.

"What did you say?" Twice now, I've startled Grace tonight, but she doesn't snap at me or make a denigrating comment about how stupid I am because anyone can see that these people are broken. Nor does she look appalled that my adoring little sister mask has gone missing in action, and I'm looking her straight in the eye, her equal.

"They're beautiful."

Grace asks, not in challenge, but with curiosity, "What do you mean?"

"They're real people with real bodies who got back into their game." I tap the picture of a man in a wheelchair. "Or got themselves into a different game."

"Real people, real bodies," repeats Grace thoughtfully. She scribbles it on her notepad the way I do in my journal. "That's not bad."

"It's the truth," I say, pleased, and scoot back so I can sit lotus-style on the couch.

Grace's eyebrows lift. "One of my friends had ACL surgery a

year ago, and she still can't sit with her legs crossed like that. Pretty good."

"Good genetics."

Grace studies me, not critically the way Mama does, looking for any minute fault in me that she can whittle away, but as if she's never noticed me before. "More like hard work." Her eyes narrow at my computer. "What are you working on?"

It takes all my restraint not to apologize with a "well, this is probably a stupid idea, but . . ." — which is a major no-no according to The Ethan Cheng Way. (Never assume failure; always visualize success.) While I open the top of my computer, I tell her, "One of my friend's little sister has leukemia. She's just three."

"Oh, that's terrible."

On the screen is the first slide, Ride for Her Life. Under the title is my manga drawing of Amanda on a snowboard in mid-flight, pigtails flying behind her like twin turbo engine jets.

"This is your snowboarding event, isn't it?" guesses Grace. "The one you talked about at our family meeting?"

"Sort of," I say, and tell her about what I learned from Dr. Martin, about how mixed-race kids have near impossible odds of finding a match on the National Bone Marrow Registry because so few minorities, and even fewer biracial people, are registered. "Plus, Mr. Fujimoro works for Baba. Isn't that a sign we have to do something?"

"So what are you proposing?"

With that invitation to give Grace the whole pitch, I run through how we can get corporate sponsors to underwrite the event, how we can charge an admission fee and command premium pricing for a VIP level, how we can sell merchandise.

Halfway through the slideshow, Grace is so silent, I'm convinced that she's formulating her yes-but-no answer. Instead, she interrupts me, "People are pretty much self-motivated. It'd be more effective if we renamed this *Ride of Our Lives*."

"How about *Ride* for *Our Lives?*" I counter. "It's more inclusive."

"Good, that's good. And we can broaden the objective and encourage people of any color to register with the National Bone Marrow Registry."

But when I get to the slide about PR, Grace says flatly, "No, that's wrong. The headline isn't about Amanda. It's going to be about you."

"What do you mean?"

"You're the heiress who fell, the one who caused the biggest ruckus in Whistler's history. The media is going to have a heyday over you." Her sharp eyes don't miss the panic that surely has to be as obvious on my face as badly applied blush. "Are you still willing to go through with this?"

Everything in me wants to shut down the computer, call this exercise a training run for the big day when I'm older and have more experience to really make a difference. But how can I let fear of getting skewered in the press stop me from helping Amanda? I can't, especially when I can still hear her nurse's bleak prognosis.

"Okay," I say.

"You sure? Do you know what you're agreeing to?"

I nod calmly, even if my hands are gripping my computer. "I fell. But I picked myself up. If companies can turn their mess-ups into triumphs, why can't I remake myself?"

Like father, like daughter in true Chengian fashion, Grace

ignores my question that she doesn't want to answer. She breaks our gaze and busies herself with tidying the photographs, her papers around her, all her excuses for not answering me. But then faintly, with her back to me, I think I overhear her asking herself, "Why not?"

My stomach growls. So I say, "You hungry for dinner?"

"Not really," Grace says, but she follows me to the kitchen, where dinner is waiting in the refrigerator, another low-fat concoction of lean protein and vegetables. Our meal is a short, quiet affair with Grace taking three bites before pushing back from the table and saying, "I've got a deadline to meet." But at the kitchen door, she pauses. "Do you work out in the morning?"

"Mostly in the afternoon."

"Good, then I'll see you tomorrow morning."

I narrow my eyes at her answer. But as Grace continues to the living room, with me following and watching while she gathers her Rude Q and A, I ask, "Wait, what about Japan?"

"Since my client —"

"The fat ass?"

"The one and the same," Grace agrees with a slight smile. "Since he decided that it'd be more prudent to use a Japanese PR agency who understands the local market, my presence is no longer required in Tokyo. So I thought I might as well stay here for the week until your parents come home." Slinging her briefcase over one shoulder and cradling Mochi under her other, Grace leaves for the guest wing, a place no original Cheng children have ever visited before.

"You're staying?" I ask, stunned.

"Good night." Without a backward glance, Grace disappears down the hall.

Upstairs in my bedroom, I reward myself, not with a victory dance but with my grandmother's obituary that I read with my covers tucked around myself. In my first quick skim in the Viewridge library, I must have missed the last sentence. Po-Po's memorial is in Vancouver, British Columbia, on Saturday. I sit up, my comforter falling off, wondering how the hell I'm going to get to Vancouver in two days when I'm still incommunicado with Age.

Ask. Grace. For. Help.

Again, those insistent, impossible words. Why is it easier to ask for Grace's help when the beneficiary is Amanda, yet so painfully difficult to raise my hand for myself?

The dragons on my alcove bed, those divine signs of the emperor, stare back at me intently, the same way Bao-mu did when she lectured me: you need say, I deserve the best.

Well, I say, I deserve to know about this missing-link family. I deserve answers.

If I'm going to ask Grace to drive me to the funeral, then I've got some Rude Q and A to prepare tonight. Rolling to my side, I grab my manga-journal, where I left it on my bedside table, and touch the *fu* character on my bedpost for good measure. Tapping my pen on the otherwise empty page of my journal, I think about all the questions Grace may have when I tell her that I need to go to Vancouver. She might yes-but-no me, but guess what? I am going to yes-but-yes her back.

Only then do I begin to draw myself and Grace, side by side in Mama's workout room, visualizing my success, which has Vancouver written all over it.

26

What was it that Robert Burns wrote, something about the best-laid plans going awry? Well, wouldn't you know it, I'm in the middle of my all-time favorite dream come Friday morning, the one where I feel like a human humming-bird, hovering in the air above the mountains, the sun warm, but the air cool when the curtains around my bed are yanked open. One could call it a rude awakening.

"Rise and shine," says Grace. She whirls around to flip open the blinds in my windows, but the only light that streams into my bedroom comes from the moon.

This is not how I pictured my negotiations with Grace to begin.

"God, Grace, what time is it?"

"Time to work out." With her hair plaited in two braids down her back and in workout clothes, she looks like Pippi at boot camp. Great, now she's taking a Grand Tour of my bed-room.

For a moment, I miss the old Grace who ignored me. But

that thought is as fleeting as last night's sleep, especially when I remember what this morning is: Victory in Vancouver. Yawning, I haul myself into a sitting position. It's tiring to watch Grace flit around my room, checking the multitiered antique Chinese wedding basket next to my desk, the upholstered reading chair in the corner. She stops in front of the silver-plated frame of herself and Wayne on some vacation they must have taken together.

I pretend I'm not paying attention as I stretch in bed, wondering how pathetic I must look to her, harboring a picture of them when I'm sure no such photo of me sullies their bedrooms.

"This doesn't feel like you" is Grace's final judgment. Her hand sweeps my entire bedroom and its priceless contents, including the bonsai Mama has displayed on my desk.

Once, I would have thought, *As if you know me.* But Grace is right. My bedroom feels nothing like me. I crawl out of bed and lean against one of the posts to get my bearings. "I told the interior decorator that I couldn't sleep in a bed that's four hundred years old because every time I closed my eyes, I saw a village of people staring at me. Do you know what she said?"

Grace shakes her head.

"She said, 'Nonsense! It would be aristocrats staring at you since this is an imperial piece.'"

"She did not."

"Yeah, she did." Shyly, we smile at each other, and I decide that it is definitely worth having my REM interrupted at five thirty in the morning for this very moment.

o o o

Half an hour into the workout, Grace isn't Little Miss Rise and Shine anymore. I swear, her face is so red, feet pedaling and hands gripping the arms of the elliptical machine, I'm afraid she's going to go into cardiac arrest, and my CPR training from my avalanche rescue class two years ago is just a tad rusty.

"Why don't we cool down now?" I say.

"God," she puffs. "How long do you usually go for?"

"About this long," I tell her, sensing that she's got enough Cheng competitive spirit to match me, minute for minute.

"Don't lie to me." Huff, huff. "Just tell me the truth."

So I do. "Fifteen minutes longer."

She groans.

"But you know," I lean over to point at the warning label on her elliptical, "it says right there that you should consult a doctor before you begin an exercise program."

"Yes, I am aware of that." Huff, huff. "My new client is, after all, in the physical fitness business." Grace looks at me accusingly while she pants. "You're not even breathing hard."

"I'm saving energy for weights."

"Okay, done." Grace presses the emergency stop button on the elliptical. As soon as she's off, she bends over so that I can see every one of her vertebrae and her ribs through her thin top.

Skinny, I realize, isn't the same thing as strong.

Me, I could stay on the treadmill for at least another thirty minutes, crank up the speed, I'm feeling that powerful this morning. That must be a sign to begin my negotiations. So I step off the treadmill and stretch beside Grace, crossing my right leg over my left, and reach for my toes.

"What are you doing next week?" I ask her nonchalantly,

because according to The Ethan Cheng Way, you shouldn't let the person on the other side of the negotiations know how much you want anything. With that small bit of knowledge, power shifts.

"You still want to go to Whistler, don't you?" counters Grace unexpectedly. But then again, I should have known that the Master of the Rude Q and A would be good at guessing.

"Actually, I don't," I say, and cross my left leg over my right.

Grace arches an eyebrow at me, the kind of expression that says, *I highly doubt you.*

Surprisingly enough, it's true. Somewhere between receiving that rejection e-mail from RhamiWare and visiting Children's Hospital, I lost my burning need to go to Wicked in Whistler. I'd rather find out about Po-Po.

According to the Syrah Cheng Road Trip to Vancouver Rude Q and A, I should be prepared to answer why she should give up her precious working hours over the weekend to spend time on me.

Grace beats me to the punch. "I'm working next week so I really can't drive you five and a half hours each way to Whistler."

"Can you drive me three hours to Vancouver instead? It'll just be a weekend trip," I say, and lie on my back. Bending my left leg, I place the ankle on my scarred knee and stretch my hamstrings. Grace doesn't stretch, but sits next to me, knees drawn to her chin.

"What's in Vancouver?" she asks.

My internal voice, the one I've squelched since it didn't lead me away from Jared but to him, now gives an impatient tsk, unmistakably impatient as Bao-mu. This Rude Q and A may work for Grace, and The Ethan Cheng Way may work for Baba, but none of that is working for me.

Facing Grace, I tell her what I want. "I just found out that my grandmother passed away a couple of days ago in Vancouver. I have to go to her funeral Saturday."

"Wait a second. Didn't your grandmother die about ten years ago?"

"That was Mama's *adopted* mother."

Grace's eyes widen, but other than that, her face doesn't change. Finally, she asks, "Why isn't your mom taking you?"

"That's what I need to find out."

Grace isn't looking at me anymore, but out the window where the sunrise is slowly displacing darkness. Telling her what I want hasn't been particularly effective. So I ask for what I need. "Can you drive me? It's important."

Grace stands up quickly, like she's brushing crawling ants off her lap, and asks instead, "Are we going to do some weights?"

Disappointed, I nod, telling myself that I hadn't really expected Grace to come through for me. Less than a day of civility does not a doting big sister make.

"So we should start on our big muscles first," I say softly. "The ones that support us. How do lunges sound?"

"If it makes my butt tight like yours, okay," says Grace.

How sad is it that the mention of my butt in the same sentence as the word "tight" works like a commercial break, interrupting my internal churning about having no way to get to Vancouver? This demonstrates two things: a little flattery can win me over, and Grace is a master of controlling conversation.

To regroup, I demonstrate the proper posture of a lunge for her, sweeping one foot in front of me, bending the back leg until it almost touches the floor.

"Keep your front leg at a ninety-degree angle," I correct her, as she lunges. "Chest up."

Out of the blue, Grace says, "You'll get a bigger turnout if you stage Ride for Our Lives in Seattle, not at Snoqualmie. Do you know of anyplace that's already set up for a snowboarding event in town?" Breathing harder now, Grace asks, "Anyplace we don't have to pay for the venue?"

"No," I start to say, but remember how over one summer, Age dropped me off at Baba's office and drooled over all the steps leading to the front door.

"Those rails are wicked good," he'd said, eyes glittering at this snowboarders' nirvana. I could see back then that he was already plotting to ride them come the perfect winter's night.

"Are you kidding?" I told him, unable to even fathom the trouble I'd be in if the headlines ever screamed, CHENG DAUGHTER, 14, ARRESTED FOR RECKLESS ENDANGERMENT AND TRESPASSING.

So now I suggest to Grace like I'm half-kidding, "Well, Dia-Comm would be free."

Instead of scoffing at me, Grace looks thoughtful for a long moment, and then she says, "Actually, the parking lot is big enough to set up a stadium and a ramp or whatever it is you snowboarders use."

"Rails. But DiaComm? Come on, that would be a no."

"Why not?" Grace swivels around so effortlessly, she'd be a natural at snowboarding. Facing me, she demands, "What symbolizes mobility more than snowboarders? Matching up snowboarders with DiaComm would be a PR coup." The way her eyes gleam at this new challenge, this new opportunity, I can tell she's fallen in love with the idea. "If you're going to do something, do it big and do it right. Remember that."

"Okay, but first, I need Baba to buy into my plan."

As if she's assessing whether I've got the guts to follow through with that — guess what, I do — Grace continues to study me, and then she nods. It's as if we share one of those sister bonds I read about in my favorite manga series, *The Shaolin Sisters,* about three girls who share the same father, but different mothers because, I swear, Grace says, "You're onto something big." Before I can react, she uses her shoulder to wipe a trickle of sweat off her cheek and asks, "So when's the funeral?"

"Saturday at two."

"We'll have to leave Sunday morning."

"Really?" I can't keep the squeak out of my voice.

"I wouldn't offer unless I meant it," she says sharply, back to the Grace I know.

"Thanks," I tell her, feeling weightless in a way I haven't since the avalanche poured down the mountain behind me. I know what has been lifted. Not my insecurity or my neuroses or my fear. But my loneliness. At a dinner a couple of months ago, a researcher whose work Baba personally funds told us that the mortality rate for single men is higher than it is for married ones. That weight of loneliness, of feeling like you don't matter

205

to anyone in the world, can literally kill you. I can't help it. I gush, "Thank you, thank you, thank you."

"You're welcome," Grace says, holding my gaze in the mirror, an unwavering look that tells me I matter and that she won't change her mind.

27

By the time Grace drops me off at school, the bell has already rung, but before I head to homeroom, I stop in at the library, where I know I'll find Lillian. Just as I thought, she's parked at the computer, devouring another jargon-laden medical article as though she's cramming for a final that's going to help Amanda.

"Lillian," I say, resting my hand lightly on her shoulder.

Despite the dark circles scooping out her eyes, Lillian shines a megawatt-smile at me. "What's up?"

"You don't have to with me," I tell her quietly. "You don't have to be perfect, not with me."

Instead of being offended, Lillian nods, her smile sloughing off her face, leaving her as vulnerable and panicked as a girl who has slipped overboard. But I'm on lifeguard duty, and I'm not letting her go down, not without a fight. So when she asks, "God, what're we going to do if the transplant doesn't work?" I tell her, "I think I have an idea."

"Syrah, not even your dad can do anything. Even Dr.

Martin said that this was our best option — thanks for having him call."

"My pleasure, but —"

"Look, I know you want to be helpful, but Amanda's got the best pediatric oncologist around, thanks to Chelsea's mom."

Mrs. Dillinger connected them to Children's Hospital? No wonder Lillian's been on her best behavior with Chelsea. I sit in the chair next to hers. "I know Amanda's getting the best care in the world, but I've got an idea for finding her a bone marrow match."

As if she's traipsed down this well-worn path from hope to heartbreak one too many times, Lillian only shrugs. "How?"

"What if we stage a fundraiser —"

"Money's not the issue."

"— fundraiser," I continue, pretending her doubts haven't interrupted me, "that will also publicize the need for more people to get tested for the National Bone Marrow Registry?"

"What are you talking about?"

"You said that the issue is that Amanda doesn't have a perfect match. And that there's probably somebody out in the world who's mixed race and matches her, right?"

Finally, Lillian turns in her chair to face me head-on, willing to listen now.

"So what I'm saying is that we draw attention to Amanda. We stage a snowboarding exhibition in her honor. 'Ride for Our Lives.'" I pull a copy of my business plan out of my backpack. "We'll invite some of the best snowboarders around, especially the ones of color. There are a bunch of Japanese riders who are absolutely kicking it in competition. I bet they'd care about this because it could be them, or someone in their family, or a friend who needs a bone marrow match. We'll offer a prize purse, and get a matching donation for the registry."

"It's a long shot, Syrah."

"I know, but so is your parents having a just-in-case baby." On the cover, I tap the manga drawing of Amanda on her snowboard etched with *Ride for Our Lives*. "All I'm saying is why not have a just-in-case plan?"

Lillian lifts her eyes from the deck of PowerPoint slides she's holding as if they're winning lottery tickets and asks, "Why would you do this?"

"Do you really need to ask? I've got zero community service hours. And a semester's worth of manga to write for the newspaper."

"Yeah, right," says Lillian, smiling, and I can tell my one tiny drop of hope is thawing her heart. "Okay, so question of the day."

Shoot them at me, I think. *I'm ready to answer any objection.*

"How are we going to pull this off?" she asks.

We, as in we are a team.

I hug Lillian and say, "You forget who I am."

There's a moment in snowboarding when a rider shifts from being technically proficient to being stylish. Her riding becomes fluid, easy, shows flair and personality. That's how I feel right this moment, like I've crossed over from being the daughter of Ethan Cheng to becoming me, Syrah Cheng, girl with guts.

While everyone else with a driver's license at Viewridge screams out of the parking lot, giddy with winter break freedom, Lillian and I are putt-putting along the side streets to

Boarder Xing, the leading snowboard shop in town, since Lillian is afraid to drive on the highways.

"So we're looking for them to review the plan?" asks Lillian, not taking her eyes off the road.

"And plant the idea that they might want to underwrite the event." I sound braver than I feel. My amped-up nerves have nothing to do with potentially seeing Age where he works after school and everything to do with me on the verge of making my first big Ask. At least, that's the story I tell myself. "Boarder Xing sponsors a bunch of the local snowboarding events up at Stevens and Snoqualmie."

"So how does that work? I mean, like, what are we supposed to say?" asks Lillian, whose stress must be channeling into her foot, which all of a sudden is pressing the accelerator. The car lurches forward. "Oh, my sister has cancer, so please give us five thousand dollars for a snowboarding event?"

"Something like that." I watch the speedometer steadily creep from speed limit to speeding.

"God, Syrah, I suck at this."

With Lillian's death grip on the steering wheel, I decide now's not the time to joke that what sucks is her driving. Instead, I say, "I'm new to fundraising, too, but think of this as a preliminary talk with the owner. She invited us to meet with her." Just as we nearly sideswipe the car in Lillian's blind spot, I warn her, "Watch out!"

Even after Lillian screams and returns to her old lady driving, we reach Boarder Xing sooner than I'd like.

No schmoozer at one of my parents' parties could scope out the store as proficiently as I do when we walk in to Boarder Xing. The store is a snowboard boutique, a mix of fashion with clothes even non-riders would crave, and that function with all the latest boards and boots to satisfy the hardest-core rider. Huge red sale signs are everywhere, in preparation for Boarder Xing's annual Presidents' Day weekend blowout. Playing on the large-screen in back of the store is a new snowboard video that I haven't seen yet with music that would be fun to ride to. At once I see that Age isn't around, but approaching us is some new sales guy I don't recognize, stocky with a scraggly soul patch. For all my nervousness about seeing Age, I'm crushed when I don't.

"You finding what you need?" asks Soul Patch Guy, all eyes on Lillian.

That would be negative, because what I need is Age. But what I want is to help Amanda. So I nudge Lillian, who is looking googly-eyed back at the sales guy, and tap into my inner Grace. All business official, I announce, "We've got a meeting with the owner."

"Are you the ones with the sick sister?"

"Amanda," says Lillian, as the interest cools in her eyes. "Her name is Amanda."

"That's tough, really tough." Soul Patch Guy sounds so mournful Amanda could be his own kid sister who's got cancer, and just like that, he lands back on Lillian's cute-boy radar. "Tracey had to step out. An emergency."

Even with zero experience in fundraising, I know this is not an auspicious start. But as I'm about to reschedule, Mr. Soul Patch says, "She wanted you to talk to the assistant manager when he comes in. Speak of the devil. Yo, Age!"

My heart squeezes at the sound of that name, which is nothing compared to the acrobatics it does when Age ambles

211

through the store's front door. His eyes find mine, shocked that I — the friend he used to see all the time — am standing in the same recirculated air as he is. Me, I'm shocked that love has commando-crawled its sneaky way inside me, no matter how much I tried to barricade it.

Mr. Soul Patch introduces Age, assuming we're strangers: "And here's the man himself, Adrian Rodriguez, head honcho here, at least when the Boss Woman's gone."

When had Age gotten promoted? What else has happened since we stopped speaking to each other?

"Syrah," he says, and idly kicks away an imaginary dust ball, which tells me that Age is as nervous as I am.

"Age."

Vaguely, I'm aware that Lillian is looking back and forth between Age and me, putting together a puzzle. That's what he and I have become, disconnected pieces that no longer fit.

Right when I start to tell him why I'm here, Age asks, "What's up?" Before Natalia, we could finish each other's sentences; now, our timing is so off we can't even get our words out right.

Pull it together, Cheng, I tell myself. So when Age gestures for me to go first, I say, "Tracey wanted us to talk with you about this snowboarding event we're planning. Why don't we sit down, since this might take a couple of minutes?" By some mutual, unspoken consent, Age and I leave a healthy distance between us on the bench fashioned out of an old snowboard at the front of the store. My pitch sputters forward, all ums, ers, and silent oopses, until Lillian intervenes, "This is all Syrah's idea after she met my little sister, who, incidentally, thinks of her as some kind of hero."

Age smiles in that crooked way of his. How can I possibly

miss him more when he's sitting next to me than I do waiting for his call? So when he says, "I can understand that," I fall back into our pattern of banter and retort without thinking, "That's because you spent so much time worshiping my snowboarding." Which makes him answer, "You wish, Gidget. It was my butt you were worshiping when I smoked you."

We smile awkwardly at each other, stuck in that uncomfortable former friend zone, well beyond getting to know you but far short of being privy to all your current secrets. We have become well-acquainted strangers.

"So what do you want?" asks Age, looking at me intently.

You. But I stick to my script, deciding that being professional is just a euphemism for being politely distant. "So I'm looking for your feedback on the plan, and I'll be honest," I tell him. "I'm also looking for your support."

Still, even though I tell myself that I'm just presenting to a potential sponsor, it's weird to be sitting here with Age. What's stranger is that we sound so businesslike, the way he asks and I answer about signage ("Yup, we are selling signs to hang on the rails and along the stands.") and sponsorship levels ("Gold level sponsorships start at fifty thousand dollars.")

Then, like a seasoned manager, Age asks, "What about press?"

"Grace is all over that," I say.

That surprises him so much, Age drops his professional demeanor: "Not a chance."

"Uh-huh," I say, laughing before I catch myself about to launch into a *yeah, can you believe it?* So I turn back to the presentation: "What do you think?"

"Impressive," Age says, his knee bouncing up and down the way it does when he brainstorms. "I don't want to promise

anything, but I'd be surprised if Tracey didn't want to participate in some way. I'll have to talk it over with her, though."

Yeah, just like you needed to talk over our friendship with
your girlfriend, I think to myself. Unfair, uncool, and totally
unexpected, but my anger burns through my thin veneer of
professionalism. And out of that opened vent bubbles my frustration: Wait a second, buddy, but I deserved the best from you.
I deserved to be treated like a great, trusted, cherished best
friend, not some bottom-fishing Z-lister who doesn't rate a
call back.

"So are there any deal breakers that we should know about?"
I ask him, sharply.

"What do you mean?"

"I'd just like to know ahead of time if there are any issues,
any concerns, that you or anyone else might have that will tank
your commitment to me?"

"She means, to Ride for Our Lives," corrects Lillian, which is
girlfriendese for *What the hell are you doing?* She smiles prettily
at Age as she stands. "Why don't we check in with you in a few
days to see whether Boarder Xing is interested? Thanks so
much for considering this. It means everything to me and my
little sister. And Syrah."

As soon as we're out of the store, Lillian says, "Well, that was
interesting. When exactly did you guys break up?"

"We didn't." I fast-walk along the sidewalk toward her minivan, my arms folded tight across my chest. "We're — or we
were — just friends." My emotions are running amok: anger,
sadness, anger, regret, anger, and above all, confusion. Where's
my manga-journal when I need it?

Lillian keeps up with me and both of us turn at the shouted

214

"Wait!" to find Age trotting to catch up. Under her breath, Lillian mutters, "Just friends, huh?"

"What?" I demand when Age is standing in front of me, which I acknowledge isn't the most effective or gracious way of sealing a deal.

"Can we talk for a second?" he asks, glancing at Lillian.

"Oh, there was a sweater that I wanted to try on," she says, and disappears back into the store.

But when it's just the two of us, Age and I are back to square one of having nothing and everything to say to each other, so we don't say anything at all. Random gum wrappers and leaves swirl along the sidewalk, not staying still long enough to give either of us the satisfaction of kicking them out of our way.

"Everything good with you?" he asks.

"Everything's great. You?"

"Yeah, great."

"You got a promotion. Congratulations."

"Thanks."

God, we don't just sound like strangers, we act like strangers. That is almost worse than not seeing Age at all. So I take a deep breath and take a risk, betting on our friendship to tell him honestly, "Actually, life sucks. Bao-mu is gone, I'm moving to Hong Kong, and you and I aren't talking. I mean, I get that Natalia isn't comfortable with me and everything that comes with the" — I swing my hands out to the side like I'm presenting myself in a royal court — "Syrah Cheng package. But I thought I was part of your package, too."

"That's just it. I was never part of the Syrah Cheng package." He stares over my head, running out of things to say. Or maybe that's what he wanted to say all along: good-bye.

Some secret girlfriend SOS signal must be radiating out of me, because in three counts, Lillian is out of Boarder Xing, at my side and bundling me into her minivan and away from Age.

"Do you know what you need?" she asks as she sticks her key in the ignition.

"A heart transplant?"

Lillian casts me a fierce look that I thought Bao-mu had copyrighted. "You need chocolate."

All the putt-putt vanishes from that girl, as if Lillian is fueled by the high octane of my heartache. No less than ten minutes later, we've covered twice as much ground as our slow drive over. She breaks her own order — "Nope, not one peep until we've got some chocolate inside us" — with a loud "Yes! Parking karma!" and swings into the one open spot in front of a coffee shop famous for its homemade organic cupcakes.

"That makes them good for you," Lillian explains, pointing out two enormous carbaholic cupcakes behind the glass counter.

"I got it," I tell her, pulling out my wallet.

"Are you kidding?" she asks, slapping cash onto the counter. "Just say, 'Thanks.' And promise to do this for me the next time a just-friend-guy breaks up with moi."

So I do. And over my emergency therapy by chocolate, we talk about, what else, boys.

"Okay," I say between mouthfuls of cupcake, "what I don't get is how to get beyond the awkward after-the-break-up phase when we were never even together in the first place."

Lillian nods sympathetically. "Yeah, like how can you know

someone so well for so long and then all of a sudden not have a single thing to say, except maybe please give me five thousand bucks?"

"Yeah!" My plate is littered with crumbs and I barely even remember eating. "What's with that?"

"Doesn't it make you wonder what you talked about in the first place? Like maybe that connection was all in your imagination and you were just counting his 'yeah' as amazing insight?"

"I don't know. Age talked," I say glumly, and pick at the crumbs.

"So can that guy at Boarder Xing."

"Soul Patch Guy?"

Guiltily, Lillian scrunches up her shoulders, as she admits, "He gave me his number."

What's amazing is that I start laughing. "Wait a sec, we went in for a sponsorship, and I come out with a broken heart and you got a date?"

"I have to be honest; weird stuff like that always happens to me." And just like that, we are in the midst of a real girlfriend conversation that jumps from Natalia's "ewwww!" newfound snowboarding passion to "awww" about Lillian's ex-boyfriend who would actually deliver care packages to her at the hospital in her old town.

"So why did you break up with him?" I ask.

"Distance. We broke up about a month after I moved here."

"At least you had the satisfaction of breaking up."

To finish the dregs of her latte Lillian tips her head back and sets the cup down on the table with a wicked grin. "You guys withered on the Syrah grapevine."

I can't help laughing. "Yeah, from a killer blight named Natalia." I sigh, looking at my empty plate sadly. "I really miss him."

"I miss my guy, too. Do you want to share another cupcake?"

Some other time, I would have said, absolutely, let me drown my sorrows in sugar. But our conversation is filling my soul up in a way that no food could. "No, I'd rather just talk."

Lillian beams. "Me, too."

28

The next day, Saturday, after our morning workout that's so early it'd be more accurate to call it night, Grace and I are Vancouver-bound. Miracle of miracles, even after nearly two hours of numbing Tibetan monk chanting (Grace's CDs, not mine), I could be peering down a steep face of untouched snow, I'm that wired. All I can think about is what's going to happen when I barge into Po-Po's memorial later this afternoon. What if the Leong family only included me in her obituary because I'm a paper granddaughter, not because they want me in their lives? After all, not one of them has ever contacted me.

More out of habit than hope, I check my cell phone, but naturally Age's self-enforced gag order hasn't been lifted. Not that he'd phone me after our talk yesterday; so why am I checking?

"That's not going to make a guy call you any faster," says Grace as I stash my phone in my backpack.

"How do you know it's a guy?"

Grace's eyebrows fly up as smoothly as a retractable roof. "It's *always* a guy." Thankfully, she returns her attention back to the road. "God, you should see some of the men Betty has set me up with. There's this one, Dale Martin —"

"Oh, God, not slimy Dr. Martin." I groan and then lower my voice, "Let me ply you with some sweet syrah, my sweet Syrah."

"Oh, revolting. But you know what the truly frightening thing is? Compared to the other men Betty's picked, Dale is almost a catch." Her hands tighten on the steering wheel like she wants to strangle him. Or my mom. I don't blame her; I wouldn't want to get set up with Dr. Martin either, even if he did call Lillian at my request and answer all her questions about bone marrow transplants and other experimental treatments.

Grace speeds up to pass a guy in a Beemer. "Look," she says, "there just aren't that many guys who are comfortable with a woman who's independently wealthy, smart, and attractive."

"Well, no offense, but you can be kind of intimidating."

"Who wants to be a wimp? Or worse, be *with* a wimp for life?" Grace shudders and presses on the gas pedal as if she could accelerate past all the climbers who've used her as a rung to their success.

"True."

Grace is on such a roll, I'm not sure how much attention she's paying to the road. Obviously, not much. She's tailing a guy in another lane who flips her off. "Jerk," she says, outraged. "Did you see that?"

"Ummm . . ."

"Case in point, guys can't be trusted. Do the money test: name one guy, any guy, you know who wouldn't freak out that you've got more money than your children's children will be able to spend in their lifetimes. Or who would sign a prenup without blinking."

I can and do. "My best friend, Age."

"Uh-huh, and why isn't he boyfriend material?" Grace waits a scant beat before continuing, "I'll tell you why. He's probably a nice guy. Right?"

Grace's "nice" sounds petrified with boredom. I laugh. "He's actually pretty adventurous, one of the best snowboarders I've seen. There's just one small problem. He's got a girlfriend who happens to hate my guts."

"Ah, the insecure girlfriend." Grace nods knowingly. "Girls can be even worse than guys when it comes to rich girls. On the one hand, they want to collect us as trophies or coast on our credit cards, but hang around them long enough, and they start tearing us down."

"That's so true!" I shriek, reminded of The Six-Pack, the ultimate clique of female collectors and destroyers. Then there's Lillian. "But not all girls are like that."

"Maybe not all," Grace grudgingly concedes. Her cell phone rings from the depths of her leather green tote bag, but instead of answering it, she doesn't even look in its direction. "But I'm absolutely right about my rich girls are a no-man's-land theory."

"Come on, don't you believe in soul mates?" Frankly, I need the possibility of romance, even if my trust fund attracts the wrong guys. Don't poor little rich girls deserve for richer or poorer, too? I grip my car seat as though I'm hanging onto a shred of hope. "I mean, you've got to believe that somewhere out there, there's one guy who's your perfect match?"

My sudden nausea has nothing to do with being carsick and everything to do with how I've pushed my perfect match into Natalia's eager arms.

"Are you kidding?" scoffs Grace, easing up on the gas pedal

because a cop is lurking in the median. "The girl you are now is different from the girl you were two years ago is different from the woman you're going to be in five years and fifteen years and twenty-five years from now. There is no way that one guy anywhere on earth is perfect forever."

But my Mr. Perfect fit the girl I was seven years ago on the playground as well as he did the one five years ago when we Chengs jumped from wealthy to obscenely wealthy and the girl I am today.

"So, what, people get married because they settle for good enough?" I ask, thinking about Mama and Baba. No matter how hard I try not to hear the gossip, it's impossible to ignore how the women snicker about Mama marrying for money, and Baba for her body. Would they still think that if they saw how tenderly Baba had held Mama a few nights ago after she learned about her mother's death?

"Trust me." Her voice hardens. "The guys who feel comfortable with us are the ones who want us for one thing. And it's not our bodies."

I dig my fingernails into my knees. The hallelujah chorus plays in my head, for she speaketh the truth about one boy in my life. But not about Age. The car is going so fast now, the trees lining the highway blur into a swath of green, the way my time with Jared has blurred into a single feeling: shame.

Far, far away, I hear Grace ask, "Hey, you okay?"

I swallow hard, blink away my tears. My robotic "you bet" is confident, clear-cutting any trace that all is not well in Syrahland.

The weird thing is, Grace's eyes narrow, like she sees right through my vanishing act. "I know we haven't been close —"

"Not close?" I repeat slowly, my voice dull in my ears. A harsh, ironic laugh escapes out of me, surprising me as much as it does Grace.

Grace flushes. "Wayne and I were . . ."

"Mean. Hateful. Choose a synonym, any synonym." God, where is this anger coming from? The same anger that spurted at Age yesterday. It's like both Grace and Age have stepped on a fracture line in my heart, one I didn't know existed, and all those layers of emotions that I've packed down, season after season, year after year, release at once. "You guys are old enough to be my parents. God, Wayne himself is a *father,* and he treats me worse than anyone would treat a dog."

"I'm sorry," says Grace softly.

At that, Mochi lifts his head in the armrest between us and yips quietly, like he's apologizing for every teeth-baring growl, too.

Once my emotions run free, I can no more check myself than I could have the avalanche I set off in the backcountry. "And then you come prancing out, all nice and 'let me rescue you' after fifteen years of being an asshole."

God, how do I stop this, stop myself? I'm out of control, wandering so far from The Ethan Cheng Way, I've lost my way.

Grace must know it, too, because matter-of-factly, she says, "I deserve that."

That simple admission of guilt and responsibility diffuses my anger, thwarting the tantrum I'm ready to have.

"But it's not me who you're mad at. Not even Wayne."

"Who?" I demand. "Who do you think I'm really mad at?"

"Your mom."

"What?"

"In the same way that Wayne and I have been mad at our dad. He left our mother and us, Syrah. We lived through years of him never being around. He was always at work so much —"

"As if he's around now."

"No!" Her rebuttal is so emphatic that Mochi whimpers. If I hadn't known better, I would have missed that telltale sign of a second emotional avalanche being released into this car. Soon, if we're not careful, the weight of our words will suffocate us. Grace's voice quiets, each syllable angular with articulated sharpness. "This was different. The only memories I have of Baba those few times when he made it home were of him yelling at us. 'You're so stupid. You'll never amount to anything.' God, anything I ever said would set off a tirade, until I stopped talking when he was around. And then my silence would make him so angry, he'd . . ."

"He'd what?"

"He'd yell even more. I know it sounds stupid, because it wasn't like he ever hit us or was a bad drunk. But I was completely scared of him and how he'd totally lose it, like he was crazy when he went into his yelling benders. God, when everyone used to say he was Prince Charming combined with Yoda, it'd make me want to throw up." She snorts. "How little they knew."

Prince Charming meets Yoda is exactly how I idealized Baba, thinking of him as suave and wise, until he yelled at me in the closet. I can't forget how his fists balled up without him realizing it. How I was so scared when his face twisted like he wanted to obliterate me, and even more scared because he lost his famous Ethan Cheng control. I turn my head, stare at the windblown clouds outside my window.

Grace takes a deep breath. "But I don't get mad at Baba, and you don't dare get mad at your mother."

No, I want to snap. *Keep your PR-pseudo-psychology-spin-doctoring bull to yourself.* But I don't, because I've got a niggling feeling that she's telling the truth. Grace turns on the blinker and we cross back into the carpool lane. Beyond the windshield I realize I can make out individual trees. But only if I look straight ahead — not behind to check out who's trying to pass me, not to the side to see who's catching up to me. But forward to where we're going.

I ask her softly, "So what's with this big sister act all of a sudden?"

"You want to know what this is all about?" Grace turns to me, her PR toothpaste commercial smile disappearing to reveal one that's melancholy and real. "I finally got it at that Evergreen Fund dinner that you aren't the girl who I wanted you to be. You should be spoiled, feel entitled, be lazy. But you're not."

In front of us, a long stretch of cars waits to cross the border. I soak up her words, closing my eyes as if that way, I can better taste the residue of our first true big sister–little sister talk and tiff.

As soft as a grace note, I hear her murmur, "You're more Cheng than I am."

My eyes snap open. "How can you say that?"

"Because you've got the guts to be a pioneer. I just toe the line."

"You've got to be kidding me. So much for being a pioneer. I totally got the yes-but-no rejection from RhamiWare. So it's not like I'm ever going to be a pro snowboarder."

Grace swivels in her seat to look me in the eyes. "Why do you really want to be sponsored? Most professional women

225

athletes are hired for their looks, not their skills. The ones who are paid the most aren't even necessarily the women at the top of their sport."

I start to deny it but realize she's not saying anything I don't already know. How unfair it is that snowboarding guys can look as skanky as they want? If they don't shower for five days, who cares? So long as they tweak out more amplitude than the next guy, go bigger and cleaner, they could be the scroungiest dirtballs on the slopes and still score sponsorships. But girls? No matter how good their tricks are, how high their jumps go, the pro snowboarding girls have got to work their sex appeal, watch their figures, stay in shape in season and out. Their bodies, not just their skills, make them marketable: boobs on boards. Just like my manga alter ego, Shiraz.

Grace says, "You could still snowboard just for the love of it —"

"But I want to be more!"

"Let me finish," she snaps — a big sister to her pesky little sister. "Why be sponsored and get paid a tiny piece of the pie when you could own the entire thing, crust, filling and whipped cream? Ride for Our Lives could be your launching pad to a whole different career, something that melds snowboarding with business with philanthropy." She pauses. "I'll be honest here. Even if you went pro, you'd never be known for your riding. Not really. You'd always be *that* girl, the one with Ethan Cheng for a dad."

As much as I hate to admit it, Grace is right.

Ahead of us, the Peace Arch links America to Canada in a great rainbow-shaped embrace. The line between us and the border is still long and interminably slow moving, but that gives me time to think about Grace's suggestion. The whole snowboarding pie. Funny, that was Jared's reach dream, but it could be my reality.

"This is another reason why having a private jet is a good thing," mutters Grace, sighing impatiently when we don't budge for another five minutes.

"I'm glad we drove."

"Me, too."

In silence, we wait until it's our turn to face the border patrol's interrogation. The young, unsmiling man leans slightly forward from within his private gatehouse and demands, "State the purpose for your visit."

"Personal," says Grace.

This morning I would have said, *Finding my family.* That's what I thought I was doing when I set out this morning with Grace. But as we cross into Canada, Po-Po's adopted country, I realize I've already found the sister I've been looking for right inside this car.

29

Richmond may be a suburb of Vancouver, but it's really little Hong Kong. I'm not just referring to all the restaurants serving up every variety of Chinese food from spicy Hunan to Cantonese seafood, and dim sum to donuts — the long, hot, and savory Chinese ones that you dip into soy milk. Almost all the storefronts we drive past are bilingual. Even the church we pull into welcomes its congregants with a sign in both English and Chinese.

The church parking lot is the one place that doesn't feel congested with people, people, and more people. There's only one other car in the lot, and Grace pulls next to it. With an hour to go before the service, why do I feel like I'm a lifetime too late?

"Do you want to drive around for a bit?" asks Grace, hand poised on the stick shift, looking ready to drive me anywhere I want to go.

All morning long, I couldn't wait to get here, but now that I'm this close to meeting a hidden branch on my family tree, I just want to hop into the backseat and watch the scenery pass me by. But watching life roll on without me isn't what I'm here to do.

"No, thanks. I might sit inside before the service starts." What I really plan on doing is scoping out a seat in the back of the church where I can leave fast if I need to and remain incognito if I want to be. "Could you come back at two thirty?"

"The service will last longer than half an hour, you know?" When I nod, Grace says, "Okay" like she understands her role as big sister: to be my safety net-slash-getaway car in case something goes terribly wrong. "I could just go in with you."

"I'll be okay."

Uneasily, Grace watches me as I get out of the car. The air is cool and moist, the sky gray but not raining. The gloomy clouds look on the verge of tears.

"I'm going to be fine," I assure her, but nod to convince myself.

That's when Grace smiles. "I know you are."

Even so, I notice she stays in the parking lot until I'm inside the church, and only then, as though she's reluctant to leave, does she drive slowly away.

From the outside, St. Joseph's Church looks more big-box warehouse than place of worship. It's bland and white with zero personality, the kind of building you'd drive past a million times without noticing.

Inside the church's narthex, the high ceiling should feel imposing, but doesn't. Somehow, between the benches and planters, the church is warm and inviting, even though no one mans the welcome desk near the entrance, which is a relief, since it saves me from explaining who I am and why I'm here.

229

Beyond the bulletin boards with notices about bible studies and women's teas I spot a placard on an easel, a collage of Evie Leong's world as beloved mother, grandmother, and wife. Pictures of her with all the important people in her life adorn the poster board. I tear my eyes away, knowing that I've never been part of even her most insignificant experiences. What I find myself looking at are my thick, heavy black shoes, not the dainty heels Mama would have me wear to school, nor the tattered sneakers I do instead. Just like my imposter shoes, I don't belong to this world. But then I hear a car honking outside, and remember Grace.

I have Grace.

Another sign announces an open-casket viewing running from one until two. Not for me, no thanks. Rearing away from the door to the sanctuary, I decide a tactical retreat to a bench in the corner is in order. Right when everyone else arrives, I'll slip inside the chapel. But just for the record, when I die, I want to burn, burn, burn until I'm microscopic ash. Age will know what to do from there, even if he's still not talking to me then. He'll sprinkle me from atop Alpental, our home mountain, so I'll have one last wonderful run.

A woman's light footsteps patter from the entrance, sounding so much like Mama that I whip around and gasp. Coming toward me is Mama, aged fifteen years and softened with twenty pounds of added weight, wearing her grief in the bend of her head. I gird myself for the inevitable rude questions when this woman finally notices me, questions I don't want to answer: *Who are you? What are you doing here? Don't you know this is a family affair?*

By this time, the woman is so close to me, retreat is impossible. If I needed proof that she may look like Mama and sound like Mama but isn't Mama, I get it. Her hair is speckled, more gray than black, in a way Mama would never permit. The woman's head lifts, revealing a face clean of makeup other than poorly applied mauve lipstick. Her gaze climbs up from my shoes to my face. Suddenly, she raises her hand to me, in surprise or supplication, I can't tell. As though she's speaking in a foreign language and doesn't want to make a mistake, she asks me tentatively, "Syrah?"

I nod once and whisper, "How do you know?"

She points. Like a divining rod, her finger leads me to Evie Leong's board. And there, near the heart of the poster, is a photograph of me and Bao-mu after I won the school spelling bee. I was there all the time, even if I didn't see it at first.

As I stare, confused, at my photograph, I feel the woman's hand on my shoulder, and I wonder briefly if, like Grace would do before our détente, she's going to say something cutting to make sure I know that I'm not part of the Real Family. Or like Wayne does, tell me that I'm not good enough, not pretty enough, and certainly not smart enough. Or like Mama, brush me off because she doesn't have time to deal with me. Or like Baba, say nothing at all.

But this woman, this perfect stranger, pulls me into her arms like I'm her long-lost beloved, and imprints me onto her body as if she wants to know me by heart.

30

My aunt — who else could she be — pulls away first. Her eyes sweep the narthex, down the pews inside the sanctuary, and even up at the ceiling. Confused, she asks in lightly accented English, not the clipped British English that Mama speaks, "Where's your mommy?"

"She didn't come," I confess softly.

Please don't make me admit that Mama would rather go antique-hunting in Hong Kong than attend her own mother's funeral. While I don't say the words, I see them in the expression that passes over my aunt's face, disappointed, but not surprised.

Squeezing my hands in both of hers, she says, "Your grandmother would have been so happy that you came."

"You think?"

"Of course."

There's a point in conversation where it's too late to ask the person you're speaking with what her name is. This is it. Besides, another family walks into the church, a stylish young woman and a man with Mama's eyes. In between them is a toddler in a three-piece suit.

"Syrah," my aunt announces like I'm a prize, a treasure she's been looking for all her life.

"Syrah?" says the man, who's got to be my uncle. He bends down to his son and points at me. "That's your cousin."

With a little encouraging push, the boy totters over to me with his arms wide open. Even if my cheeks flame with embarrassment from all the attention, I have to admit I love hugging the boy close. That is, I love it until my gaze falls on a girl who looks my age, except she's beautiful in the sleek, sophisticated way that Mama is.

Who am I kidding to think she's going to welcome me with open arms, not when girls like her, The Six-Pack, can't stand who I am and are jealous of what I have. Their envy seethes within them the way it does me when I see Grace and Wayne together.

Miracle: the girl grins, and as she approaches me, she blurts, "Thank God you've come." My "what?" goes missing in the minuscule space between that first pronouncement and her next: "You don't know what it's been like to be the only girl in this family. Finally, someone else to share the torture." Short breath. "Oh, my God, you have no idea what it's been like. 'Your hair is too long.' 'Your hair is too short.' 'You should wear some makeup.' 'What's that gunk on your eyelids?'" A roll of her (makeup-free) eyes. "I mean, it's been enough for me to want to run away from home."

I've memorized all the names in the obituary and venture a guess, "You're Jocelyn?"

"Oh, sorry!" Jocelyn's smile looks anything but sorry. Glee, relief, love, that's what I read until I notice her swollen eyes, lids so puffy she must have spent the last couple of days crying.

I haven't.

The million questions that have been ping-ponging in my head since I discovered that my real grandmother lived just one hundred eighty miles from me demand answers now: what was her voice like? What made her laugh? I want to know all about her. All about them. And know why. Why Mama was given away. Why no one ever called me.

But in the continuous white noise of Jocelyn's enthusiasm, I am mute.

"Did you know that our birthdays are just two weeks apart? You're older," she tells me. "Which makes you the second oldest cousin in our family. Did you know that?"

I shake my head. How do I tell her that I don't know anything at all, not even who this first aunt is? So before Jocelyn can dart off on another conversation, I ask.

"Oh, that's Marnie, the oldest auntie. Can't you tell? My dad may be the oldest son, but Auntie Marnie's the oldest child, and that just bugs both of them like you would not believe. You know, he likes to be all he-man in charge, and she just wants to be all in charge. Boy, you missed a fight when Po-Po was sick."

I missed more than a fight. I missed an entire family history.

"And then," says Jocelyn, pausing dramatically, "there are The Boys." So many boys are streaming around the church, playing hide-and-seek between the pillars and the bulletin boards, they must be multiplying. Laughing because she knows exactly what I'm thinking, Jocelyn places her hand on my arm and lets me in on an important secret: "The key is to establish

your dominance upfront and early. They're like a pack of dogs."
A group of adults descends on us. "Get ready," she warns.

Auntie Marnie sends her a chastising look. "You need to share Syrah."

"But I just got her!"

The way they're talking about me as if I'm the new must-have toy of the season should make me feel mildly offended. After all, it's how I feel when strangers whip around for a good look at me once they figure out who I am. Or so-called girl-friends ask to "borrow" a sweater only never to return it.

But I'm not offended. Not at all. Not even when The Boys use me as their "base" when hide-and-seek morphs into tag and they nearly knock me unconscious.

And especially not when Auntie Marnie smiles tearily at the chaos of our family. "Po-Po would have been so happy right now."

The service is long, and anything but boring. It's a crash course in my family history. Po-Po's sons and daughters share stories, like how her driver's license was revoked (for speeding, of course), and how afterward, she resorted to biking and was riding around up until three months ago. Not bad for an old woman.

Before I know it, I'm tearing up just as though I've known and loved her my whole life. Auntie Marnie hands me a tissue.

Po-Po's drawing teacher, a young woman in a peasant dress, shares this story: "When Evie walked into our first drawing class, all the students assumed that she was the teacher. She

235

smiled like a little girl and said, 'Only if you want to learn how to erase.'"

How can I laugh when I'm crying because I lost out on knowing this woman? I concentrate on the poster-sized photograph of Po-Po and a man I'm assuming is my grandfather, he looks so much like Mama, as thin as my grandmother is round.

Right at two thirty, the door behind the congregation opens quietly, and I know before I turn around that Grace has crept into the church. From where I'm nestled between the Chus and Leongs, I look over my shoulder to smile at her. And when I face the front again, Uncle Patrick pats my arm like I belong right here, in the front pews with the family.

Auntie Marnie is the last to speak. How she toys with her gold necklace, pulling at the pendant, reminds me of Mama. "Life wasn't always easy for my mother, but she always said that you must live with your eyes looking forward, never backward. But now that she's gone, I think we have to look backward to understand the woman she was, the family we are now." Marnie pauses to compose herself, riffling her notes on the podium. "When the Communists took over China and killed my father because he was a man of many words, Mama knew she was going to be removed from us and taken to the country to work in the labor camps with all the other intellectuals. Her first thought wasn't about her welfare, but ours, her children's."

My focus pinpoints on to Auntie Marnie's mouth, so I won't miss a single word. Next to me, Uncle Patrick shifts uncomfortably in the pew, as if this is history he doesn't want to revisit.

"I will always remember the night before the Red Guard came to take her away. She sat down on the bed that all the girls had to share now that we were reduced to living in one room, with strangers in the rest of our home," says Auntie Marnie. "She said that my job was to ensure that our family survives. And to do this. . . ."

Jocelyn slips her hand on top of mine. A warning? A comfort? It doesn't matter; I prepare for the blow.

Auntie Marnie swallows. "Mama's one regret in life was that she asked her best friend to take her baby, just a few months old, to Hong Kong." Unerringly, Marnie finds me in the church and looks deeply into my eyes. She could be talking to me alone. "Mama thought that I couldn't take care of so many children on my own. But as soon as that baby was gone, she knew she made a mistake. Her tears. I will always remember her tears. But it was too late. Mei-Mei was gone, to a better place."

A better place. Only when Jocelyn hands me a fresh tissue do I realize I'm crying harder than before, and she keeps her arm around me. I don't know who I'm mourning for. Marnie because her guilt has coiled around her as tightly as wire forcing a bonsai to bend. Po-Po because she never overcame her losses, no matter how many amusing stories all these people are sharing about her. Mama because she was given away. I know how all three women have felt — guilty, bereft, and abandoned.

The light streaking into the church reflects all the colors of the stained glass window, Jesus ascending to Heaven. A better place. That's how Marnie described Mama's adoption. Her relocation might be a more accurate way to describe it, since I can still hear Bao-mu's voice sharpen with dislike when she had spoken about Mama's adoptive parents, her useless uncle and his vindictive wife. It makes me wonder if that "better place" in Hong Kong damaged Mama in ways no one but she could see. In ways no one better than I could understand.

After the service I'm surrounded by so much noisy family, whose *Syrah, you need to meet so and so* and whose *Syrah, how is your mommy doing* and *why isn't she here* and *what is your daddy doing now that he's retired* questions, and their *Syrah, you need to hear about how your grandmother loved to go hiking* stories begin to blur.

More words are heaped on me with everyone maximizing this moment to make up for years of silence. I start to shut down, overwhelmed, wishing that I was alone with my thoughts. Or alone with Age. Or just alone.

But I smile and nod, smile and nod, smile and nod.

I feel a touch on my arm, look up, and see Grace. With her tall, ultra-lean body, she stands out in this crowd, an elegant skyscraper in a Chinese village.

A good hostess even at this memorial, I introduce Grace, "This is my half-sister."

"You're Syrah's sister?" asks Marnie, delighted to find another niece to dote upon.

Half-sister, I'm expecting Grace to correct. Instead, she says, "Yes, I am. And you are . . . ?"

And just like that, Grace spearheads a conversation so I'm free to "mmm hmmm, wow, uh-huh" tune out.

Later, our car joins the caravan driving to Auntie Marnie's home for the wake. Aside from Grace asking me once if I'm doing okay, comfortable silence is our official language.

o   o   o

If Mama were in charge of this wake, she'd have designated Auntie Marnie's kitchen as the sub-par command central and berated the poor event coordinator for not providing enough table rounds for all the guests, not utilizing a unified color scheme, not using china and silver but paper plates and disposable chopsticks. She would never have permitted something as low-class as a potluck, and worse, would have been horrified that people are leaving their hodgepodge platters wherever there's free counter space rather than displaying the food like untouchable art.

But she's not in charge of this wake.

There is no event coordinator.

And Betty Cheng is a no-show.

The difference between The House of Cheng and The Home of Leong?

Let me count the ways.

The only antiques in this home are ones that have been well-used over time, not pristine museum-quality pieces. The knick-knacks in the display case are misshapen clay animals made by little hands, not priceless porcelain formed and glazed by master ceramicists from centuries past. The people milling around and pushing homemade food on me talk of family, not family fortunes.

The Boys want to know what I do for fun in Seattle. As I tell them about snowboarding, I feel myself thawing. The trick is to focus on their eyes and their questions, and I can almost forget

I'm at a wake for a grandmother I desperately wish I knew, surrounded by people I don't know.

"Tell us about your scariest jump," says one of The Boys, which one, I couldn't say.

The scariest jump was the one I took to get away from Jared. But that's not a story for innocent ears. So I tell them about the different tricks the pro snowboarders can do, the ones I used to do, the ones I want to do. I tell them about how being on top of the mountain makes everything else seem less important. And I tell them about how it feels to move faster than the wind, aimless but powerful and, above all, free.

When I finish my story, I catch Grace watching me wistfully, like she wishes she could feel aimless but powerful and, above all, free, too.

How long I talk, I don't know. What I talk about, I don't remember. At last, after what feels like the five hundredth conversation with yet another relative, my brain freezes, unable to make one more mindless comment, and my cheeks rebel from smiling a moment longer. I make my way through pods of people. Not until I'm halfway to the front door does it occur to me that I'm escaping.

Looking from one side of the hall to the other, I swear, I could be back at Children's Hospital. Instead of acrylic signs that broadcast to the world who's made major gifts, these photographs — black and white, color, sepia — are a mosaic of family memories that I have no part of. And I realize why all this talking has been so taxing.

What strangers want from me is access to Ethan Cheng and a free pass to mine our Gold Mountain. What this family wants is access to the real Syrah, the girl who's been wandering aimless and lost on that same mountain.

A wave of fresh air rolls over me as soon as I open the front door, surprised that it's still light outside. I check my watch. How can it be only five when I feel like I've been talking for an eternity?

"Syrah?"

I turn around to face The Boys. Beyond them, what looks like the entire Leong family has gathered to stop my flight.

One of my boy cousins says, "If you're going snowboarding, we're coming with you."

"Snowboarding? Who's going snowboarding?" asks Auntie Marnie, jostling her way to the front of her pack. I swear, this woman's hearing is as keen as Bao-mu's.

I don't get a chance to answer, *No, of course I'm not going snowboarding. Just outside to sit by myself for a while.* As if my pause were the last morsel on the dining room table, The Boys pounce on it. Now I know why Jocelyn lumps her cousins together into one big noun. They talk over each other and answer as one.

"She's got tickets to Wicked in Whistler —"

"A snowboarding competition . . ."

"The biggest one in Whistler . . ."

"Duh — of course it's in Whistler. Wicked in Whistler . . ."

"Can we go?"

"It started yesterday."

Auntie Marnie claps her hands together. "Quiet! I can't think! All you boys do is make noise."

I second that notion.

"No one is leaving," announces Auntie Marnie. No wonder Jocelyn says our eldest aunt has the leadership gene, which is the polite way of saying she's Bossy with a capital B. "You," she says, pointing to the rest of the family, "have food to eat, and you" — she points at me — "have something to see." She takes my arm and orders, "Come."

A closed door down the hall could be any other in this house, but I know it's Po-Po's room. Auntie Marnie opens the door gently, as if she doesn't want to wake the sleeping person inside. "Come in, come in," she says brusquely when I hang outside the door, feeling like an intruder.

Without waiting to see if I'm obeying — proof that she's used to everyone jumping at her every command — Auntie Marnie removes three enormous scrapbooks from the corner bookshelf. "This is what I wanted to show you." She points me to a reading chair, switches on the lamp, and places one of the albums on my lap. Heavy and substantial, it weighs me down so I don't float away the way I've felt I was going to all afternoon.

Underneath the first photograph of a chubby baby is Chinese writing that I can't read. I look up at Marnie, knowing the answer before I can form the question.

"Your mother's name."

"Betty?"

"No, her Chinese name." Auntie Marnie squats down in front of me.

I shake my head. "She doesn't use that name." Nor do I since mine, Zhen Zhu, meaning pearl, makes me feel more asset than beloved daughter.

"Oh." Marnie smiles at me sadly. "It's Yu."

That one-syllable name sounds emphatic rather than harsh. My hand automatically touches my throat, to where Mama's pendant always rests on her neck, and I translate, "Jade?"

Auntie Marnie nods. "Our mother wanted her to know that she was treasured. Jade is so precious in our culture, almost magical in its powers. We never forgot your mother."

The problem is, my mother must have wanted to forget that name. Auntie Marnie cocks her head at me. "Can you read Chinese?"

I shake my head. "I can only understand it."

Nodding, she points to the single Chinese character that makes up Mama's name. "See," she says and covers the tiny dot that lies like a pearl at the corner of the character. "That means 'wong.' You know wong?"

"King?" I ask.

"Not king. More like the family clan leader. Jade is that, the chief, plus this dot." Auntie Marnie gets heavily to her feet as though the weight of the past is almost too much to bear. With one finger, she circles Mama's name, a tender caress before leaving me alone with Po-Po's memories. "Maybe one day, you can give these scrapbooks to your mommy."

Aside from the one baby picture, there are very few photographs of Mama's childhood, three or four of her as a toddler and no more until she's six, maybe seven. I recognize Wei-pou's stern face that matches her upright posture in a hardback chair, Weigong standing at her side, looking more servant than partner. Two plump boys are positioned in front of them, and standing to the back by herself is Mama, so tiny she's just two eyes peering uneasily over Weipou's shoulder, an interloper in this family portrait. In another picture of just Mama and her two brothers, her expression is more browbeaten than any homeless child in the Evergreen Fund slideshow.

"Oh, Mama," I murmur, running my finger across her pinched face, wishing I could smudge the not-good-enough expression away.

The next page skips forward a few years to Mama at boarding school, standing next to other girls who are all white. Even without the cheongsam, Mama looks every bit the outsider, with her arms hanging awkwardly at her side. But there's a luminosity in her eyes that wasn't there in her Hong Kong pictures and relief in her smile, as if she knows she's in control. And free. By the time she enters Cambridge, she looks almost like the Mama I know: gorgeous, confident, perfectly put together, not a wrinkle on her skirt, nor a blemish on her blouse.

As I skim through this first scrapbook, I could be watching one of those time-stop documentaries where plants burst from seed to full bloom on the count of three. The next scrapbook begins with Mama's wedding announcement in the *New York Times,* articles about Baba's company, photographs of my parents at various functions, and then there's me, me, and more me. I recognize every photograph: they're copies of pictures that Bao-mu took. I always thought it was so weird how she was never without a camera. My first successful foray on the potty: *CLICK!* My first dance recital with all of three shuffle-steps: *CLICK!*

I may not have been known, but I was loved. And so was

Mama. Without having to study every page, I know it. And I know it because the third book, more empty than full, is waiting for Mama's life and mine to fill it.

If Mama had any inkling of how much she was cherished, would that change anything? Randomly, I flip from page to page, picture after picture of bone-thin Mama. Then as now, she's emaciated, like she's not worthy of food.

Suddenly, I'm so tired, my eyes go out-of-focus. It's as if hands lead me to the bed where Po-Po had slept since she moved to Vancouver. Considering that I normally sleep in a bed used by four hundred years' worth of people — doing who knows what and please don't tell me — I have no problem lying down and closing my eyes. I keep one hand on the scrapbook I've carried to bed, as if I could soak up the love that went into clipping every one of those articles and gluing each picture down in this ultimate brag book about two little treasures, one Jade and the other Pearl.

31

I wake to The Boys thudding around their indoor track of a living room.

"Shhh!" I hear one of the aunties shushing them. "You'll wake up Syrah."

I smile then, thinking how great it is to wake up in a house full of noisy life. As soon as I pull my hair back into a messy ponytail and wipe the sleep out of my eyes, I head downstairs toward the scent of potstickers frying in the kitchen. Suddenly, I'm homesick for Bao-mu, who always foisted a container of the fresh dumplings onto Age whenever he came over to visit, telling him, "You not cook tonight. You study!"

"Syrah's finally up!" yells one of The Boys, zooming around me. I swear, there's got to be an easy way to remember which one is which. Give me enough time, and I'll figure it out. "Is this how fast you go on your snowboard?"

"You're way faster," I assure him.

"I'm faster than Syrah!" he bellows more victoriously than a first place winner at Wicked in Whistler.

Laughing, I follow my nose to where the Leong sisters are seated around the kitchen table, a well-oiled potsticker production line.

By way of greeting me, Auntie Marnie looks up from the long strips of dough that she's slicing into one-inch segments and asks, *"Chi bao le ma?"* Funny, isn't it, that her greeting — a standard Chinese one, *have you eaten yet* — is a question I'd never hear out of my own mother's mouth, so concerned is she that I don't gain an unnecessary ounce?

With a dough-caked hand, Auntie Marnie motions me over to the empty chair, unaware of the drifts of flour flaking with her every movement. Quickly, she bustles to the stove, where she wipes her hands on a kitchen towel and lifts the cover off the frying pan, sizzling with potstickers. "Almost done."

As I sit in the one remaining empty spot at the table, I wonder where Grace is, since she's not in here with the rest of the women. Auntie Marnie reclaims her seat across from me. Next to her, Auntie Yvonne rolls the cut-up dough in her palms before flattening the balls with a tiny rolling pin into pancakes. Jocelyn drops a mound of pork and cabbage filling in the center of each skin before folding the edges over into fat crescent moons.

That's where the production line hiccups. Jocelyn nods at the growing stack of pancake skins in front of her. She whispers to me, "They're way too fast."

"No," teases Auntie Yvonne. "Your young hands are too slow."

While the conversation rolls ahead in rapid Mandarin, I take my place in the production line as Jocelyn's backup helper. Just as I did with Bao-mu countless times over the years, I pick up

247

a doughy skin, dollop some of the meat into the center, dip one flour-dusted finger into the bowl of cloudy water, and wet the edges of a skin. I fold over the dumpling, and the way Bao-mu taught me, I crimp the edges.

"Just like Pi-Lan!" cries Auntie Yvonne, delighted. "She is such a good cook."

Surprised, I ask, "You know my Bao-mu?"

"Of course." Auntie Marnie pops up to check on the pot-stickers, moving them around with long chopsticks in some order only she understands. "She was your po-po's best friend. Pi-Lan was so sad that she couldn't make it to the memorial. But the baby came home from the hospital yesterday, and she had to be there to help."

Then it comes to me. Bao-mu was the one who brought Mama to her new parents. That's why her photos were in Po-Po's scrapbooks. So why did she come back to take care of me for all these years?

As I pick up another pancake skin, I notice Grace hovering by the kitchen door, as if she wants to join us but doesn't know how. It's the way I feel around the girls at school who seem to speak another language. In this case, we do. Grace doesn't speak Mandarin.

"Grace, hurry, we need reinforcements," I tell her in English, then dust the flour off my hands and grab the extra chair tucked under the telephone nook.

Pretty soon, Grace is shaping The Son of Blob in her hand. "What's the trick?" she asks me quietly, embarrassed at the miscreant in her hands.

"It's all about putting the right amount of meat on the skin,"

I tell her. "Too much, and it oozes out. Too little, and you're eating the Pillsbury Doughboy."

Auntie Yvonne squashes another ball into a large medallion-sized pancake and looks at me in the same way Bao-mu does when she embarks on a fact-finding mission. As if she's merely relaying information, Auntie Yvonne says casually, "Pi-Lan said your mommy bought her a big house in California."

It's hard to say who's more surprised, me or Grace. On Bao-mu's last day at The House of Cheng, I had visions of Winston Churchill sending his allowance to his nanny after she'd been cut off penniless despite years of service, and I worried out loud to Bao-mu about her retirement. She had brushed off my concern: "You not worry. I be lots okay."

"Pi-Lan told Po-Po that your mommy took three trips to find her the perfect house. Three thousand square feet, four bedrooms, and a housekeeper," says Auntie Marnie proudly, as if she were the one who'd arranged it. She carries a platter from the stove to the island, steaming with dumplings. "All furnished."

Three trips to San Francisco? When had Mama found the time? Suddenly I remember the emergency shopping expedition tacked on to her last D.C. trip. Only Mama wasn't shopping for the newest "it" shoes or the season's "must-have" pieces, but for Bao-mu's future. There is a whole life that Bao-mu and my mother have kept secret.

As if we're all preschoolers, Auntie Marnie orders us, "Go wash your hands, and then we'll eat."

Soon, Auntie Yvonne is scooting the platter that we're sharing family-style closer to me. "Eat," she urges. "Eat."

Under the doting eyes of my aunties, I choose one, which gets a fast rejection from Auntie Marnie: "No, no, that one is too skinny. You take this one," and she hands me the plumpest, choicest dumpling. I take a careful bite, and close my eyes. Hot, savory juices flood my mouth. When I open my eyes, Auntie Marnie is watching me closely, weighing my love for her in my response.

It is so delicious that I want to shove the rest of the dumpling into my mouth, but restrain myself to careful chewing and enthusiastic nodding.

"Good?" Auntie Marnie demands.

The ultimate compliment would be to tell her that these are better than Bao-mu's, but I'd feel too disloyal to do that. Besides, the potsticker is too hot in my mouth for an answer, a verbal one anyway. So I spear another with my chopsticks, which is all the answer Auntie Marnie needs, and she smiles, satisfied. That is, until she notices at the same time I do that Grace isn't eating.

"You need to taste," commands Auntie Marnie, using her chopsticks to nudge the potsticker closest to Grace toward her. "This is good for you."

"I'm not really hungry, thanks," says Grace. Her eyes dip to my aunt's rounded stomach, and I can read her mind: if Marnie thinks she's the poster child of good-for-you cooking, Grace isn't buying. "Ample" would be one way to describe Aunt Marnie. "Fat" would be my family's. It's not that her seams are bulging, because they aren't. She's just curvy like I am, in a way that stick-thin Chengs aren't supposed to be.

"The other day I was at Children's Hospital, visiting my friend's little sister. Cancer," I say amid the aunties' sympathetic clicks, sounding like a pod of concerned dolphins. "And none of the kids on her floor could eat. I just felt like it was so, I don't know, disrespectful not to eat when I can."

Auntie Marnie nods, understanding me. "To stay healthy, you need to eat. Not too much, not too little. This was one of your po-po's favorite things to make with us girls growing up," says Auntie Marnie, looking sadly at the plump potsticker at the end of her chopsticks.

"No, she liked eating them," corrects Auntie Yvonne.

Auntie Marnie shakes her head and says authoritatively, in what I've already identified as her eldest sister, I-know-best-tone, "No, no. It's the talking part she loved best. She always said that we brought our secrets to the kitchen table."

"And she devoured them like they were fat potstickers!" says Auntie Yvonne, laughing.

The lure of these fresh potstickers is irresistible, even to Grace, who selects the tiniest one with her chopsticks, nibbling at its end. I don't say anything, and I keep my eyes off Grace. I know what it's like to have every bite scrutinized and not feel worthy of the most minute morsel. But I hear her chewing, and take another bite myself.

Auntie Marnie sighs. "I wish Mei-Mei was here right now."

There are many places I can picture Mama: on the jet, at a fashion show, in her gym. But sitting at a dirty table with dough and raw minced pork on her fingers, I think not. Then again, maybe I've dismissed Mama too quickly. Maybe she would be at home here with her hair pulled into a careless ponytail, the way she was at a daycare for homeless kids. And I wonder what Mama is doing now, whether she's eating anything in Hong Kong, stealing a bite here and there. If she's thinking about her

251

mother. What she would do if she knew I was here, surrounded by her sisters.

"She should have come yesterday." Auntie Yvonne's mouth purses disapprovingly. "You're supposed to honor your mother. No matter what."

A little accusation goes a long way. Mama should have come. It's what I've been thinking since Mama left for Hong Kong. She should have come to her own mother's funeral. She should have come with me.

"Aaah," Auntie Marnie sighs, a sound loud with guilt that all but says, *what can we do?* "We gave her away."

Auntie Yvonne sets down her chopsticks, ready to fight. "What could we have done?"

Softly, Grace says, "I don't think I would have come if I were Betty."

Just then, The Boys clamber into the kitchen, following the scent of these little pieces of our hearts, dumplings served up as morning dim sum. "We want some, too!"

There are only a half dozen left, and instead of brushing The Boys off, Auntie Yvonne smiles indulgently at them and bustles to get them clean plates and forks, telling them in her actions that they are worthy. The doorbell rings, and Auntie Marnie orders The Boys, as if there's safety in numbers, "Open the door and then come back to eat."

Obviously, no one dares to flout one of Auntie Marnie's orders, and The Boys leave together, one giant mass of noise and dirt.

"Your father's good to her?" asks Auntie Yvonne, who's abandoned all pretense of politeness.

"Auntie Yvonne!" cries Jocelyn, rolling her eyes. She leans

toward me. "Consider yourself an official part of the family. All questions are fair game now. Just wait."

"She's always been part of our family." Auntie Marnie spins around indignantly to face us. "Syrah is a true Leong."

"No, she's not," says a voice, sharp with an accent that sounds a world apart from this little home in Richmond. Standing in the doorway, faces grim, are Mama and Baba.

How many times have I imagined them so hell-bent on being with me — to catch my soccer games, dance recitals, spelling bees, snowboarding competitions — that they'd cancel meetings, reschedule appointments, turn down lucrative speaking engagements, and surprise me with their appearance? Only now that they're ready to take me away (why else would they be here?), I don't want to go.

"Mama?" I say at the same time that Auntie Marnie steps uncertainly away from the stovetop and toward her. She breathes in disbelief, "Mei-Mei?"

Words waiting to be said for nearly forty years come rushing out of Auntie Marnie in a spate of hot and sour Mandarin: how they made a mistake and sent Mama away, how their mother would have been happy that the family is finally reunited. But Auntie Marnie has no idea that Mama doesn't speak Mandarin. That with her every word, she's widening the unbreachable emotional gap between them, the one that yawns with so much more distance than the scant four feet that separates them here in this kitchen.

Arms crossed, Mama answers in Cantonese, her words burning like the forgotten oil on the stovetop: I. Am. Not. Your. Little. Sister.

Her older sisters look bewildered first at her, then me. Baba, ever in control, commands, "Syrah, get your things."

Even with everything going on, I notice that our father doesn't spare a single glance at Grace, who's standing so straight and immobile, she could be a longtime military cadet.

"Now?" I ask. "Wait, what are you doing here?"

"My business in Hong Kong finished early. So I'm able to make it to the meetings in Whistler after all," says Baba. "But when we went home to pick you up, you weren't there."

Mama folds her arms over her chest and stares at me as if I've betrayed her. "Bao-mu told us where you were."

Bao-mu, Mama said, not Pi-Lan, her given name. Mama called her "substitute mother," *Bao-mu,* the way I do. Hearing that nickname on Mama's tongue makes me wonder whether Bao-mu was Mama's surrogate mother, too? Is that why Bao-mu continued to take care of me long after she should have been enjoying her retirement?

"I couldn't believe it when Bao-mu said she was sure that you were here," Mama continues. Accusingly, she says, "Marnie told her."

Of course, Bao-mu knew I'd find a way to Po-Po's funeral. Instead of being mad at her, I can understand what she was trying to do: mastermind a reconciliation of sorts.

However brilliant Bao-mu is, she doesn't account for Auntie Yvonne undermining the peace process. In English, my aunt demands, "How come you're so mad? You were the lucky one who got to live with the rich uncle. We visited your house after you got sent to the best boarding school in England. It was a mansion. You had servants. A cook. A driver. We barely had enough to eat one meal a day."

Auntie Marnie puts a warning hand on Yvonne's arm. If I'm expecting Mama to stop this the way she does any heated argument or political debate at her parties — with a gentle well-placed, self-deprecating comment — I'm wrong. Dead wrong.

Mama's tone is seething. "Lucky?"

"Stop, stop, this is all a misunderstanding," says Auntie Marnie, tears welling up in her eyes.

I'm expecting Baba to run the same interference with Mama, because, after all, Chengs do not show public demonstrations of emotions. Instead, he stands behind her, the way Mama stood behind Weipou in that family portrait. One big difference: Baba has her back in this battle. Mama looks lethal in her wealth, armed in her expensive tailored slacks, handmade sweater, and sunglasses swept on top of her glossy hair.

"How can you deny it?" asks Yvonne hotly. "Marnie was sent to the country for five years. Me, I worked like a peasant for two years." She lifts up her left hand and wiggles her ring finger, the one missing its tip. "I lost this threshing rice while you were enjoying Hong Kong." Her hand with the decapitated finger gestures at Mama. "And look at you now."

"*Bu yao qiao le,*" I plead for them to stop. Glancing over my shoulder, I'm startled to see The Boys clustered behind my parents, transfixed by the sight of adults fighting. "*Hai zi men zheng zai ting.*" The children are listening.

Only when Mama breathes in do I realize I've spoken absent-mindedly in Mandarin, the language of the sisters she wants to deny. Not the Cantonese of her lonely childhood in Hong Kong. The funny thing is, no one other than I can speak both languages. Only now do I have an idea why Bao-mu insisted I learn Mandarin even after Mama forbade it. She must have thought I could bridge the Cheng-Leong gap one day. Sure, I can translate word-for-word what's being said between these two enemy camps, but I don't want to. The words, their implications, are that ugly. Besides, anger, hurt, and blame are a lingua franca we all understand, that don't need any translation. All I have to do is look at The Boys, who are staring wide-eyed at the adults fighting worse than any children.

Baba orders me sharply, "Go get your things." When Grace approaches me, he snaps at her as though she's a disobedient child, "I want to talk to you."

The last thing I want to do is leave Grace alone to face the wrath of Baba, but Marnie says, "Syrah, listen to your parents."

It's a dismissal I don't expect. Head down, embarrassed and angry, I hurry to Po-Po's bedroom and gather my belongings. It doesn't take long to roll my few clothes into tight cylinders, squeezing out the air the way Mama taught me so I minimize wrinkles, maximize space.

"Are you okay?" asks Jocelyn from the bedroom door.

I nod, glance around Po-Po's room for any trace that I was here, and don't find any. But then I see the scrapbooks, too big to fit in my backpack.

"I know it's a pain, but could you send me these?" I ask.

"Of course," Jocelyn says without hesitation.

The immediacy of her answer undoes me. I throw myself into her arms, leaving no doubt that whatever our shared history, we are family. Love is a lingua franca, too.

32

When two funeral marches are broadcast back-to-back on a classical station, the meaning should be pretty obvious: play dead. Call me a slow learner or a girl with a death wish, but two hours of silence is about all I can take.

So I ask my parents, "How long have you known they were in Vancouver?"

There are no recriminations, no accusations, and definitely no answers. To say it's silent in the car would be inaccurate. Instead, no one changes what they're doing: Baba cycles through his voicemail while driving, Mama studies the latest Christie's auction catalog, and me? I go back to staring out the window at the snowdrifts as if I haven't spoken up at all.

The music dum-dum-dums its way into my thick skull. What did I expect? Effusive explanations from the King of Control and his Queen of No Comment?

According to the road sign, Whistler-Blackcomb, British Columbia, is just ahead. Five and half hours from Seattle, three from Vancouver, and at the start gate of my imagination ever since my parents bought Chalet Cheng. Now that I'm finally here, why do I want to lunge for the steering wheel and turn us back to Richmond?

The windshield wipers sweep back and forth through the thick falling snow like they can't decide which side they want to be on: Cheng, Leong? Richmond, Whistler? Mama, Po-Po?

Highway 99 spills into Whistler Village, and instead of winding up the mountain to our chalet, Baba turns into the village and pulls up to the newest boutique hotel. A valet in a faux-fur-lined parka rushes to greet us, his feet leaving potholes in the new snow.

"Why are we here?" My question may as well have been rhetorical, given the likelihood of either parent answering.

Amazingly, Baba says mildly, "A quick meeting," like there hasn't been a two-hour stretch of silence in our car, or that he and Mama haven't SWAT-team extracted me, a prisoner of war, out of the Leong enemy camp. News flash: this prisoner wants to go back.

The urge to brag about Baba has Mama breaking her self-imposed code of silence, too. "Your father has to greet Nokia's other directors who are here."

"So bringing me to Whistler really had nothing to do with me, did it?"

My question is ignored, Baba too busy handing over keys to the valet and Mama too busy smiling and thanking the valet, who solicitously holds out his hand for her. The person who needs a helping hand isn't Mama, or me, but Baba. As he approaches the front doors, he slips on a patch of salt-covered ice that still doesn't provide enough traction. Immediately, Mama abandons her helpless female act, shakes off the valet as if he's a cheap Old Navy jacket, and leaps over to Baba. Before I can reach him, Mama catches Baba's arm so he doesn't fall. She asks, "Are you okay?"

"Fine, fine," Baba says, shrugging off her concern. He drapes his arm back over Mama, back to being the one taking care of her. And that is how they walk inside the hotel, two against the world.

The fireplace, the focal point in the lobby, is made of enormous boulders, like the spillage of an avalanche. The runoff point is where the Nokia people are gathered; you can tell, since they're the only ones dressed in business attire, looking ridiculous in this lobby that could double for a fashion runway of Gore-Tex, there are so many girls in here. With three good hours of riding left in the day, they're inside? What I would do to grab their gear and go.

You could set the Big Apple's New Year's ball to the countdown taking place the moment the corporate suits spot my parents. Three, two, one! Happy billionaire, everyone!

"Ethan! Betty!" shriek the wives, sounding every bit the middle-aged versions of The Six-Pack, as they cluster around Mama.

Mama is in her element, all "Wonderful outfit" and "Where did you get that?"

Over the hustle of business and bustle of shopping tips, I hear the one voice that makes my brain cells nosedive to the bottom of my heart. A group of snowboarders struts into the lobby, loud, raucous, jostling each other. But I don't see any of them, not a single one except for Jared Johanson.

Whoever said that time heals all wounds obviously hasn't experienced fatal injuries. It's been, what, over half a year since I last saw Jared, and there it is again, that fluttery feeling. I obviously suffer from short-term memory loss. For all my swagger in androgynous snowpants and all my hiding in baggy jeans and enormous sweatshirts, I'm still all girl. A girl who got stuck in whiteout conditions of my own making and ended up with such a bad case of emotional vertigo, I didn't know which end was up.

God, even now, I know what I see: an up-and-coming snow-board star with eyes the color of silver pine who is currently basking in the attention of adoring girls, otherwise known as pro hos. And I know what my inner ear is hearing, *Bad news, stay away. Stay far away.* So why is my heart strumming fast as a hummingbird's? Why am I hoping that he'll turn around and see me? Why do I want him to stride over to me, put his arms around me, and confide that he hasn't been able to stop think-ing of me, either?

"Syrah!" calls Baba.

Wistful thinking is more dangerous than beautiful snow crystals, because Jared turns around. Jared sees me. Jared starts to stride over to me.

Cowardly me, I hide behind my parents' coattails and slip with them into the VIP boardroom, glad when I'm inside.

But as the door closes behind me, I catch and keep Jared's gaze. As if Grace is coaching me, I spin my situation into its proper light. Don't think of this as running away; think of this tactical retreat as my first inspection run, the slow cruise around the course before Race Day, when I'll talk to him.

With a *click*, the door shuts on Jared. I gather my strength, put my game face on, and smile at the executives gathered to fête Baba.

33

Chalet Cheng perches on one of the best vertical rise mountains in North America, above the older million-dollar townhouses and the new multimillion-dollar condos. Even though I've been here just once, I can navigate to our chalet blindfolded. On the left is the vast Italianate villa that looks out of place on this street of log mansions, on the right a metastasized bungalow. And secluded at the end of the road is Chalet Cheng, a timber-frame lodge set atop blue-green river rocks. Windows the size of minivans frame the sunrises over Wedge, Armchair, and Mount Currie on clear mornings. At night, Rainbow Mountain glows in the sunsets, earning the peak its name. I breathe out, feeling like I've made it home.

Once inside, Mama and Baba head immediately to the library for a glass of wine. The only place I want to go is my bedroom, but I stop by the hand-peeled log of red cedar that runs from the bottom floor clear on up to the third, feeling dwarfed beside it. It's the same feeling I get standing on top of a mountain: awestruck that I could possibly exist in a world this massive.

The contractors spent three months looking for the right log, and were just in time to salvage this thousand-year-old tree from being turned into paper.

I start up the staircase that bends around windows etched with totem figures. As I near the second floor, Baba walks into the entry and looks up at me.

"We have a business dinner tonight," he says. "A number of snowboarders will be there. You're more than welcome to attend."

Visions of Jared dance in my head. I'm not ready to face him yet.

"Thanks, but I'm really tired," I say, and continue up the stairs, past the second floor, which is reserved for Wayne's family. For a guy who barely acknowledges my mom, he certainly helps himself to the perks she provides, down to the perfect shade of green she picked because she knew it was his favorite color.

But then again, I think as I drop my backpack in my own bedroom suite on the top floor, I never thanked Mama either after she spent a good two weeks poring over color swatches, fabric samples, and furniture designs to create my room.

From my window seat, I watch as the last of the sun dips below the ridgeline, and Baba's car pulls out of the driveway and disappears down the dark street.

My cell phone rings, and for a brief, stupid second, I think Jared's calling me. I dive into my backpack, scrambling for the phone, wondering what, if anything, I should say. By the time I grab the phone, reality sets in before caller ID does. Of course it couldn't be Jared. Why would he call when he never did after my accident?

"Syrah? It's Lillian." Her voice sounds unsure, not knowing

whether she's welcome to step over the decimal point that separates her from me.

"Lillian? What's up?"

"Hey, I'm sorry I'm calling during your vacation, but I . . . ."

I know what it's like not to have anyone to talk to. "Stop.
What's going on?" And then I guess, "Is Amanda okay?"

"We had the baby —"

"Oh, my God! Congratulations."

Lillian's voice is a mishmash of emotions. "Zoe is absolutely
yummy. You've got to see her. But . . . her tissue isn't a match
after all."

"Oh, no." I drop back down to the window seat and clutch a
pillow to my chest, a feeble shield against what I know this
means.

"You know this was a possibility all along and my parents
didn't want to do any in vitro testing and risk Zoe. So now . . .
unless we find a bone marrow donor who matches Amanda,
we'll have to use the stem cells that the doctors harvested from
her. It's not ideal. Even Dr. Martin says so."

"There still isn't anybody who matches her?"

"Nope."

"God, this is so unfair," I say. "So when's the procedure?"

"Two weeks, if everything goes as planned."

"Two weeks," I repeat faintly. Inside, I'm thinking: no way, no
way. There's no way that I can pull off Ride for Our Lives in
fourteen days. Aside from one lame Ask at Boarder Xing with
Age, I haven't done any others.

As if she knows what's going on in my mind, Lillian says,
"You know, I didn't call because I wanted or expected you to
pull a Cheng-style miracle."

But those are the magic words. The Cheng name creates miracles, whether it's securing a private premiere of *Attila* from Hollywood or snagging five million dollars in three phone calls the way Mama did for the Evergreen Fund.

"We can do it," I tell Lillian.

She snorts, a little sound of disbelief that I've heard all my life from Wayne, the one that cuts down my dreams with a *You just try, little girl.* You know what? I'm tired of that snort.

"Okay, there's one thing you have to do," I tell Lillian, more forcefully than I intend. Call me a hypocrite, but knowing that I'm going to have to talk to my parents about Ride for Our Lives makes me think twice. "Let your parents know what we're planning, because we'll need their support."

"I don't know, Syrah. Even if we pull this off, it's no guarantee that we'll find a match."

"No," I agree. "But don't underestimate The Tao of Cheng."

When we hang up, I think about how Lillian and her family are confronting something they can't control or fix, no matter what they do. Or how much money they have. My big angst today was being pulled away from Auntie Marnie and my family when the truth is, I can always return to them. As soon as I turn sixteen, I'll get my driver's license. My car is already waiting in the garage, even if I pretend the Mercedes sedan isn't there because I don't want anyone, especially The Six-Pack, to know.

And this afternoon, I got all worked up just because I saw Jared, a boy who created a messy mogul field in my past. But here's the thing: Jared can't create a single bump in my future if I don't want him to.

34

In the preface to *The Ethan Cheng Way,* Baba quotes from Sun-Tzu: "One who knows the enemy and knows himself will not be endangered in a hundred engagements." I figure, considering Sun-Tzu's *Art of War* has been in print for 2,500 years, there's got to be a reason why military strategists still study him.

But before I figure out what I want to say to Jared, I've got more pressing business to attend to. After I send out a flurry of e-mails to potential sponsors — including RhamiWare and Boarder Xing — I get in touch with Meghan, Mama's event planner extraordinaire, who volunteers to handle the event logistics, right down to finding contractors to erect the scaffolding for a ramp and install a rail for the event. For a disease that kills indiscriminately, cancer also unifies in the oddest way: Meghan's best friend in high school died of the same leukemia that Amanda has.

"You sure you can arrange this on such short notice?" I ask her.

"Oh, sweetie, I've done much bigger events on much shorter notice," Meghan says, laughing at my event planning naiveté. "You just figure out when and where, and I'll have this baby running."

By the time I get off the phone with Meghan, it's ten at night, and I'm feeling like Ride for Our Lives may actually happen. Chalk up one more lesson from The Ethan Cheng Way that is completely right: surround yourself with only the best people. Which means that it's finally time to do some housecleaning in my personal life. Only then do I begin sketching out how I want my conversation — the one and only skirmish I want with Jared — to unfold. You could call this my manga version of Grace's Rude Q and A.

Figuring out his questions is the easy part. After all, I've been listening to them for the past half-year. So you over me yet? Can I meet your dad now? Did you honestly think that I liked you? The problem is, I don't have answers to the harder questions, the ones I should have asked myself all along:

Question: What was I looking for that I thought I'd found with Jared?
Answer:
Question: Why didn't I say No?
Answer:
Question: What do I need from him now?
Answer:

Mother Nature calls; procrastination beckons. I go to the bathroom, realize I've forgotten to eat dinner, and head downstairs.

The light from the open refrigerator door illuminates Mama, standing with her back to me, foraging furtively, her silhouette barely there. Watching her lift the top off a plastic container and slip out a single cold *shu mai* makes me want to cry. No, I decide, it makes me want to sit her down at the table and force-feed her and ask her how the hell can she go to a four-hour dinner, prepared by the best chef in Whistler, yet allow no more than two or three morsels to pass through her lips? A few scant pounds separate her from being that prospective student at my school, the Skeletal Girl who broke off the edge of the muffin, nibbled on those few crumbs, and called that her big meal of the day.

In the dark hall, I collect myself. Breathing in, I close my eyes and exhale loudly, partly to announce myself and partly because I'm as nervous as I would be going into the no-mistake section of a mountain.

When I round the corner, Mama is taking a glass out of the cupboard, the refrigerator now closed.

"I was thirsty," she says, as if she has to explain why she's in the close vicinity of food. She pushes the glass into the water dispenser in the refrigerator door. "What are you doing up so late?"

"I didn't eat dinner," I say. *Like you.*

Mama frowns. "This is the worst time to eat. Food just sticks inside your stomach."

"My body will survive." The refrigerator is stocked, thanks to the house manager, with a half dozen bottles of wine, cheese, cold cuts, and Chinese take-out containers. I grab the largest one and sniff. Baba's favorite peanutty noodles.

Mama recoils. "Don't eat that!"

"Why not?"

The only voluptuous part of Mama's body that she actually likes is her pouty mouth. Now, those lips are thin with displeasure when I place the container on the island, not in the refrigerator where it's safe from temptation. "First Marnie, then Yvonne, and now you."

"Mama, do you know how much they want to know you?"

"So you're taking their side."

"No, I'm just trying to understand." I shake my head, thinking of all those scrapbooks Po-Po made, the ones I wish I had right now to prove to her how much she was loved. "They talked about you during the funeral. Your sisters are so proud of you."

Mama looks away from me, her perfect face cold.

"So was your mother. Po-Po had pictures of you all over her bedroom."

"You shouldn't have gone there," she says quietly.

"Why not? I don't understand."

"Because they gave me up when I was inconvenient. Lo and behold, now that I have all this" — her diamond-covered hand flings out to take in the length of the kitchen, this entire lodge, all the way down south to The House of Cheng in Seattle — "suddenly they want me. People will use you if you let them."

"Not all people, Mama. And not if you don't let them."

"You're too young to understand."

I know I'm venturing into the fracture zone of Mama's heart, where a single misstep can release a slab of hurt. But I can't stop now. "This all happened during the Cultural Revolution, right?

What would have happened if you stayed in China instead of going to Hong Kong?"

"I would have rather stayed in China, dirt poor, reviled, motherless," says Mama, her eyes hot. "My uncle —"

"Weigong?"

Mama nods. "Your . . . adopted grandfather, he was a nice man, but he had no control, no power. My aunt, your weipou, hated that I lived with them."

"Oh, Mama. What happened?"

Mama takes a sip of water, which turns into a gulp, like she's trying to fill herself up. Wiping a drop of water off her upper lip with the back of her hand, she says, "When I was five, she told me every bite I took was one out of her own children's mouths. So I had to eat after they finished their meals. In the kitchen with the servants. It was never enough. Every night she locked up all the cupboards. Not even one crumb would be left on the tables or counters. I got used to hunger."

Five, that was old enough for me to remember slights like Wayne leaving me behind while he took his kids and Grace to get ice cream whenever they visited. Old enough to know that he and Grace didn't want anything to do with me, but not understanding why. No wonder Mama doesn't think she's worthy of food. Like mother, like daughter, I haven't either.

I grip the kitchen island, needing her happily-ever-after. "But then you went to boarding school in England, right?"

"Only because England subsidized half of the cost. The other half, I won through a scholarship." She lifts her chin proudly. "It's how I got into Cambridge."

"And that's where you met Baba."

She nods. That much, she's told me. Baba was a guest lecturer in her economics class at graduate school. He was impressed with her questions, she his answers. Supply met demand, a match made in an economically fiscal heaven.

Mama dumps her glass of water into the sink and says briskly, "It doesn't matter now. It happened so long ago."

"Is that why Weipou never liked me?" I ask her quietly.

Setting her glass down on the granite countertop, Mama laughs bitterly. I remember how Bao-mu told me that everyone had to destroy their art and valuables before the Red Guard stormed into their homes. More than art was destroyed in the Cultural Revolution.

"It wasn't you, Syrah. It was *me*. She couldn't stand that I survived."

"You succeeded, Mama."

Smiling slightly, Mama nods. "Oh, she hated that I married Baba. But she didn't understand that he made me richer than all this."

I shake my head, not understanding.

"I know how everyone talked, still talk: 'Betty, what a gold digger.' Especially the wives of Ethan's friends, who worried that I would put ideas in their husbands' heads, set a trend of trophy wives." Mama bats at the air with her left hand, the one with the diamond so massive she could knock out somone's teeth with the right move. "What no one accepts is that you can't choose who you fall in love with."

That, I understand. Even though I knew Jared was a player, a guy who bragged about how much he liked women, that still didn't stop me from falling in serious like with him. And unbidden, I see Age, the boy I've been afraid to love.

Mama fingers the large jade pendant that she always wears as her talisman. Jade. Yu. Her Chinese name.

"Your necklace . . . ," I say.

"This was the first present your father ever gave to me. The stone of heaven." Mama holds it out to me, but I know the shape of the pendant, its etching by heart, the crane that stands for longevity. Forever, I had always assumed it meant that she wanted to be immortal, not knowing that Baba meant for their love to last forever.

Mama releases her pendant, which drops heavily to rest between her bony clavicles. "What your weipou never understood is that I would give this all up, every bit of it, if I could make your father younger."

I glance at her sharply, thinking about how many things I would have traded with our Cheng fortune: friends who wanted me for *me,* siblings who didn't assume that my life was golden, parents who didn't jet off at every business opportunity.

"You'll be diapering your own babies at the same time I might be doing that for your father. No, all the money in the world doesn't make our relationship sensible." Mama swipes the counter with a dishcloth, soaking up all the excess drops. "What I found with your father is something Weipou couldn't stand."

Without knowing it, Mama has mothered me in the way I needed most tonight, because it occurs to me that even knowing I shouldn't trust Jared, I couldn't help falling for him. I'm not stupid for forgetting to apply The Ethan Cheng Way, run the cost-benefit analysis that would have warned, *keep away.* If Mama had done that, she wouldn't be with Baba. Even if I had done that, I couldn't have stopped from responding to Jared's attention.

"So," I say softly, as I heat up the food in the microwave, "in a way, going to Hong Kong was the best thing that ever happened to you."

Mama is so quiet I'm afraid I've sloughed off too many of her memories. But then she murmurs, surprised, "In a way."

35

On Sunday morning, the sun creeps across my bed toward me through the open slats of the wood blinds, and as it does, so do all my unanswered questions about Jared. Not until after breakfast, when I'm brushing my teeth, does an epiphany rock me. Sure, I could shoot questions back at Jared when I finally face him: what was the big idea of using me to get to my dad? You jerk, how come you never called me?

But would any of his answers make a difference to me now?

Grabbing my manga-journal from my bed, I bring it with me to the window seat, pulling the blinds all the way up. In the bright sunlight, I begin at the beginning, the way I needed to with Mama last night.

The first pages of my journal show Shiraz splayed in a benched cliff. She can't move. And in a hyper-close-up, she looks up. The next three panels are zoomed out, not just of any mountain, but one enormous Bold Mountain, all craggy-faced with bulbous cornices of snow. And here, trapped in an ice-clad hell, my rescue fantasy begins. Leg broken and in storm conditions, Shiraz makes it down the mountain by herself without the help of a single macho ski patrol guy.

Just as Dr. Bradford denied me a brace, telling me that it would end up being a crutch I relied on, I know it's time to retire Shiraz, my personal knight on a shining snowboard. She's a crutch I don't need anymore, as wide-eyed and large-chested as she is.

These are Shiraz's thoughts and actions, not mine.

So I walk to my desk, rummage for a new notebook, but find the diary I had been keeping a few years before the Accident, the one I thought I lost after my one and only visit to Chalet Cheng. As I flip through it, reading my words, I could be visiting an old friend I haven't seen for such a long time that I've forgotten her. But you can't completely erase the people you love out of your heart, no matter if they're taking care of a great-grandchild five hundred miles away or they've stopped talking to you.

Leaving a few pages between the Old Me and the new, because I'm not sure how to bridge the two, I start on a blank page, unmarked as a fresh powder field. Before I figure out what I want in my future — and what I want from Jared — I need to face what happened that night so many months ago and why. Taking a deep breath, I begin to draw.

I draw how I went to Jared's room.
How I watched him lock the door.
How the lights went off. How I wished I could turn off the moon.
How I didn't say a word, not even when his pants came off.
How he told me what he wanted me to do to him. How he said it wasn't really sex when he pushed me to my knees.

Back off when you feel pain; that's what my physical therapist told me when I was rehabbing my knee. I flex my fingers, which have been gripped tight around the pen. Who cares that The Six-Pack are so cavalier about sex that heart-to-heart conversations are more intimate to them? For me, that night with Jared was a big deal, and when it comes down to it, what I think and how I feel about it is all that matters. I want to stop now, run downstairs, and gorge on pancakes slathered in butter and thick maple syrup to make myself feel better.

But the only way to purge this pain is to binge on it, not on calories. To remember. So I continue to draw.

How I skulked to my room alone afterward, feeling more naked than I did in his room.

How the next morning I overheard Jared cackle to another camp counselor, "Syrah's my free pass to paradise, man." How he laughed like he had won more than his Olympic gold, more than his starring role in a snowboard movie, and a heck of a lot more than me.

How I felt more filthy than rich, especially when the first sweet nothing out of his mouth when he saw me was, "So when can I meet your dad?"

How I finally told him no, when I should have said no eight hours earlier. How he told me that I was blowing what happened all out of proportion since he had a girlfriend and wasn't planning on breaking up with her anytime soon. How all we were doing was having fun.

How I left him to have fun by himself at the base of the mountain. How I thought — and hoped — he'd stop me, beg me not to do anything crazy. But of course, he didn't, not when

I took a chairlift up by myself, not when I hiked past the SKI AREA BOUNDARY sign. And not when I went into the back-country, where it's so cliffy and rocky, none of the campers were allowed there, buddy or no buddy.

Even now when I'm safe on this window seat, simply journaling, those mountains, those fierce, majestic mountains outside my window, make me shiver as I remember how desperately I wanted a way out of my life. Sighing, I continue.

How I can't remember riding down any part of the mountain, not a single foot, before the snow broke under my board. How I mistook the roar of the avalanche that I set off for a rifle shot to my heart.

How the snow chased me down the mountain the way my guilt and shame did: relentless, overwhelming, unstoppable. How I couldn't outrun the snow any more than I could my memory of Jared.

How somehow — call it fate, call it luck — I ended up in a benched cliff, twenty feet down, ten feet across. How I looked up and saw that I was eighty feet from the next level of ground. How I couldn't have moved even if I wanted to because my knee couldn't bear my weight any more than my heart could bear the weight of my guilt.

How I wanted to die, I hurt so much.

How I began to think about Mama and Baba. Bao-mu. And Age.

How I wanted to see them all again.

How the search-and-rescue effort for me became a search-and-recover mission after the ski patrol spotted the avalanche, calculated my chances of survival after three hours of being buried in cement-like snow: ten percent.

How Baba and Mama infused another million dollars into my search, which brought in more volunteers and avalanche dogs onto that mountain than any in Whistler's history.

How a dog bounded over to me as if I was a ball he had found.

How I've felt guilty and unworthy and ashamed ever since ski patrol piled me into the toboggan like I was an idiot for riding in terrain way above my level.

And that leaves me with answering the hardest question of all: why did I go where I shouldn't have been? And finally, finally, I put a name on it:

How it all began because I felt unloved, unwanted, unnoticed.

I draw through Grace's first call. And her second, hearing the phone ring only when I finally set down my pen, exhausted but exhilarated that I survived. As I write *Exhuming My Past* at the top of this section of my manga, I answer, "Hey, Grace."

"Syrah, I've been calling and calling you," she says, sounding annoyed.

With those words, I don't need to ask Grace why she's calling. I know. The same way Age used to, and Bao-mu still does, Grace is checking on me. And I know that even if I felt used up and burned out and lonely after my night with Jared, I have never been truly alone.

"You called at the perfect time," I tell her.

"How's that?"

I cross out the title, because the past isn't and shouldn't be dead and buried. It's a living presence that affects me as much as it does Mama, Baba, Grace, and even Wayne.

"I was getting ready to do some battle," I say.

"What?"

"Excuse me," I correct her with a smile. While I may not need a knight to rescue me, I do need a Round Table of trusted advisors. "So what do you wear when you think you're going to run into an ex for the first time?"

"Anything that makes you feel strong," says Grace immediately, and forcefully as only women with tons of experience do. "Think power outfit."

It's easy to picture Grace in one of her power suits. Put her in business clothes and even the mighty media would quake. Considering all I've got are the black pants that I wore to Po-Po's funeral and a pair of jeans, what I'm feeling is a severe power shortage. But that's my problem, not Grace's.

Unless I want to totally freeze in the snow outside, jeans it is. But downstairs in the mudroom, as I bend over to put on my clunky black shoes, I spot my gear hanging in my locker, not the boy's jacket that Mama detests or my wide-legged androgynous snow pants, but the body-conscious, never-before-worn snow jacket and pants, hot pink and vibrant orange, that Mama had specially designed for me before my accident.

And there, there waiting on the heated floor like a pair of faithful dogs, are my old boots, a little scuffed, a lot worn, and infinitely more beautiful than any strappy heels.

After all the gear is zipped and buckled, reluctantly, I take a good, long look at myself in the mirror and am surprised to see someone I like. These last couple of months, I've holed myself up, waging a Cultural Revolution of my own, attacking my Four Olds: Old Culture, Old Habits, Old Ideas, Old Family. Most of all, I've been purging Old Me.

"Welcome back," I tell my reflection.

"Syrah, you ready?" calls Mama from down the hall. "Did you find —" And then she walks into the mudroom and does a double take. "You look beautiful in that color."

"Thanks for packing this," I tell her, meaning it. And I throw my arms around Mama, who doesn't feel nearly as breakable in her fur coat. "You don't know how much I appreciate it."

When I strut out to the garage, I do feel beautiful. Maybe Mama and Grace have a point about power clothes. All I know is, put a parka on this girl, and she might as well wear a sign, traffic-cone orange so that everyone stops to look.

DANGER: GIRL IN GORE-TEX AHEAD.

36

Take four hundred of the best professional snowboarders from forty countries, add a couple thousand onsite viewers and a hundred million more who'll be watching the coverage on TV, and you're talking Wicked in Whistler. The competition is being staged on Blackcomb Mountain, which has been turned into a parade of parkas by the time we arrive. Here I thought being an hour early would be enough time to stake out a front-row position to stalk Jared, but by the gaggle of girls parked beyond the finish gate, I'm about two hours too late.

Tall lights around the half-pipe stick out like gangly giraffes past the Nokia yurt where Baba and Mama want to visit to check out which phones appeal to the kids here.

"I'm going to walk around," I tell them.

"Remember, you can watch from the VIP stands or in the tent," Mama reminds me, her teeth chattering in the cold. Reason number 542 why a little body fat is a good thing: free insulation in winter.

"Maybe," I tell her, then wave them off and trudge through

the snow to the base of the mountain, where I can join the crowd gathering around a large, fenced-off area.

Even with my parka and my natural layer of body fat, I'm cold in this wind, and I cross my arms around myself, not that that does much good. Inside the enclosure, a bunch of guys wearing thick black jackets walk around, headsets on, looking official and important. Off to the side are the ramp and rails for the jam session later this evening, where a thousand bucks will be given out every half hour to the rider with the best moves. On the other side is a large stage capped with an enormous screen. Above it all, loud music thumps, pumped in from the speakers set atop towers.

Personally, my favorite event is the slopestyle, where the riders take a course that's a little bit of everything: some jumps, some rails, and a whole lot of palm-sweating fun. That event's not until the afternoon, and anyway, I'm here to look for Jared, who competes in boarder cross, which pits four riders at a time as they race down a course of turns, jumps, and mogul fields. Let's just say this isn't exactly the cleanest of events, not when snowboarders get rewarded for cutting each other off as they race to qualify first for the semis and then the finals.

One of the men in black motions to a cameraman with a shaky cam on his shoulder. A couple of snowboarding hotshots have arrived, including Jared. I can identify every single one in his group: Hideo, who starred in the last Mack Dawg snowboarding movie; Jorja, who's been dominating the snowboard scene in Europe; and Erik Johanson, Mr. Fame and Glory, one of the giants in snowboarding and Jared's older brother.

The girls in front of me are jostling to get an even better position at the fence, hoping to attract the attention of both the snowboarders and the cameraman. I stay in my spot. The reporter first talks to Erik, then moves on to Hideo and Jorja, before returning to Jared's brother.

Finally, the reporter turns to Jared, a footnote in this news piece, the first thing that'll be cut if the segment ends up too long. "So, are you going to follow in your brother's footsteps and win your first world championship the way Erik did when he was eighteen?"

Erik sidles off as though he doesn't think his brother's answer warrants his time. I can see the irritated sweep of Jared's gaze over to his brother before resting on me. His fifteen seconds of fame are over, drowned in the "Erik! Erik!" of the girls who've jockeyed their way to an open spot on the fence down the way, and the cameraman pans their apple-cheeked good looks.

"Hey," says Jared, approaching me. It's one thing to prepare my talking points and another to have Jared on the other side of the fence, so close that I have to look up, up, up at him. How can his eyes be greener than I remember? "So, stranger."

"Yeah, it's been a while," I tell him, wondering how on Earth my hands could possibly be sweaty (sweaty!) when it's about twenty degrees out here.

He grins like he knows that I'm nervous.

I grin like I'm not, even though I feel like I'm losing my footing on an uneven, gravelly path, one that leads directly to old fantasies. Looking at the freckle by his mouth makes me forget everything — everything that I wrote last night and practiced this morning — everything except how just one of his kisses made me forget that I am Syrah, Ethan Cheng's daughter, and believe that I was Shiraz, the snowboarding chick. It was such a heady transformation that, I swear, I feel the ghost of a tingle on my lips. And I remember how he nudged me back against the wall, pressed into me, and how I smelled evergreen on him, as if he were part of the mountain.

"You caught me at a good time," says Jared, his gaze flickering to the cameraman who's walking away. And just like that, I wonder why I'd want to be with someone who's constantly posturing to make himself look more important than he is. No matter how being with Jared made me feel, when it comes down to it, I'd be just another data point to prove his greatness.

The wind stops blowing, but I don't need to brush my hair out of my eyes to see Jared clearly for the first time since he bedazzled me on these very slopes. I'm no more girl on the fast track to a pro snowboarding career than he is the man of my dreams.

Sure, I could leave now. But I've got a few things to say. And according to The Ethan Cheng Way, confrontations are best in your place of power. If you can't have that, opt for neutral grounds. Since I'm at a disadvantage on snow (I mean, who am I kidding? I'm not the one competing today), I ask him, "You want to grab something?"

For a moment Jared looks surprised, but then his natural self-assurance asserts itself. Either that or the prospect of a free lunch.

"For sure," he says easily.

I meet him at the gate and we approach the enormous VIP tent. Jared looks at me expectantly, but when I continue past it, he has to ask more directly, "Are your parents in there?"

I know that's Jared-code for: Take me to your patriarch.

"Yup," I say. When the choices are 1) parents potentially barging in on us in the VIP tent or 2) paying for food in public,

I know exactly what scenario I want. So I guide-dog us to the day lodge at the foot of the chairlifts.

Next to me, Jared asks, "So you doing well?"

"Doing great." Yeah, if great means on the verge of hyperventilating because I've forgotten what I want to say to him and a gaggle of girls are staring at him like he's the dessert du jour. Unconsciously, his eyes flick over at them, checking them out. I'm grateful for my gear, which, I do have to say, acts like a fashion power surge, especially when I overhear those same girls shifting their attention off him and onto my "cute outfit."

"Actually," I tell Jared, "I feel fabulous."

"Great, great," he says, opening the door for me. "Now, me, I've been crazy-busy. God, this season already, I've been to Europe three times, San Candido, Kreischberg, Berchtesgaden. Some guys want to start filming in Aspen this spring." Weary sigh before The Jared Johanson Report continues, "Then a photo shoot with Burton."

Five more data points into his greatness, I'm feeling distinctly unimpressed, and I move up in line for my hot chocolate.

"So you might be wondering what's going on with my gig at . . ."

Actually, dude, I'm not. That's when I realize Jared is delivering his own carefully crafted answers right off his Rude Q and A, the one he thinks he needs to memorize, because in his head, everyone compares him to his big brother and finds him lacking.

I remember what he told me once: "I want that final, I want that podium."

Instead of awe or adoration, I feel nothing but pity for Jared. And that sets me free.

I tune back into his do-re-mi-me-me-me serenade. "And then this summer, I don't know, I thought I'd chase the snow . . ."

His tune hasn't changed, so in bemusement, I fix myself a cup of hot chocolate.

See, Baba might quote Sun-Tzu all over his book, but as brilliant a military strategist as he is, Sun-Tzu is just not what I'd call a nice guy. I mean, can you trust someone who lops off the heads of two women just because they giggled? So Mr. Sun-Tzu might be right when he said, "Warfare is the greatest affair of state, the basis of life or death, the Tao of survival or extinction." But that's the thing. I'm tired of experiencing life as survival, like we're animals in some dingo-eat-dog documentary. Either Mama gets food, or Weipou's kids do. Either Baba can love me, or he can love Grace and Wayne. Either Age can date Natalia, or he can be friends with me.

That may be the Tao of Survival. But it's not the Tao of Syrah.

According to my way of navigating the world, I don't have to cut Jared down to size to claim victory. Why do that when I can pull a Mama instead?

Fifteen years of watching the master of the social brush-off finally comes to good use. The second Jared stops for breath, I smile politely at him and say, "I'm so glad you're doing well. It's been wonderful catching up. Good luck to you!"

Before Jared can blink at me in surprise, his tray laden with an early lunch of turkey sandwich, power bar, and bottled water, I set down the money for my drink and my drink alone, and tell the cashier, "One hot chocolate, please."

But, gosh, being the good girl is so darn boring. Maybe every girl needs a little Sun-Tzu in her life. Smiling brightly, I say, "Oh, one thing."

"Yeah?"

"There is no such thing as a free lunch. And by the way, I would never have been your free pass to Paradise."

For a moment longer, I stare at Jared so that I'll remember him clearly, not like I was riding to him with the sun in my eyes and he's some hazy figure who I thought would rescue me from me. But like he is right now: tall, dark, and totally dumbfounded.

Oh, my god, I don't need you, I think and grin when it finally dawns on me. I don't need to be a pro snowboard girl who's featured on the covers of magazines and in countless ads. I don't need to reel in an up-and-coming star and stand at his side while everyone congratulates him on his drool-worthy tricks. I don't need to be less than I am to make everyone else feel better than they are. And I certainly don't need to buy myself into anyone's good graces.

I am good enough as I am.

"Goodbye, Jared," I tell him, and hand him my hot chocolate, empty calories that I don't want or need anymore.

Feeling lighter than I have felt in a long, long time and bathing in my own alpenglow, I fly across the snow and make my way to the VIP tent.

37

After the closing ceremonies on Tuesday, you would think that I could find a spare moment to talk to my parents about Ride for Our Lives in the five hours it takes for us to drive home. But this time, when I present my plan to them, I want to be prepared, completely buttoned up in the Chengian way. Besides, I want to savor this time with them, and I ask Baba random questions about his childhood. After a couple of stories, like the one about how he and his two older sisters used to torment their grandfather by hiding his slippers, Mama shyly shares one of her own.

"I used to love to catch frogs," she admits.

"You're kidding." This comes from Baba and me at the same time.

"Not the big, scary, buggy-eyed ones, mind you. So don't think about ordering any for our ponds," Mama warns Baba. "The little, tiny ones. They were so precious and delicate, I hated the thought of anyone stepping on them."

My mother, shopper of Chanel and champion of pygmy frogs. Who knew?

"Was this in Hong Kong?" I ask.

"Yes, of course. Weipou would swat me when I came home dirty, but . . ." Mama's voice trails off before she turns around to smile naughtily at me. "It was worth it."

Too soon, the front gate to our house opens. The thing is, tonight, as the gate shuts behind us, I don't feel corralled the way I usually do, but invited into a special sanctuary. It's a feeling, I decide, I could get used to.

When the landscape architect told Mama that traditional Chinese gardens are a perfect mix of yang — everything that's public and rational and open — and yin — all that is private and emotional and hidden, I thought, *Alright, boys, let's just flush another six digits down the drain.* But he did have a point. Not everyone belongs in my private, emotional, hidden heart. No wonder Mama and Baba only invite the people they most trust and admire to our home. Selectivity isn't snobby; it's necessity. How else are they supposed to keep themselves sane and keep human leeches at bay?

The driveway wends down to the house in the feng shui way, bending and twisting, always a surprise around the corner. Just like life. Which is why I really ought to write a letter of apology to that landscape architect for scoffing at him. I'm on visit 1,095, give or take a couple dozen, and it's taken all this time to finally appreciate the symbols Mama layered into The House of Cheng. Those craggy boulders excavated from China? They're auspicious. Those bats on all the upturned roof eaves? They convey everyone who ventures within our walls with the Five

Blessings: longevity, wealth, health, virtue, and peaceful death (admittedly morbid, but infinitely practical).

As we approach the main house, I ask, "Can you let me out here?"

"Why?" Both my parents swivel around in their seats, surprised at my request.

Ridiculously, I'm close to crying, because I finally, really and truly, feel like I belong in The House of Cheng. I tell them, "I just feel like using the front door."

A large box from Vancouver waits on my desk, occupying so much space the bonsai and my new snowboarding magazine perch precariously close to the edge. Wrapped inside a blanket that still smells of Po-Po's bedroom are her three scrapbooks.

Surrounded on the floor by this semicircle of memories, I can't decide what to do with these scrapbooks. Sure, they belong to Mama, but considering that we haven't mentioned her mother, the funeral, or Vancouver since our kitchen talk in Whistler, I have no idea what she'll do with them. Burn them, toss them, or, like me, shelve them up high where she'll wish she could tuck them out of sight, out of mind the way I tried to forget *The Ethan Cheng Way.* Somehow, as I lift an album to my lap, so heavy I need both hands to manage it, I don't think Mama will get off as lightly as I did if one of these guys fell on her head. I smile, thinking about Bao-mu's commentary on that sign: *You might as well break head, you forget your past.*

I'm steaming in my jacket, so I leave this three-volume encyclopedia of Mama to hang up my hot pink parka in my closet.

There, on the wall, is the picture of me and Age, snowboarding buddies.

Question: When did *avoid* turn into a *void* in my heart?

Answer: When I was too afraid to commit. Too afraid to say, *Yeah, baby, we might as well go for it since everyone, even strangers, thinks that we're a couple, we're that close.*

For the first time since I pinned up our photograph, I take it down and study it. Not just look at it, but scrutinize it until I vibrate from remembering Age's voice and missing his presence. With Age, I never had to work at being anyone but who I was. And the funny thing is, regardless of what I did with Jared that night at camp, I've been more naked with Age, fully clothed and just talking.

As I hold the picture in my palm, I can see Age saving every little scrap his mother gave to him — the last notes she slipped into his lunchbox, the how-to guide for staying sane with two little brothers. And especially the videos she made during her last bout of chemo, condensing a lifetime of maternal nagging into ten hours of tape. What girls want (which took a good hour and a half and didn't cover half the subject since we girls don't always know what we want). How to get ready for a date (do not shave if you don't know how). And what it means to be one of the good guys. Age didn't need that lesson.

If he were on speaking terms with me, I know Age would find some pithy saying, which would reduce down to this: give the scrapbooks to your mom.

So I wrap my arms around these great books, ready to shepherd them to Mama's office, when I find her standing in the living room, dressed to go out to dinner in heels and Armani, and testing the dirt in her bonsai planter with a frown. Hearing me as I approach, Mama shakes her head in exasperation. "The housekeeper forgot to water this."

"I have something I want to show you." I lead Mama away from the miniaturized pine tree and over to the sofa, where I place the scrapbook with the most recent pictures in her lap, hoping that the top layer of her emotional scar tissue isn't as sensitive as the wound itself. As her tour guide, I open the book, and point to the picture that changed our lives. "Do you remember the day DiaComm went public? Who knew?"

"Who knew?" Mama repeats softly, flipping through a few pages in rapid succession, past the photos of her and Baba accepting the Seattle First Citizen Award, announcing a matching grant for Children's Hospital, breaking ground at The House of Cheng. Incredulously, she asks, "Did you make this?"

"No, not me," I say, and as I replace the scrapbook with the one that begins with her wedding photographs, I tell her, "Your mother did."

Shock radiates through her body; she flinches. Abruptly, Mama whips her head around to me, unable to fathom what I've told her, and then looks away hastily because she can't handle the fact that it's true.

"Aunt Marnie gave these to me on the night of your mother's funeral," I tell her. "Po-Po wanted you to have them."

Mama's arms are crossed protectively over her chest. She's not touching the scrapbook or looking at the pictures.

"See, Mama," I say, wanting her to remember the happy moments in her past. "Your boarding school, right?"

"I felt free there," she says so softly, I have to strain to hear her.

"Like how I feel on snow," I tell Mama, wanting so much to

connect with her. "Free. No one knows who I am on the mountain."

"No one knew me at school. I remember lying down in bed that first night when all the other girls were complaining about how uncomfortable the mattresses were, and I remember thinking that I could sleep well for the first time because I wasn't afraid."

After we study another photograph and another, the time feels right for me to lug the last scrapbook onto my lap and open to her baby picture.

"You were even beautiful as a baby, Mama." Like Marnie before me, I trace her name, written in Chinese, the same character whether Mandarin or Cantonese. "Yu. You are *wang.* See?"

"*Wang.*" The way Mama says that Cantonese word for *leader,* as though it were a revelation, I know she's never noticed any of the hidden meanings, the secret symbols, of her name.

I wrap my arm around Mama's bony yet strong shoulders, trained and conditioned to bear a heavy burden. No matter what, I won't let go; my sturdy body won't let her fall down simply because her stepmother didn't love her the way Mama deserved to be loved. As we sit there, I silently turn the pages, each photograph whispering, *Remember? Remember?*

"Mama, don't you see?" I tell her, pausing on the photograph of her graduation from Cambridge. "You were always treasured. You were always Yu."

This is what I've wanted to hear from Mama's perfectly lined and colored lips: that I've always been cherished. It's strange to hear those words coming out of my mouth, stockpiled as they have been inside me, emergency provisions stashed there by

Bao-mu who always believed in me, always loved me. Always knew that one day I'd need to share them.

With those words, so simply and easily given, Mama's body relaxes, and she leans into me. And as she remembers, picture by picture, I learn how much I've been treasured, too.

38

With winter break in full swing, I've got at least ten hours each day to dedicate to Ride for Our Lives. By mid-morning the first day back home, my hsuan has morphed into command central, notepads of lists and notes everywhere. After I get off the phone with Meghan, who, true to her word, has figured out most of the logistical details — "It's the least I can do for everything your mom's done for me" — I know that if I were up in my bedroom looking into my ghost-detecting mirror, my eyes would be gleaming, I'm having so much fun. But I don't have time to preen and instead pick up the phone for my check-in call with Lillian.

"How are the babies?" I ask.

"Zoe isn't sleeping, and Amanda's bouncing off the walls. So it's chaos here, but no one's got the heart to tell Amanda to pipe down, not when she's going to be quarantined for a couple of weeks, you know."

"So when's her chemo starting?"

"Tomorrow." Lillian laughs mirthlessly. "It's crazy, isn't it? Dr.

Martin told me that they have to basically kill the patient in order to save her."

"Like avalanche control."

"What?"

"Sometimes you have to set off a couple of small avalanches so you don't have a huge one."

"I hadn't thought of it that way." After a moment's pause, Lillian continues, sounding a fraction more upbeat, "So I need some good news. Anything. Please tell me you were wicked enough in Whistler for the two of us."

"Well, if you really want to know . . ."

"I do."

"I was."

"No way!" Lillian shrieks.

"Way!" I shriek back. And then I give her the abridged version of my past. While I'm not ready to provide full disclosure about Jared, something tells me that I'll spill all to Lillian when the time is right. Still, we do the "ewww" girlfriend shriek together when I get to the part where Jared starts bragging about all his accomplishments. And she does the "you did not!" scream when I tell her about my "no free lunch" comment to him.

"But I need your advice on something," I say, pacing a circuit from the door to my light table, past the bathroom door, and then around the sofa.

"You? You, Miss I'm-No-Free-Pass-to-Paradise? You need my advice?"

I laugh. "Well, there's this other boy. . . ."

"God, Syrah, how many are you juggling?"

"It's not that." But then I realize, it is, sort of. "It's my best friend."

"Let me guess, that guy at that board shop? I knew you had a thing for each other!"

"Wait, wait — he's dating someone else, remember?"

"Who is so freaked out by you that she's signed, sealed, and delivered a restraining order on you," says Lillian.

"Something like that."

"And now you've finally realized that you want a free pass to his paradise."

"Lillian!"

But we're both laughing, and it is almost worth having Age be dating Natalia just to have this conversation with Lillian. Almost.

"Seriously, though, what do you do when you love somebody enough to set him free, and he never comes back?" I stop doing laps around my studio to stand by the window overlooking an arched bridge.

"Well, why don't you tell him how you feel?"

"Definitely not an option. Let's just say I've seen what happens when someone comes between a couple." Fifteen years of being blamed for breaking up a family is all this girl can take. But then it occurs to me that Bao-mu might be on the right track. While I'm not about to take Age away from Natalia, I can ask for his friendship. "How about if I let him know that just because he has a girlfriend doesn't mean he can't have a girl who's his friend, too?"

Lillian is quiet, and I know it's not because she's tuned me out but that she's weighing my idea. Slowly, she says, "I think that's great. You're not telling him to break up with her and you're not coming between them. But I still vote for telling him how you feel."

After debating other possibilities ("putting a feng shui curse on Natalia is not an option"), circling back to Amanda ("let me know if there's anything I can do") and Zoe ("when can I meet her?"), and giving each other a pep talk, since there's still so much to do for Ride for Our Lives (omigod!), I know as far as Age goes, I have to do what I'm comfortable with.

At my light table, I begin to draw a letter manga-style for Age, inviting him to participate in the amateur snowboard rail jam at the event, unless he's afraid that I am going to whip his burly-burly butt in the competition. Then, abandoning all bravado, I write the truth, plain and simple and unadorned with any pictures: Age, it would mean so much to me if you just showed up. And then I attach VIP tickets for him, his dad, and his little brothers. And one for Natalia, too. I just hope that he'll read that as a sign that I want him to be my front-door friend.

One day, our timing will be right, the stars will align, and Hong Kong will be a distant memory. And when that time comes, I'll tell Age everything. As I'm about to seal the envelope, I stop, because the hallmark of our friendship has always been about telling each other things we can hardly admit to ourselves. Like how I've been a closet snob, too spineless to stand up to my parents and introduce them to Age, the boy who has always had my heart.

So I rip out the pages in my manga-journal, the ones that I wrote back in Whistler with the blow-by-blow account of The Jared Episode, and slip them inside my letter to Age. I don't want to hide that old history anymore, at least not from Age.

39

With my PowerPoint slides saved onto CD, Rude Q and A memorized, and power parka on, I'm armed, ready, and puffy. According to the daily schedule Mama left on the kitchen table for me this morning, my parents are home this evening, which means it's time for me to persuade them to support Ride for Our Lives. From the sounds of the argument I can hear yards away, a battle is being waged inside Baba's studio-study.

Baba's voice, stinging, rings into the dark night. "Could you please explain to me how it is possible to lose thirty-five million dollars in a single quarter?"

Through the windows I see everyone arranged in their normal pecking order: Baba at the head of the table, Mama to one side, Wayne to his other, Grace next to her brother and Mochi on her lap. There wasn't a memo about a family meeting on the kitchen table, in my inbox, or on my door. Could I possibly have been so disastrous at the last meeting that I've been dropped from the cc line?

Wayne rattles off numbers, using data to brace his deficit: "Sales were up fifteen percent —"

"But did you even look at their competitors?" demands Baba. If my dad is the emperor of the Cheng dynasty, then Wayne must be his eunuch, whose sole, emasculated purpose is to serve.

That truth hits me as hard as plowing head-on into a tree. Wayne is living my nightmare where all the possibilities for what I do with my life dwindle down to just one: adding to the Cheng coffers whether or not he yearns to do something different.

Through the window, Grace shakes her head at me in silent warning. I divine her meaning: danger, danger. Stay out while you can.

Wayne's shoulders are hunched over, human origami, so that he's as small and unnoticeable as possible while Baba rails at him. What should be sweet payback for years of being the big butt of Wayne's cutting comments is painful to watch. Especially since I remember how Grace told me that she can only remember Baba yelling at the two of them, virtually nothing else from her childhood.

To create a diversion, I step inside the office.

"Syrah, do you need something?" asks Baba mildly, like he hasn't just been berating Wayne.

Maybe it's Baba's gentle tone, the way he normally speaks to me, that makes Wayne's eyes go as cold and flat as a snake's, his Chinese horoscope sign. Or maybe it's just me. Whatever it is, Wayne snaps, "This is a private meeting. We're discussing some important issues."

"Yes, I know." My hands feel cold and sweaty as I look at Baba, not Wayne, for permission. "I can come back later."

"Actually, we're finished," says Baba.

While Baba leans back in his chair, Wayne glowers at me. Instead of feeling intimidated, I feel sorry for him, this grown man who can only make himself feel like a bigger and better version of himself by whittling me down.

"What do you need?" asks Baba.

Quickly, I pop the CD into his office computer and project my PowerPoint presentation onto the large screen on the far wall. My manga drawing of Amanda on her snowboard is practically life-size. I swallow. Looking directly at my family, I tell them what I want: "I need your help."

"'Ride for Our Lives'?" Wayne throws down his pen in disgust. "What? I thought we went over this already. We're not subsidizing your career."

"Aren't we subsidizing yours?" I counter softly, but my gaze doesn't waver off him. However sorry I feel for Wayne, I won't play the adoring little sister to his bullying big brother, and I definitely won't be his willing punching bag anymore. It's as if Bao-mu is by my side, not letting me forget that I am a Cheng, too, because in a voice that sounds so confident I don't recognize myself, I say, "This has nothing to do with jumpstarting my career. It's about saving lives for kids like Cindy and Jack."

At his children's names, Wayne's comeback dies, just as I knew it would when I scripted this Rude Q and A yesterday in my hsuan.

"Mr. Fujimoro, who is an important DiaComm exec, may lose his three-year-old daughter, Amanda, because they can't find a bone marrow match for her. She's mixed race like Cindy and Jack, so it's virtually impossible to find a donor." I forward to the next slide with a pie chart. "As you see, minorities account for only eight percent of the National Bone Marrow Registry. Internationally, the numbers are even more pathetic. The chances of finding a donor match for biracial populations drop drastically because of the unique makeup of their DNA." I focus on Wayne. "Which means that if Jack or Cindy ever got a disease like leukemia, unless they're a good match for each other, they might not survive."

"So what's your recommendation?" asks Baba, just like I knew he would.

"We're moving to Hong Kong so you can help define the vision of the mobile world in Asia. Like Grace says, what better expression of mobility" — I smile at Grace for giving me those words — "than world-class snowboarders? You saw for yourself how many people were pushing to get into the Nokia tent at Wicked in Whistler. And Nokia itself sponsored that event because of its large reach outside the hardcore snowboarding community."

"So you want to stage an event?" asks Mama, cocking her head to the side, already envisioning it.

"That's exactly right." I play footage from the evening rail jam session at Wicked in Whistler. "We could organize a snowboarding event, a contest, and bring together the best of the best riders, focusing on the ethnic ones."

"What's the payoff?" Baba asks.

I nod because I was expecting that question and summarize the next slide. "With your new role representing American telecom interests in Asia, you have the opportunity to build on your reputation as a visionary in mobility and create a strong public image for your industry. You'll be the original mobile pioneer talking to the next generation of mobile users."

In the perfect Hollywood world, an inspirational score would swell as my family falls out of their chairs and surrounds me, declaring that I'm brilliant. Rather than tell me that I'm a little sister worth having, Wayne says, "You're just exploiting our name."

No translation necessary. Regardless of what I do, I'll never be good enough for Wayne. Which hurts. Stupid, I know, but I haven't prepared contingency plans for this particular objection. Then, like the sign I need right now, Mama toys with her jade pendant. *Yu*, the stone of heaven, its Chinese character made up of the word for leader, *wang*, and one tiny dot. That dot may be as small as a pearl, but it's as powerful as a period, that full stop at the end of every sentence in my journal. And that's what I picture now, my pearl of wisdom and power and confidence, because I refuse to topple over from Wayne's verbal push.

Like any *wang*, I take a chance, veer off-slide, off the groomed tracks of my prepared speech, and speak from the uncharted backcountry of my heart. Without needing Baba's book, I quote from *The Ethan Cheng Way*: "'Use whatever strengths you have.' What does the Cheng name stand for? Paving the way, removing impossible obstacles, improving people's lives."

At this point in my presentation, I thought Baba would turn to our resident PR expert and ask Grace for her thoughts, collect all the input before making a calculated decision. Costs versus benefits, risks versus rewards.

But instead, Baba checks in with Mama, placing one hand on top of hers. "What do you think?"

Without hesitating, Mama asks me, "How important is this to you?"

"More important than anything I've ever done. Amanda is running out of time."

Like a team, my parents nod, and just like that, the Chengs are in. *That's it?* I think. All I had to do was ask? But as I see Baba nodding to himself while he looks at the last slide, the one listing everything I still need help with, I know that it's also because I came prepared and I knew what to ask for.

"Unbelievable," Wayne mutters under his breath, and collects his papers. "First, this makes no sense on any level — financial, personal, and medical — to get involved. And second, when does this need to happen?"

"A week and a half now," I answer.

"Impossible."

"Mama's event planner, who agreed to help with this event pro bono, says it's possible," I reply. "And she's already made a lot of headway."

"It's definitely possible," says Mama confidently. As *Business-Week* put it, where there is a Cheng, there is a way. As if to prove it, she's already flipping through her Day-Timer, every day blocked out with back-to-back appointments and meetings. I can hear her mind whirring, reprioritizing me to the top. "Not a problem."

"I have work to do." As Wayne leaves, harrumphing out the door, a boy locked in a perpetual temper tantrum, I gaze after him wistfully. I think we all do because none of us speaks in the dead silence until Baba says, "You know, Wayne has a valid point." I hear the Voice of Reason in Baba's tone. "The chances of finding a donor even with this are very slim."

"I know." My Voice of Hope counters, "But so were the chances of you finding me in the snow."

Satisfied, Baba nods, and Mama asks, "What do you want us to do?"

"I thought you'd never ask," I say with a big smile. And then, at great length, I tell them.

40

My internal body clock wakes me the next morning at 6:29. Why do I have to wake up now, be tantalized with the unrequited hope that Age will call and tell me he finally understands why I pushed him away? I wait another minute. No such call. If my letter couldn't convince him that our friendship was worth resuscitating, nothing will. Crushed and defeated after waiting another full thirty minutes for a call I'm not getting — I'm a slow learner, what can I say? — I head downstairs to find Baba reading the *Wall Street Journal,* and Mama nibbling tiny bites of cottage cheese out of a bowl while poring over a Sotheby's auction catalog. Odd because at this time of the morning, Baba's usually working and Mama working out.

"So your sixteenth birthday is coming up," Baba says while I fix a bowl of oatmeal in the kitchen. Over his newspaper, he's watching me so intently I think he's about to interrogate me about my goals and objectives for the next year. Instead he asks, "What's on your wish list?"

"Nothing," I tell them as I carry my hot bowl to the table and sit next to Mama. Last year, I had so many birthday wishes: a snowboard championship, a trip with Mama and Baba, a détente with Grace and Wayne, a girlfriend. More or less, I've gotten them all. What I never thought I'd have to wish for was Age.

"Then how about this?" With a secret smile, Mama slides a piece of paper across the table to me. There's a number written on it, and it's followed by a lot of zeros. Six to be precise.

"What's this?" I ask.

"The Cheng Family Foundation matching fund for Ride for Our Lives," says Mama, whose smile blooms full on her face.

"You're kidding." When I finally look up from the paper commitment, I catch my parents exchanging pleased looks. But when they start laughing like they're the ones who won the financial aid lottery, I realize it's not pride but pleasure I'm witnessing. Just as I'm about to jump up and down and thank them, Baba holds up one finger.

"There's a catch," he says.

There always is with Ethan Cheng. But I know that I'm about to learn an important business lesson. I'm game.

"You need to solicit the same amount from other donors," says Baba as he flips the page in his newspaper.

How am I supposed to drum up another million dollars? I slump to the back of my chair, but then I know. The answer is staring me straight in the face. Betty Yu Leong Cheng, the woman at Baba's side. Raising a mere million dollars is nothing for my mother, who has been known to raise a heck of a lot more than that for the Evergreen Fund in just three phone calls.

"According to *The Ethan Cheng Way,* always learn from the best," I tell Mama now. "Can you help me with the pitch? You are the rainmaker."

Mama swallows another dainty bite and points her spoon at me. "You mean, a snowmaker."

"What?"

"Excuse me," she corrects me automatically. "I secured a few snowmakers. At no cost."

"Mama, you're amazing!"

The way Mama claps her hands together, grinning, she looks like a little girl who has just been told that she's a beloved treasure. Maybe that's all we need. Not fame and fortune for endorsing products, whether it's a cell phone or a snowboard. But to be endorsed unconditionally by the ones we love most in the world.

"So, if I were you," begins Mama, pausing for another bite, "I would start with the Dillingers. They're good for at least a hundred thousand."

"Mama!" I'm shocked that she's talking about fundraising in such a crass un-Betty-Cheng like way. But this isn't business; it isn't even pleasure. It's about Amanda and all the other kids who are waiting for a donor to give them their chance to live. So I ask, "Who else do you think I should hit up?"

"You two are dangerous together. I can just see it," says Baba, shaking his head fondly at us. "This is going to be the most effective fundraising campaign the National Bone Marrow Registry has ever had."

"How can you say that?" I ask.

"Your great-grandfather was part of the group who came to the Gold Mountain to build the railroad," says Baba, lowering the business section to the table. "A few years after those men built the railroad, which radically changed commerce and transportation, they were excluded from America." His voice may sound even-keeled, but I sense the outrage behind his words. "You just never know when your luck will change. So you don't have to be the best or the smartest or the richest person in the room, but you have to be the hardest worker. Never giving up is how you make your own luck."

"Surviving," I say.

"Survival," corrects Baba. That word rings with the same steel as the railroad tracks that my great-grandfather must have hammered. Survival — I wonder if that's what propelled Baba through his career. That need to work himself to the top. Or was it to prove that he was more than the grandson of a manual laborer? "It's why we named you Syrah."

"What? I don't get it."

"The syrah grape grows in France's Rhone River valley, where it has to endure intense summers and then the winter wind, the mistral," explains Baba.

"It's a survivor," says Mama.

A survivor like my mother, who thrived despite Weipou's best efforts to starve her spirit, and like my father, who eked a legacy out of nothing to honor his own manual-laboring grandfather.

"Remind me to tell Lena that the guest quarters need to be prepared for the Leongs." Mama raises her eyebrows when I drop my spoon and Baba coughs. She demands, "What?"

"Excuse me," I correct her with a smile, "but since when are the Leongs visiting?"

"Since I invited them to Ride for Our Lives." Unconsciously, Mama runs her jade pendant back and forth on the gold chain, so that the crane runs amok, uncertain which way to fly. "It's just one night."

"Thank you," I tell Mama, swinging around to their side of the table to hug her first, and then Baba. "These are the best birthday presents ever."

When I settle down in my seat again to finish my now-cold oatmeal, Baba shakes out his newspaper, Mama goes back to reading about the next Tang horse on her acquisitions list, and me? I savor the traces of their loving smiles as they glance at me when they think I'm not looking.

41

Muscle memory is the only thing that gets most students and teachers through the first day of school after a long break. In my first period English class, I learn that lethargic brains are to homework what atrophied hamstring muscles are to exercise. Now, me, on the other hand, my brain has worked through my vacation, all pistons whirring as I try to keep track of everything that needs to be checked on and checked off before Ride for Our Lives. With only six days left before the Big Day on Sunday, I have zero seconds to spare.

My hand shoots up the moment Mr. Delbene asks in journalism, "During our long vacation, I hope that some of you spent a few minutes thinking about our newspaper. Anyone with a new idea?"

In the back of the room, Chelsea mutters, "What is she? The Lillian Fujimoro clone?"

Why bother responding when I don't really care what Chelsea thinks and I'd rather focus my energy on what's important: Lillian.

"I think we should publish a special edition newspaper to galvanize" — love that word! — "support for Lillian."

"Why?" asks George, looking around and only now noticing she's missing. "Where is she?"

"With her sister in the hospital."

"Yeah, probably throwing another party," Chelsea snipes.

"Actually," I say, "her little sister needs a bone marrow match if she wants to beat her leukemia."

"I had no idea," says Mr. Delbene.

All is quiet on the Chelsea front. Instead, her mouth is open, guilt-stricken into silence. So she had no idea either, even though her mom was the one to hook the Fujimoros up with the best pediatric oncologist in town. If her mom hasn't communicated this to Chelsea, chances are something is broken in the Dillinger home, and Chelsea, as much as I don't want to admit it, might be another girl who's slipped overboard without anyone noticing, too.

"So what's your proposal?" asks Mr. Delbene, who's rocking up and down on his feet the way he does when he's excited.

That's my opening to tell everybody about Ride for Our Lives and then show them the copies of my first-ever manga column.

"So what if we distributed this via e-mail to everyone in school and ask them to forward it? Through a little viral distribution, we might just reach someone, somewhere, who'll be the perfect match for Amanda. What do you think?" I ask, growing more and more uncertain as I wait, wait, wait for people's reactions.

Finally, George says, "This is brilliant." And then, as if this were his idea in the first place, he says, "Blog meets service learning. You know, most kids our age don't read the newspaper."

If I've ever doubted The Ethan Cheng Way, I don't anymore, not when I now have conclusive proof that Baba is right yet again. See, according to him, visionaries are so ahead of their time that they often get vilified for their forward thinking. It takes people a little time to come around, but they usually do.

"Manga meets service learning meets social commentary," I correct.

"Right, that's right!" says George, nodding as if I'm the one who's finally catching on.

After class, Mr. Delbene asks me to stay behind. While I wait for him to speak, he tacks my manga-column on the bulletin board and reads the working title, "'A Fine Whine,' huh? Not The Syrah Cheng Way?"

"Nope, that's been done before."

He nods as though he understands that sometimes we have to step off the well-grooved tracks and find our own route, however bumpy it is. "I can't wait to see what you come up with next."

That makes two of us, Mr. Delbene. I can't wait to see what I come up with next, either.

42

Tell me that I woke up this morning on the set for a new horror movie, *The Night of the Living Leongs,* because surely zombies have replaced that entire branch of my family. The Boys standing outside The House of Cheng have their mouths shut, hair slicked down, and shirts tucked in, and in no way do they resemble The Boys of Richmond. My aunties and uncles file inside, dumbstruck tourists visiting a five-star haunted hotel, half-expecting that they'll be picked off one-by-one. Even Mama, she of the perfect quip for every social situation, is uttering monosyllabic replies, like her conversational talents have been vaporized.

So it's up to me to be the convivial host-slash-translator-slash-tour guide.

"Come in," I welcome everyone, and lead the Leongs to the living room, where dim sum stations are set up. "You must be starving."

One of The Boys whispers, "Our whole house fits in this room."

"Yeah, a kid came in here about a year ago and he was never seen again," I whisper back, loud enough for the rest of The Boys to hear.

That seems to loosen them up; at least it gets a round of "nuh-uh" going among The Boys.

Kids down, adults to go. They're standing around, gawking. Not that I blame them. It's not every day that you step into a house that has more precious Asian art than most museums. Even Jocelyn looks subdued, and I start to worry that maybe she hadn't been envious of me back in Richmond because she had no benchmark, no conception of what billions look like. But then she intercepts my SOS and says, "Auntie Marnie, the present."

With that prompt, Auntie Marnie's natural bossiness asserts itself. "Yu," she says in an authoritative voice. "Mama wanted you to have this." From her cavernous purse, zipper broken and marred with a faint blue ink mark, Marnie withdraws a yellow silk envelope, snapped shut. She urges it on Mama, who simply holds it gingerly in her hand as if it's a small-scale version of Pandora's box that she's loath to open. Well, that just irks Auntie Marnie, who commands, "Open it."

With shaking fingers, Mama pulls out an apple-green jade bracelet. Even to my untrained jewelry-appraising eyes, I can tell that it's hardly as valuable as the piece Mama wears around her neck. So many conflicting emotions must be running through Mama that I wouldn't be surprised if she dismissed the gift, but slowly, with everyone watching, Mama works the bracelet, carved out of solid jade, over her left hand. At last, it slips over the birdlike bones of her wrist, and when it does, everyone smiles.

"Perfect," pronounces Auntie Marnie.

At that moment, Baba walks in, briefcase in hand, unaware that the Leongs, even The Boys, are staring at him with star-struck awe: the great Ethan Cheng, the man whose face has graced sixty-two magazine covers, is standing right here with them. His eyes are only for Mama. When he reaches her side, she looks up at him and smiles tremulously, holding up her tiny wrist. "Look, Ethan, look at what my mother left me."

"It's beautiful," Baba tells her, and then greets the Leongs as if they were his family, too.

In the middle of the introductions, from across the room, comes a loud crash followed by an equally loud chorus of "Oh, no!" The Boys are standing amid a fallen bonsai and its shattered pot, mouths agape with horror at what they've done.

"*Aiya!*" cries Auntie Marnie, rushing to them as she simultaneously launches into a tirade of Mandarin, scolding The Boys for being so clumsy.

"It's okay," I tell Auntie Marnie, even though I'm panicking inside: *Oh, no, they destroyed one of Mama's perfect, precious bonsai.* Mama is staring, staring, staring at the tiny pine tree, lying like roadkill, thrown feet away from the broken porcelain.

Auntie Marnie first tells the boys to stand back and then continues her chastising in Mandarin, "Didn't I tell you to be careful here? Aaaah, you boys are like ants on a hill, running up and down all day long. Now look what you've done."

"It was an accident," says Mama, interpreting Auntie Marnie's Mandarin correctly. "Just an accident. It can be replaced. Really," she says slowly, "nothing important was broken."

As relieved as The Boys look at that, Auntie Marnie is still glaring at them, so I don't hear a single protesting peep from them when I suggest that they follow me downstairs pronto. After I leave them in the theater, bouncing up and down on the couches as they watch a cartoon with Jocelyn, I return back upstairs to find Auntie Marnie still lamenting over the bonsai.

Just as I'm about to tell her to forget about it, Baba stops me with a gentle hand on my arm. Only then do I see the miracle unfolding within The House of Cheng: this broken vessel is mending our fragmented family.

"What a waste," sighs Auntie Marnie, her hand full of jagged pieces of pottery that she's salvaged from the floor.

"The pot was too small anyway," says Mama, taking the shards from her. "No, no, what's going to waste is all this food." And then in halting Mandarin, Mama asks, *"Chi bao le ma?"*

It's a greeting, a new start in our family history. "Let's eat," I agree, following Mama's lead, as we urge plates on my relatives, on Baba, and finally on each other.

43

On Sunday, the morning of the event, Mama and I set a world record for female preparedness in the Cheng household. Mama has us on a timer; I'm not kidding. Seventeen minutes is all she allots for us to breakfast, shower, and steal into the car, all without waking up any of our extended family. Like conspirators, we're giggling as Mama reverses out of the garage, looking like a teenager in her pigtails and après-ski outfit. My new red jacket — the result of the "You need to wear bright colors on TV" pronouncement by Auntie Marnie, which was seconded by Mama — is not for the fashion shy.

"We did it," I say, and pull out the minute-by-minute program we created with Meghan a week ago. "I was sure one of The Boys would wake up."

"You wore them out yesterday."

"Our toys wore them out." For once, I don't feel guilty about our largesse, not when I can share it with the people I love.

Niceties dispensed with, we get down to business for the rest of the drive over to DiaComm. It's still so dark, I need to use the mini flashlight Mama packed for this purpose. The lake we're crossing over on the 520 bridge is flat black.

"I can't believe today's the event," I tell Mama.

"You've been working nonstop. How're you feeling about your speech?"

"Like I'm going to throw up." Last night, Grace casually mentioned that my appeal for bone marrow donors would be broadcast to thirty million viewers worldwide over ESPN, and as she said, "That's not counting the pickup on the news . . . if you give a good enough sound byte."

"You'll get used to it," Mama says, as if I'll be speaking at more of these fundraisers in the future.

We arrive to a DiaComm that has undergone a miraculous transformation, from parking lot to Snow Park. No sooner does Mama get out of the car than she marches to the snow blowers. Apparently, the shape of the snow is not quite up to Cheng standards.

"Shouldn't this be smoother?" she asks, pointing a dainty finger at a lump.

A thin guy with a goatee takes his shovel and whacks down the offending bump.

"Is your mom always like this?" he asks me when Mama moves off to meet with the vendor who'll be selling Ride for Our Lives T-shirts, proceeds benefiting the bone marrow registry.

"Like what?"

His bushy eyebrows lift meaningfully before he attacks another bump. In a way, I'm no different from Christine, who denounced Bao-mu publicly during the Cultural Revolution. Haven't I put down Mama whenever I could, whether it's in my head or in my journal? Written her off as a socialite fluffhead? Haven't I been denouncing Mama, figuring if I couldn't have her, I didn't want to be like her at all?

For the first time that I can remember, I defend Betty Cheng, socialite, philanthropist, adopted daughter, reunited sister, and beloved mother: "Yeah, she's always on top of everything. Isn't she amazing?"

Three hours before the event starts, the pro riders begin arriving to practice. It's a who's who of snowboard superstars, both guys and girls who are regulars in all the riding magazines. Some are Olympic medalists, others are video stars. Whatever career track they're on, the snowboarders here are at the top of their games.

Surrounded as I am by these celebs, the only person I'm focused on is Lillian. She looks nervous and hopeful and afraid, just the way I felt on the way to Vancouver, desperately wanting the Leongs to accept me but unsure whether they would.

"This is so much bigger than I thought it was going to be." Lillian gestures to the stands that are already congested, the VIP tent for the corporate sponsors, the pro snowboarders milling in the staging area around the ramp, the booths for Children's Hospital and the vendors, and the tent housing the National Bone Marrow Registry. "I can't believe you pulled this all off."

"We haven't yet," I correct her. What counts isn't the pomp, but the results. Will people, especially minorities, register their bone marrow?

"Are you kidding me?" Lillian's about to go on, but she looks over my shoulder, mouth widening, as she gawks, not at the snowboarders, but at all the press, the celebrities of journalism who've turned out. The business press is hovering around Baba, ready to capture every business bon mot springing out of his mouth.

Then, grinning at Lillian, I hand her a press pass. "Have fun hanging out with the big boys."

"You Chengs are amazing." She slips the long cord over her head and looks at her badge, hanging like a medal on her chest. "It's so official." Throwing her arms around me, Lillian says, "Thank you."

I know she's thanking me for more than the press pass, and instead of demurring with an "It's nothing," I hug her back with a "You are so welcome," and honor my own hard work to pull off Ride for Our Lives. Then I tell Lillian about the editor of *Snowboarder* who tracked me down earlier, not exactly groveling, but definitely apologetic for writing about how rich dilettantes like myself were hazards on the slopes.

"Ewww!" shrieks Lillian, just the way I hoped she would.

"I told him he could make it up to me by featuring Ride for Our Lives — on the cover. I'm so shameless." Isn't it funny how once I accepted my body, I've learned to love throwing my weight around?

"Can I quote you on that?" she asks. "You know, I've got that article about you that I need to write."

As co-chair, my job is a lot more than meet-and-greet duties. I'm supposed to work the crowd, make sure that the VIPs are taken care of, that everyone and everything is in place. Luckily, we've got Meghan, the event planner extraordinaire, who is managing most of the behind-the-scenes logistics. Like now. With her walkie-talkie to her mouth, Meghan orders the espresso cart moved over two feet. Why, I don't know, but with this event in her good hands, I welcome Mobey and B.J. at the entrance, where they're standing awkwardly, staring at all the riders and Mount Cheng, the twenty-foot ramp built on top of scaffolding that runs down to a twenty-foot kinked and curved rail.

"Hey, guys, you came!"

B.J. throws his arm around me. "This is unbelievable."

"Thanks," I say, and can't help asking, "Where's Age?"

The guys exchange a look, one that tells me that Age isn't coming. Uncomfortably, Mobey keeps staring at the ramp and mutters, "He made other plans."

Those other plans are Natalia. We all know that.

"Here," I say, "let me show you guys around," and lead Mobey and B.J. to the tent that Mama had set up for the pro riders.

"All this loot is free?" asks B.J. in wonder.

"Yup. You know my mom," I tell them proudly. "If the presenters at the Oscars can haul home fifty grand of goodies just for reading a teleprompter, then so should 'our' snowboarders." That means, of course, the latest and greatest cell phones with a free one-year plan, free music, free games, and yes, free manga for all the participants.

"God, I gotta be a pro rider," moans B.J.

"Hey, is that Jared Johanson?" asks Mobey, gawking dazed-and-amazed at the ESPN and *Sports Illustrated* photographers who are camping out in the staging area. Beyond them, Jared is standing next to his brother. My heart, I am glad to report, doesn't break at the sound of Jared's name. Not the way it does at Age's absence. *Muy* adult of me to invite Jared and ask him to round up his buddies, I have to say.

"I can't believe all this," says Mobey. And then he punches me in the arm as if I'm one of the guys. I punch him back, glad that I am. He says, "I knew you'd be more than a snowboard girl."

More than a snowboard girl. It's true. You'd think that it'd be all bittersweet and heavy sighs being this close to my old dream. But I don't feel more than a twinge of wistfulness, the same way I feel when I see pictures of our old house. Snowboarding gave me a place in the world, and going pro was something tangible I could strive for. Somewhere along the way, having fun gave way to courting fame and proving my worth.

Striding toward me now is a man on a mission to save his job.

"Hey, hey, Syrah Cheng," Ralph of RhamiWare says, and I can't help but replay his snub in my head, how I was too much of a liability to contemplate being sponsored. Ever. Now, with the full-force of the Cheng family behind me, not to mention with the camera crews and journalists teeming, I've proved that I can draw a crowd. And according to Ralph's accounting, that catapults me to asset status.

Age has a point about keeping snowboarding pure; it's a passion, not a job. Once you're on the payroll, you become a corporate marketing tool, a cherished one so long as you're good for the bottom line. If I doubted it before, now I've got confirmation. I don't need a sponsorship, or want it, if this is the measure of success.

So when Ralph says, "We need to talk about getting you on the Am-ster team," I know exactly how to answer his offer to join RhamiWare's amateur riding team.

"Thank you so much, but I'm going in another direction," I tell Ralph in my yes-but-oh-aren't-I-polite-when-I-say-no way. As The Ethan Cheng Way points out, never burn bridges, especially when I've got the second annual Ride for Our Lives to plan, and guess who I'm going to hit up for an even more generous contribution?

"Really?" Ralph looks crestfallen.

I gesture to Mobey and B.J. "But I have two friends you really ought to watch." My walkie-talkie crackles and Meghan's familiar voice beckons: "Eaglet, fly home. Roger that?" Smiling, I respond, "Roger. Eaglet is on her way."

The best charitable events, Mama explained to me when we called on the Dillingers a week ago, are the ones that build to an emotional pitch. They connect people to the cause and show how their participation matters. And that tiny, minuscule little task is what I'm supposed to accomplish with my speech.

Watching my parents kick off the event from the side of the stage with me is Lillian, who is so green, she matches her beanie. My hands are slick as footage of Amanda rolls, ending with a close-up of her big hazel eyes. The crowd applauds, so loud I have to cover my ears.

"Lillian, you're up," hisses Grace.

"Oh, God," Lillian mutters. Looking as panic-stricken as I feel, Lillian begs, "Go out there with me."

"Nope, it's your moment," I tell her.

Naturally, Lillian is flawless as she talks about how important it is for her little sister, who just wants to be able to snowboard, to get a bone marrow transplant. From where I stand, I can already see a couple of people breaking off to wait in line at the Bone Marrow Registry tent. I hate to say this, but Lillian has just jeopardized her newspaper career. She's got future anchorwoman written all over her.

"And now," Lillian says, grinning, "I am privileged to introduce the girl who started this all, Syrah Cheng!"

If I thought that toast at Baba's birthday party was bad, it's nothing compared to making a fool of myself in front of thirty million viewers, more if I have the right sound byte.

"Omigod, Grace," I mumble.

"Go," says Grace, all no-nonsense, and she gives me a gentle but brisk push that would make Bao-mu proud. As I step onstage, she whispers into my ear, "You're going to do great . . . Mei-Mei."

Mei-Mei. At last I hear that word. Two syllables, one sound, that's all, yet that "little sister" propels me onstage with pride and confidence as I approach Lillian and my parents, who are waiting for me.

My eyes skim this vast audience collected here in the Dia-Comm parking lot — the Leongs in the front, kids from my school, my crew — and land on Jared. From the stage, I can feel his hunger and remember what he's coveted: *I want that final. I want that podium.* Funny, isn't it, that it's me, Syrah Cheng, who's standing at this podium.

With a shock, I realize it's not so funny, because I belong up here.

My words, my ideas, and my actions — those are what I want my legacy to be, not my snowboarding. Here's the thing, my grandfather was killed in the Cultural Revolution for his words because they were that powerful. I pause, filling my lungs with the cold, clean winter air, before I share my words: "It took a three-year-old spitfire to teach me the difference between being a victim and being a victor." When the applause stops, I talk about how with one insignificant test, we can make a significant difference in someone's life. "Hundreds of people are waiting right now for a bone marrow match. Think about it. They could be waiting for you." As I look toward the tent where an even longer line is now queuing, I say, "Thank you so much for getting tested today. In tandem with Ride for Our Lives, blood banks are open in San Francisco, Los Angeles, Chicago, and New York, waiting for people to register."

Unscripted, my parents come to stand on either side of me. Baba, future telecommunications ambassador to Asia, announces, "The same is true in the major cities throughout Asia: Tokyo, Taipei, Hong Kong, Seoul, Shanghai, and Beijing. Blood banks will be open during business hours for the simple test."

My eyes are wide with shock, especially after Mama takes the podium and adds, "The Cheng Foundation will pay for all costs to register on the bone marrow database, regardless of race or color, for the next thirty days."

"You're kidding me," I whisper, my eyes filling up with tears. "I had no idea."

My parents beam at me, leaving an empty space in front of the podium for me. Instead of panicking since I haven't prepared, I remember Grace's advice on speeches. Hook them with a great first line and end with a bang.

"You know," I say, "this great woman — who happens to be my beautiful and brilliant sister, Grace — says, 'If you're going to do something, do it big. And do it right.' That's The Grace Cheng Way. So please help us do something. Let's do it big and do it right, and find that donor for Amanda."

Under the flash attack by the photographers, I bolt out of my inner circle onstage and grab Grace's hand, hissing at her, "If I'm getting photographed, so are you," and drag her with me to stand in the middle of Mama, Baba, and Lillian. Afterward, I ask one of the photographers, "Could you please send me a copy for my scrapbook?"

"Make that two copies," says Mama before she goes hand-in-hand with Baba to the bone marrow registry station, where they stand in line to get their DNA tested with a cheek swab.

A tune debuting from the new Mack Dawg snowboarding video soundtrack — Grace's brilliant idea — crescendos, signaling the start of the jam session. In groups of ten, the snowboarders take two runs each with Erik Johanson, Jared's big brother, kicking off the session to deafening cheers.

Snowboarder after snowboarder hits the rail, riding it from its kinked edge to the rounded staircase rail in the midsection and ending on the up-and-down ledge. The veterans are all doing something cool, but the best thing is that they're having a great time and all for a good cause. I mean, they're smiling even when they fall. It's the same way Age snowboards, as if there's nothing more important than enjoying the ride. When was the last time I felt that way, or the last time I allowed myself to just revel in the moment instead of chasing after my pro-riding dreams?

The Boys can't believe the tricks that all these riders are throwing down. They keep gripping my arm and asking, "Can you do that?" and "What about that one?"

Honestly, I've got to laugh. All these guys, who live and breathe snowboarding, are in a totally different league from me. Honestly, I was always good, but not good enough to go pro. And that's perfectly fine, because I'm good enough for me.

The event winds down to the amateur jam session, where local kids are invited to have a go on the rails for a donation. I wave to Mobey and B.J., who are heading my way, looking as pumped as the old guard.

"Where's your board?" asks Mobey, pausing in front of me and my parents.

"I'm on hostess duty, so I'm living through you guys today. You better be good," I tell my crew of two.

"Chengs don't live vicariously," says Mama, horrified.

"Excuse me?" I say.

"Take your snowboard," says Mama.

"My snowboard?"

Materializing next to me is Meghan, holding a new Vera Wang snowboard. Who would have thought that a designer known for her couture bridal gowns could fashion something as kicking as this iridescent mother-of-pearl snowboard? "Mama," I gasp as the snowboard shimmers in the light, "this is gorgeous."

"Betty," says Baba, his mouth turned down into the "no" position.

"Oh, Ethan," says Mama, touching his arm and smiling

winningly up at him. "Nothing in this world is totally safe. You run more risks gallivanting around the world without a body-guard."

"I don't know about that," says Baba, somewhat sheepishly, but he nods his approval at me.

What Age told me was true; when it comes down to it, I don't need my parents' blessing to do anything I truly want. Not really. But their unspoken "yes" feels awfully good.

It's my turn on deck, and as I trudge my way up the stairs on the scaffolding to the top of the ramp, my name — Go, Syrah! Go, Syrah! — reverberates, more war cry than chant, thanks to The Boys, whose arms are thrashing in the air with each syl-lable.

"You pack your own cheering squad, Sarah?" asks the official at the top of the ramp, squinting at the name badge around my neck.

"Syrah," I correct him. "As in my dad's favorite wine."

His eyes widen at his gaffe. "You're Ethan Cheng's kid?"

"And Betty Cheng's."

The yelling below gets louder, if that's possible. The Boys have progressed from waving their arms to full-body slamming each other, and I can almost hear Auntie Marnie threatening them if they move one more time, they're banished to the car. Jocelyn and Auntie Yvonne have unfurled a banner with my name on it, and behind them, on their own bench, sit Mama, Baba, Grace, and Mochi. First thing this morning, Bao-mu called, telling me, "You do great! Tell everybody, just get tested for blood. It only cotton swab. They not feel." I'm at peace with

Wayne's absence, knowing that whatever he's dealing with are his issues, not mine. Age's no-show is harder to accept, maybe because it's my issues that are keeping him away.

Now that the official at the top of the ramp with me knows who I am, he looks uncomfortable, like he's in the presence of a social better. Here's the thing. Even with my trust fund, I'm just a girl, no better or worse than any other.

So I read his name tag, meet his eyes and tell him, not unctuous, not condescending, but truthfully, "Hey, Scott, thanks for helping today."

"You're welcome," says the official, flattered that I noticed him. Isn't that all we want? To be noticed and needed?

When the wind picks that moment to rush hard at me, knocking off the official's cap, I hear Bao-mu: *See, that sign. You, survivor, just like your name.* I'm not the Old Syrah anymore; I left her somewhere up in Whistler. And I'm not Shiraz; as cute as she was, she's only a paper doll when it comes right down to it. The New Syrah is stronger, wiser. A sweet, savory and sassy survivor.

"You ready?" Scott asks, his eyes meeting mine.

Am I ready? My hands are sweaty. I feel like I'm going to pass out, since my family is watching below, never mind some of the pro riders who are curious about all the amateur upstarts and the press who want to see Ethan Cheng's kid. This on-the-edge feeling is familiar. I realize what it is: nerves before an adventure whose ending I have no way of predicting.

"Yup, I'm ready," I tell him. And then in the VIP stands, I see a beanie, red and well-worn and being waved in such large, sweeping arcs, there's no way I can miss its owner the way I have so many opportunities. Grinning, I think to myself, my parents have a point. I could get used to the view from atop Mount Cheng. From where I stand and what I see, joy so expansive fills me until I can almost believe I'm already flying down this ramp and soaring toward Age.

Hong Kong is six months away. Six months. Anything can happen if I'm open to the possibilities. Just look at all that's happened in the last half year. Heck, the last two weeks.

I nod and tell Scott and myself and everyone who's watching me, "Ready or not, here I come."

In snowboarding, there's a fine line between overthinking and underthinking. How many times have I visualized this moment in my head and in my manga-journal? Trusting myself, I simply drop down the ramp. The chants of my name fade into the background, and all I hear is the scream bubbling inside me, not out of fear, but fearlessness. The wind rushes on my face as I pick up speed, sliding down my Gold Mountain. This is my mountain, my home mountain, the one I will keep returning to, the one I'm so lucky to have.

With my arms spread wide as though I'm embracing every possibility, I leap into the air and hit the rail, perfectly balanced on those scant three inches of iron. I know exactly what I'm aiming for: the snow glittering like hope. I read once that snow isn't actually white, but every single color in the spectrum. Our brains just can't comprehend what we're seeing, so we distill it down to one understandable hue. I slide along the rail and let out my exultant scream. And in front of me, the snow catches the sun and refracts it into a billion pieces of good fortune.

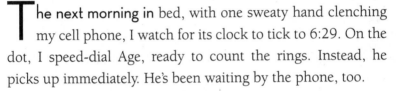

44

The next morning in bed, with one sweaty hand clenching my cell phone, I watch for its clock to tick to 6:29. On the dot, I speed-dial Age, ready to count the rings. Instead, he picks up immediately. He's been waiting by the phone, too.

"Hey, it's me," I say.

"I was just about to call you," Age says.

With those words — proof that Age being at Ride for Our Lives yesterday wasn't just some strange fluke — I release my breath. Then, in a confident manner that would make Grace proud, I tell him, "I know."

Age laughs. "What? Am I that predictable?"

"Trust me, when it comes to guys, nothing is predictable."

"Right back at you. So what's up?"

"I figured it's my turn to check in on you."

"Hunh," says Age, but I can tell he's pleased.

More relaxed now, I lean back into my pillows. "So in the spirit of me checking in, what are you doing today?"

"Grom duty. My dad's working on a deadline."

"Cool, then you can bring your brothers over for lunch. I've got in my hot little hands that new Mack Dawg video we can watch afterward."

Without losing a second, Age says, "Noon, your studio."

"Noon, the main house," I correct him.

"You sure?"

"Dude, you're part of the Syrah Cheng package." I bite my lip, remembering how Age responded so caustically and honestly the last time I said this.

But Age answers right away: "Good, because, dude, you're part of *mine*."

"Good," I say.

"Good," he repeats.

"Then you won't mind if I get that in writing?"

Age starts laughing again. And I press the phone closer to my ear, because I was way off on how much I missed his chuckle, the way it builds and then recedes, a wave I can count on, day in and day out.

"You Chengs," he says.

"What?" I ask, all innocent. "So some guy gave me this great new manga-journal yesterday that I need to fill with something." Next to my pillow is the notebook Age handed me after the event. On the first page, he's inscribed a poem I've read and reread so many times that I could quote it with my eyes closed.

As earth stirs in her winter sleep
And puts out grass and flowers
Despite the snow,
Despite the falling snow.
— Robert Graves

"Some guy, huh?" says Age.

I open the journal to run my fingers over Age's slanting scrawl, all angular ascenders and descenders, the ridgeline of a beloved mountain. "Yup, just some guy who I really missed."

He's silent for a moment before shooting my words right back at me: "I know."

"You are so . . ."

"Intelligent? Insightful? Unbelievable?" he prompts.

All of the above, I want to say, but settle on the truth: "Welcome." And then I grin when Age um-er-uhs his way through a simple see-ya, so I know he's feeling just as jittery as I am — in that good and oh-so-wonderful, I-am-aware-of-you way.

Hanging up, I place the phone next to the manga-journal and gaze out to the garden, still smiling. Like Mama's peonies that bloom every year, I survived despite the snow, despite the falling snow. With one leg outstretched, I hug the other, the scarred one, to my chest. My friendship with Age may or may not become something more, but I know that it, too, will survive the winter of other boyfriends and girlfriends and Hong Kong.

I reach to my bedside table, where I've stashed my original manga-journal. After my manga marathon at Children's Hospital, there aren't many empty pages left, but I only need a few for my final drawings of Shiraz. The thing is, I can't leave my girl unfinished.

The big question in *The Ethan Cheng Way,* the one you have to answer before you can begin to formulate a plan is this: what do you want? The only way I know how to answer that is with more questions of my own, which may not be what Baba intended. But it's what feels right to me.

So propping my journal on both knees now, I draw a hall with door after door, each an open-ended invitation, a possibility. Manga author? Columnist? Snowboard gear designer? Publicist? That's how I want Shiraz's future to be. And mine. Endless questions. Infinite possibilities. In the center door, I finally write, *Ex-pat in Hong Kong?*

That's all we can do: be prepared to spring on all the opportunities life presents us — on powder days, in business, and especially, in love.

When no more doors can fit on the page, I add the three tiny scars on Shiraz's kneecap, a constellation tattooed on her, forever reminding her of what she lost — and found — on her mountains. I close my journal, rest my hand on the cover, giving it a benediction. As far as crutches go, Shiraz was an excellent one. But I like me better.

I pick up my gift from Age, my new notebook, the perfect container and mirror and psychoanalyst for my thoughts, dreams, and fears. On the cover is a bottle of (what else?) syrah, the best varietal, don't we all think? I flip the book over, ready to begin once again in authentic manga style. Isn't it funny that what the Japanese authors consider their first page is our happily-ever-after last one? When you think about it, it's not a bad way to approach life. What appears to be an ending — heartbreaking wounds that you can and cannot see — may just be a beginning, a start of a brand-new adventure.

I take a breath and begin to draw my new beginning, my new adventure, starring me, Syrah, on this page as white and unblemished as newly fallen snow.

o   o   o

A few days later, I wake to the scent of soy sauce eggs and remember that it is my birthday, sweet savory sixteen. I trace my fingers around the dragons in my alcove bed, the ones swallowing their tails. And finally I understand what Bao-mu has been trying to tell me all along. You have to swallow your past and learn from it before you can move on. It's too late for me to get to know Po-Po, but I can learn everything I can about her, my parents, Grace, all the rest of my family, and Bao-mu, who is waiting for me downstairs.

Without wasting another moment, I fling out of my bed and race down the steps so fast my orthopedic surgeon would cringe . . . or rub his hands in glee that I might be a repeat customer. At last, I reach the kitchen, and there, in front of the stovetop, stirring a pot like she has never left The House of Cheng, is Bao-mu. Her hair may be dyed black and permed curly now, but she is my Bao-mu, all dressed up in the tangerine-colored cashmere sweater she's saved for special occasions. Like our reunion now.

I swallow my first instinct to cry, *You're home,* but Bao-mu's home is down in California in the house my mother bought for her to be near her own family. So instead, I call out, "You're here!"

"See-raah," Bao-mu says, remorse on her face as she turns to me. "I too late for you snowboard!"

"No," I assure her, and wrap my arms around her. "You're never too late. I have a video of it."

She tried her best to come, and in my book, that says it all.

"How go? You do okay? Your mommy said you okay snowboard now. That true?" asks Bao-mu.

Instead of answering, I take her hand, so little in mine, and lead her toward the kitchen table. After I pull out a chair for her, I go to the stovetop and spoon two fragrant eggs into tiny bowls, one for her and one for me.

As I set the bowls on the table, I notice that it's snowing outside, twice in this miracle season that was so slow to start.

"Look!" I point out the window as the gathering flakes skim and settle on the ground.

"So beautiful," she says, beaming. "For your birthday."

Bao-mu doesn't have to tell me that these are a sign. The most gorgeous snowflakes, the ones with all the intricate shapes and patterns, drop the farthest from the sky. They don't just survive their 40,000-foot descent. They revel in their fall, that harrowing, sweeping adventure that shapes them. Literally.

What's the point of reducing life to a question of survival, as if our time on Earth is some ordeal to be endured? We all deserve more than that, me included.

Sitting across from Bao-mu so that I can look her square in the face, I tell her, "Bao-mu, you were wrong. Life is adventure, not just survival."

I pick up her hands, mine cupped underneath hers like a safety net. With my thumbs, I rub her dry knuckles, hands that are swollen with arthritis but would still pull me up if I fall. In Mandarin, I say, *"Wo jiang, ni ting."* Let me talk so you listen.

acknowledgments

I challenge any writer to claim a better editor than mine, Alvina Ling, the "dear genius" and guardian angel in our relationship. She wields her mighty blue pencil with an insightfulness that humbles me, and then bubble wraps me with such strong belief that I can tackle the tough questions she poses. As well, heartfelt gratitude goes to my Little, Brown family: Gail Doobinin (creative art goddess), Megan Tingley, Connie Hsu, Rebekah McKay, Tina McIntyre, Elizabeth Eulberg, Andrew Smith, Christine Cuccio, and David Ford.

This book would be languishing on my hard drive if it weren't for Steven Malk, my beloved agent-therapist-buddy, and the wonderful Dana West and Lindsay Davis.

If my first novel was one for the girls, this is for all the men I've been blessed to call friends: Drew Guevara, who has always made me feel like his cherished buddy; David Hornik and Ben Golub, who taught me about loyalty; and the incomparable Sanjay Sarabhai and Kennell Jackson, both of whom I miss dearly.

This is the book that Seattle's telecommunications giants, the yes-but-no guys at Ignition, and my management team at

Microsoft built. Special thanks go to Coach John (Stanton) for brilliantly constructing Ethan's life and the history of the cellular industry, Steve Hooper for his exemplary leadership, and Adrian Smith for explaining how these cell phones work in the first place. Pete Higgins, you are my hero of heroes for your unfailing support spanning continents and career changes. Between you, Robbie Bach, Hank Vigil, Liz Welch, Melinda French, Patty Stonesifer, and Alex Loeb, I received a far better education than any MBA program could have given me about business, integrity, passion, perseverance, and generosity — plus, we had a rocking good time at Microsoft.

Blessings to the divine Diviners — Peggy King Anderson, Judy Bodmer, Katherine Grace Bond, Janet Lee Carey, Holly Cupala, and Dawn Knight — who have sustained me throughout the telling of Syrah's story with chai tea, kettle corn, and pom-poms. Janet S. Wong, you are truly your namesake, a treasure and leader among friends. My dearest Kelly Sheiner, without that day in San Francisco with me in my leg brace and you burgeoning with baby, both of us watching runners wistfully, I'd never have had the idea for this book.

Props to the snowboarding community who've been generous with their time so that I would tell this story right: Deb Friedman, Alexis Waite, Suzi Riggins Boone, Rhami Marshall, Susan Waite, Whistler ski patrol, the Canadian Snowboard Federation, and most especially Sam Shin, who lives the difference between passion and calling. I hope I did you proud. A shout out to Dr. Neena Kapoor who answered all my questions about biracial bone marrow transplants, the caring staff at Children's Hospital & Regional Medical Center in Seattle who showed me real life on the *third floor*, Linda and Cameron

Myhrvold for hosting me at Whistler, Bei Guan for sharing her family story with me, and Dr. Lawrence Holland for fixing my knee.

Family is everything, as Mama (my real-life one) always says. So I am thankful for all of mine — the most wonderful mother in the world, Ann Chin-Hong Chen; my Baba, Bob Teh-Nan Chen, who is integrity personified; my way talented siblings, Sue Lim, Will Chen, and Dave Chen; my smart and spunky aunties Lillian and Janet; and the most supportive in-laws you will ever find, Bill and Robbie Headley. No wonder Robert turned out to be such an amazing man. Most of all, to my kiddie-links, Tyler and Sofia, may your lives always burst with a billion pieces of good fortune.